Lie Beside Me

A NOVEL BY

JUDITH DONATO

Devon Grove Press

D1248966

Library of Congress Number: 2012921489
Devon Grove Press, Wayne, PA

Cover design by Strategic Eye, Inc.

For Mark, Annie & Spencer
And
Mom & Dad

Prologue
The Card

1

Kate McAllister was blind.

This was not true in the medical sense. Her vision was keen and sharp. She was one of a handful of people in her circle that didn't need reading glasses dangling like a noose around her neck, at least not yet. It was the bedroom's fault. Its pitch-black, not-yet-adjusted-to-the-light darkness caused Kate to fear she would stumble or crash into something as she made her way toward the bed. The small slit in the curtains, the one she had been meaning to sew for the past two years, wasn't throwing its usual blade of moonlight and her only guide was the rhythmic sound of her husband's breathing. He turned over without even a sigh. It was a sign sleep had set in, the kind of sleep the End of Days could not disturb. Michael would sleep through Armageddon. Kate would be lucky to grab an hour here and there. Sleep was one more thing on the list of things that had eluded her over the past year.

Michael had gone to bed earlier, so she navigated carefully around the furniture. She bought the Ethan Allen "Georgian Court" collection over twenty years ago with her first royalty checks. This furniture of powerful men and women with its deep cherry patina and rising bedposts made her feel successful. Solid cherry settees, end tables, butler's trays, and foyer plant stands filled with expensive faux flowers decorated the Philadelphia Main Line homes she visited as a child.

When she was growing up, people who didn't need to worry if there was enough money left over at the end of the month to pay the electric bill had this furniture. Now, she had it too. Countless hours of dusting and polishing kept it looking fresh off the showroom floor. It was hers, bought with her own money and brought to the marriage like a circle of friends who supported her and stood by her in good times and in bad. The nightstands, the dresser, and the imposing Philadelphia highboy were strong and powerful allies that wouldn't bow to passing trends.

You couldn't kill this furniture if you tried, and Michael tried. Each night he tried by bouncing his keys carelessly onto the vanity. He tried by insisting his water bottle wasn't leaving a ring on the nightstand and the spare change he dropped didn't scratch the dresser. Stain sticks and wood putty repaired the small imperfections that only she noticed. The furniture refused to decay. It refused to die.

The floorboards creaked under her weight. Kate stopped. It was a natural reaction, a moment from every movie she'd ever seen where suspense is built on the sound of a floorboard surrendering under the weight of the oncoming intruder. But she wasn't an intruder. This was her home and he wouldn't hear her. He rarely did. The TV was off, an unlucky circumstance since the forty-two-inch plasma could light a runway. Their bedroom door had opened without a sound. She oiled the hinges last week when he was away. They had been silent for days but Michael didn't notice. He hadn't noticed many things for many months.

Something she ate earlier hadn't agreed with her. Kate had been careful with her diet since early last summer, but a cocktail reception at Michael's office offered too many of the foods she had denied herself since joining the gym. Kate's rule had always been to never walk past anything wrapped in phyllo dough and the party tonight was no exception. Too often denial had become her companion. She used to smother it with Hostess Snowballs and Ring Dings when the kids were small. Extra helpings of fettuccine alfredo kept it drowning in heavy cream and butter. The five pounds after Laura was born turned into ten when she had Jake.

"Did you notice how much weight Colleen dropped?" Michael asked at the party.

"Yeah, she looks great." Colleen was Michael's secretary and up until that moment Kate had never had reason to resent her, but it wasn't Colleen's fault. Kate had been working out three times a week since last spring and was down eight pounds, but that didn't warrant a compliment from her husband.

The dog watched with curiosity as she made her way toward the bed. She slid under the covers and looked up at the ceiling. Kate was tempted to move her body into Michael's but he wouldn't feel her next to him. She settled in and soon the lists started, the rat-a-tat counting off of things she had to get done drumming through her head. Thanksgiving was ten days away. She and Michael were hosting the dinner. Kate rejected the current media buzz that it's everyone's favorite holiday. "It's less commercial." "It's much more relaxed than Christmas." Those relaxed people are the ones who aren't up at dawn to spend the better part of the day basting two turkeys. They linger over coffee in front of the Macy's Thanksgiving Day parade; so when they show up at your door with a regifted bottle of wine, they are perfectly rested from a leisurely morning. Kate loved having friends and family with her on the holiday, but was overwhelmed at the thought of feeding a small army. Hosting Thanksgiving dinner felt like swallowing low doses of arsenic. It's slow, painful, and no one wants to go near it. The weeks of preparation exhaust even the most seasoned hostess. But it was traditionally "Kate's" holiday, so she'd smile her way through the grease and the gristle, drink too much wine and secretly be thrilled when the last folding table was carried back out to the garage the next day.

This year would be a little different. Laura was making her first trip home since their teary drop-off at Vassar in late August. Except for a quick visit over Parents' Weekend, the only communication with her daughter was by text, phone, Skype, and email. Kate was curious if Laura would seem more mature and independent to her.

Where was it? Kate rolled over on her side and suddenly couldn't remember where she stored her great-grandparents' carving knife. Was it in the pantry or did she box it up after last year and put it in the basement? Electric gadgets that whirred with twin-serrated blades could never replace this carving knife that had been passed down for generations. She lacked her ancestors' skill. Her father was once a perfectionist with it. He carved with precision, meticulous in every slice, each cut that separated the wing and thigh from the cavity was smooth. Nothing tore away or left a ragged edge. Nothing was wasted. Every piece had a unique form and shape set by his careful hand. He took his time, making sure the temperature was perfect so the breast didn't fall apart. His hands moved with a surgeon's grace. The first cut was the most important. The first cut determined the success or failure of the entire carving. The aroma of fresh roasted turkey and the soft spray of steam and heat still filled her with nostalgia for those holidays.

Kate's technique was choppy, always impatient to get the job done. There were things to pull from the oven, salads to toss, soup to be ladled. So she hacked and sliced, laying out pieces on her mother's platter, the one with the hand-painted turkey, chipped and cracked from years of use. She loved that turkey platter not for what it is but for what it had been to her and her family for so many years – a place that sparked memories of all of them around the table.

Michael rolled toward her and swung his arm gently across her breasts. His head nestled against her neck and his warm breath enveloped her. His body heat triggered the one thing Kate dreaded more than the insomnia. In seconds every cell under her skin was flush and inflamed. Her neck, face, arms, and legs were covered with a thin film of perspiration that would eventually evaporate and leave a chill. She wanted to throw back the covers and stand under a cold shower, but it would be over in a few minutes. She'd wait it out. Michael's fingers played across her nipple as he inhaled. A low moan came from his lips as he whispered softly into her ear, "Marilyn."

2

Michael McAllister was a runner. He began soon after college and rarely missed a morning except for the occasional Sunday when he slept in while his wife and kids went to Mass. He loved being the first one up, when no one was demanding his time or attention. He stretched quietly. The dog lifted his head from his oversized cushion. "Want to come with me, Dex?" Michael's voice was soft, but the dog showed no interest and drifted back to sleep. It was a cold November so he layered his clothing, selecting a tight-fitting turtleneck, warm socks, thermal pants, and a wind suit.

He went to the kitchen and started the coffee. Kate would be up in a few minutes to make sure Jake didn't sleep through his alarm. The pattern had been the same for as long as Michael remembered. He slipped on a hat, deactivated the security alarm, put on his gloves, and stepped out the back door.

He was hit by a blast of crisp autumn air. It already felt like winter. He bent his knees and lifted his lower leg to the back of his hamstrings to stretch his quads. Michael then leaned over until his hands almost touched the driveway as he loosened his back muscles. He jogged slowly toward Conestoga Road heading for Valley Forge Park. His route was always the same. He'd enter the park by the Memorial Arch and loop through the fields to the running trail, circle around Washington's Headquarters, cut back through the meadow to Overlook Drive, then sprint by Route 23 past the chapel and cemetery on his way home.

Michael's feet pounded the ground rhythmically on his way to the arch. They had what his father would call a "hard" frost last night. The kind that gets into the ground so deep it erases whatever day the calendar says it is and marks the beginning of winter. Nothing grows after a hard frost and whatever is left in the ground dies.

On brisk mornings like this or the most sweltering August day, Michael could see his life in sync with his breathing and the steady movement of his body. All of the external junk that littered his inbox and his Blackberry along with the mountain of paperwork and voicemails at the office all faded to nothingness. All he knew was the trail and the tall grass as his legs pumped toward the same destination day after day. His route never changed, or rather Michael never bothered to change it. If he were looking down from one of the traffic helicopters that often interrupted his solitude, he would see a man running in a circle.

He looked past the majestic oaks and noticed the clearing for his house off in the distance. Kate would be going about her morning routine by now. He considered tacking on another half a mile. He wasn't ready to go home. It was getting harder to keep up the pretense. He disguised his restlessness in the language of complacent domesticity. His life was peaceful and comfortable, but like his morning run, the scenery was always the same. And if there was one thing Michael desperately needed, it was a change of scenery.

He picked up his pace once he reached the cemetery. Michael glanced at the worn headstones. Some had been weathered to half their original size and the names and dates were barely visible. Men and women from another century were now long forgotten. The bare facts of their existence – the day they were born and the day they died would eventually be erased forever. Lives that once had meaning and purpose now had neither. Michael headed along the country road toward home. He didn't have the luxury of time this morning. He had to shower quickly and get to the office. He was leaving for Dallas in a few hours. The trip was with a major client who planned to launch a new drug in the fight against HIV/ AIDS. Michael's firm was awarded the marketing research piece of the project and he was personally overseeing it. The job was financially lucrative, which meant his firm would beat last year's sales numbers, but that wasn't the real reason he looked forward to this trip. Dallas was Michael's turning point. It was where he would stop running in circles. He had been planning his escape for months, and if he had one regret about the decision he was about to make, it was that Kate had no idea what was coming.

3

That Tuesday morning Kate Marino McAllister followed her usual routine. Jake was stumbling around upstairs getting ready for school as she poured herself a mug of coffee. Kate enjoyed the simple pleasures of her daily routine and knowing what to expect each day. She embraced the sameness of Michael waking up a half hour before her each morning and making coffee as carefully as he did everything else. He filled the water level to the exact amount and measured each scoop like a scientist. But this wasn't an ordinary morning and Kate's predictable pattern had been upset. She was agitated and on edge, questioning if she had heard Michael correctly last night. It had been more of a low, humming sound than his actual voice and barely above a whisper at that. She wasn't paying close attention because her mind and body were overheating at the time. Kate entertained the thought that he had said Melvin or Milton, which was disturbing for completely different reasons. But her ears were as keen as her eyes, and she knew without question the name her husband called in his sleep was "Marilyn."

She threw Jake's lunch together and mourned the loss of making the extra sandwich for Laura, who had forever evaporated from Kate's morning ritual. Michael came home from his run winded but with the glow of perfect health. The cold November air wafted off his clothes and chilled Kate.

"Morning." He kissed her cheek as she slathered mayonnaise across a slice of bread. He grabbed the orange juice from the fridge.

"How was your run?"

"Good. Mind if I check the scores?"

"My computer's up."

"Thanks, Hon. How's the coffee?"

"Perfect."

Michael moved to Kate's office. His clipped conversations and long silences weren't new to his wife, but they seemed more frequent lately. She followed him to the office, not sure how to start a conversation about last night. The screen lit Michael's face. The small lines that had crept in around his eyes were barely visible.

She wanted to ask, "Who the hell is Marilyn?" But what came out was, "What time do you leave today?"

"For Dallas? Around three. I thought I'd catch up on things at work, then come back and pack."

"Mom!" Jake was in the kitchen. "I'm late."

"You're not late. Grab a bagel." Kate wanted to find an opening with Michael before he left.

"You mind driving him this morning? I've got a ton of things to clear up before I leave for Texas," Michael said.

"No problem."

"Come on, Mom!"

"You sure?"

"Yeah, it's fine," Kate said.

"I'll go say goodbye to him." Michael went to the kitchen as Kate grabbed her coat and purse still trying to place that name. She didn't know a Marilyn. She couldn't remember having ever met one or heard Michael mention that name until a few hours ago. She mentally ran through his employees, clients, even the wives of his tennis buddies, but there wasn't a Marilyn in the bunch. She drove Jake to school while Michael showered. Jake hopped out of the car before she came to a complete stop. Kate couldn't help herself from watching him lope into the school with a group of boys. Before she could pull away, Cecile Peterson flashed her lights behind Kate. She pulled up and out of the way of the other cars so Cecile could come up to her window.

"I was hoping I'd run into you this morning," Cecile said.

"I'm kind of in a rush to get home. Michael's leaving on a trip."

"Jake tells Sam Michael's barely home these days."

"Business is good," Kate said. Cecile reminded Kate she volunteered months ago to chair the annual Book Fair. As last year's chairperson, Cecile had a stack of folders and order forms in her car that Kate needed to review and a list of meetings she needed to schedule before the holiday craziness set in. She reminded Kate that although the fair was months away, they had to get an early start if they were going to exceed last year's numbers. The Book Fair was beginning to sound a lot like Thanksgiving. Kate loaded her trunk with Cecile's files and contacts and finally headed home.

By the time she dumped everything in her office, Michael was already dressed and on his cell phone. He gave her a quick kiss on his way out the door. Michael had moved his company from Philadelphia to the suburbs when Laura was in middle school because he missed too many afternoon games and parent/teacher conferences over the years. His ten-minute commute gave him flexibility on those rare weeks when he wasn't on the road. Kate thought of calling him as soon as he got to the office, but she wasn't sure this was the kind of conversation they should have over the phone.

She usually began a rough draft of her biweekly column for *Newsbreak* magazine on Tuesday mornings, the same day the dry cleaner dropped off the laundry he picked up last week. The doorbell rang at exactly nine thirty.

"Here you go, Kate." He handed her the clump of wire hangers and Kate handed over the nylon bag full of this week's cotton shirts and wool slacks.

"Thanks, Stan. Got a bill for me?"

"Next week. They're slow down at the store." It was always the same, a few quick pleasantries then a cheery goodbye. Kate placed the crisp, plastic-covered clothes in the center hall closet. When he got home, Michael would move the dry cleaning upstairs and sort what belonged to whom. Life with Michael was good in that married-forever, you-know-what-to- expect, kind of way.

Kate smoothed out the plastic bag against the winter coats and spring jackets that jammed the closet. She noticed a small, brown manila envelope stapled to one of Michael's suits. It was that same small size they put Laura's wisdom teeth in after she had them taken out this past summer. Michael probably left a credit card or spare change in one of his pockets. They had the most honest dry cleaner in suburban Philadelphia.

She snapped off the little envelope and returned to her desk. What would her column topic be this week? Global warming? Washington gridlock? The price of milk? Kate had a love/hate relationship with her column. She loved the ones her readers adored and tried her best to ignore the ones that were dissected in the letters to the editor section. She already covered the "sending your child off to college for the first time" angle. She'd written countless pieces on marriage, relationships, pets, and mortgages. She was blocked; her ideas were caught in the traffic jam of old topics, revisited ones, and those that hadn't occurred to her yet. Her coffee was cold. She returned to the kitchen, taking the little envelope with her.

She topped off her mug, the one with the picture of Laura and Jake smiling in front of Cinderella's castle from a trip to Disney World a few years ago. Kate ripped open the little envelope. She blew into it, reached in with her thick fingers, and pulled out a business card. It was from a woman named Marilyn Campbell, a partner in an advertising firm called Lewis, Kramer, DiMayo & Campbell. She had never in her life met a Marilyn and now twice in less than twenty-four hours the name and its owner invaded Kate's life like a rude houseguest. Michael dealt with several advertising agencies, mostly in Philadelphia and New York. He constantly complained that they tried to control every aspect of a project. Kate wondered if Marilyn Campbell was one of those advertising pests he couldn't stand. Maybe that was why she was disturbing Michael's sleep and her business card had been forgotten in his dry cleaning. She flipped the card over mindlessly and saw a handwritten note. "Loved last night. Love us. Call me soon. M."

Kate read it again, but was more intrigued by the smell of the card than the words written on it. She lifted it to her nose but didn't recognize the perfume. How long ago was last night? Kate couldn't remember when Michael last wore that blue, pin-stripe suit. The handwriting was beautiful, with a distinctive scroll, and done with an expensive pen. Kate knew pens. It was one of the few things she collected. Fountain pens, cartridge pens, even cheap early ballpoints. This one was pricey, probably a Montblanc. But it was the perfume Kate couldn't identify. She passed it under her nose one more time. It was strong and seductive and evoked a sad, unsettled feeling in her.

The card said, "Love us." She searched to find the gray area in Marilyn's words. Maybe she'd write about gray areas this week – from the innocent ones that are often confused for a real problem – to the ones that aren't gray at all and can turn an ordinary, seemingly boring Tuesday morning upside down and shoot it right to hell. She was getting ahead of herself. She needed to slow down her overactive imagination and be analytical. But Kate was never analytical. That's what she loved about her job. She wrote about her opinions and her unanalytical observations of life and the world because it was difficult to argue with either. She went with her gut on all kinds of topics and this time, she didn't like what her gut was telling her about Marilyn Campbell.

Of course, there was the obvious explanation. Michael probably took Marilyn and a bunch of coworkers out for drinks after working on a big account together. He was constantly on the road and Kate lost track of which client matched up with which city. Sometimes advertising people were along; often they were not. Life on the road is the nature of his business. No travel, no money. Once the kids were older, Kate often enjoyed the time to herself. She would take Laura and Jake out to dinner or the movies, but since Laura left for school, Jake's idea of fun was go-kart racing or rock climbing. Kate had no patience for noisy indoor tracks or watching her son climb up a vertical wall with nothing between him and the ground but a harness securely fastened by a nineteen year old with a bad case of acne and job burnout.

She was losing focus. Kate reexamined the card. Marilyn wrote, "Call me." Michael probably needed to call her for work. But if they were working on a project, wouldn't he be calling her anyway? Why would she need to remind him? Kate flipped the card through her fingers. Michael wasn't the type of guy who collected personal notes and business cards from women, but how did she know this? Kate believed he was where he said he was and didn't pay a lot of attention when he gave details on people and projects. With cell phones, there was no need to leave a paper trail of names, numbers, hotels, and flights. He probably had this woman's number in his email contacts so he could reach her a half-dozen ways. That's why the card was a problem. What was its purpose? Every possible avenue to someone's workplace or doorstep was right there on your computer, but for some reason Marilyn Campbell thought Michael needed a souvenir. Kate put the card in her top desk drawer and tried to concentrate on her column, but like <u>The Tell-Tale Heart</u> it kept beating louder and louder, refusing to be ignored and stay out of her sight and subconscious. She busied herself by opening bills and coupon offers, but the card beat in Kate's ears until she finally took it out and put it on her desk. It stared back and haunted her like Poe's nemesis.

By her third mug of coffee, Kate decided Michael couldn't keep track of a double-life and her first guess was probably right. Michael was upset about something at work and that's why he said that woman's name. Kate had a column to write. Her deadline was Black Friday, the day after Thanksgiving. She needed an early start if she was going to pull off the dinner and keep her editor happy. The magazine wanted the piece first thing that morning so they could turn it around quickly for a weekend press run. She had a file cabinet full of ideas, but she didn't want to sort through it. She walked around the first floor, put on music, and tried to motivate herself with a couple of quick jumping jacks but the card kept drawing her back to the office. And in the end, all she really wanted to do was sit at her desk, drink cold coffee, and stare at that card.

Kate came to a decision. She wouldn't grill Michael or flash the Marilyn Campbell card in his face the minute he walked through the door. She hated making a scene. Most of the time she was like her father. Despite the stereotype of the stern Italian-American patriarch, he never lifted a hand to her or her sisters or raised his voice in anger. He believed in talking things out, unlike her mother who wielded a wooden spoon like a Samurai.

Her husband wasn't due home for a few hours, then he was on the road until Friday afternoon. Kate had plenty of time to put this mystery to bed. She'd get over her aversion to logic and reason, conduct an unemotional evaluation of the facts and per-sonalities involved, and come up with a sensible and reasonable explanation. There was only one problem; the woman with the whispered name, perfect penmanship, and scented card smelled like trouble.

Part 1
How They Began

4

Kate Marino was named after her mother's favorite actress, Katharine Hepburn. Maryann Marino was the daughter of immigrants and was drawn to the actress' all-American, independent spirit. Kate had seen dozens of pictures of her parents when her father was still in the Navy. Her mother was tall and had striking reddish, blond hair and Caribbean-blue eyes. Nana would tease her that the Germans must have crossed the Italian border and had their way with someone in the family a few generations earlier. Those rogue genes were not gifted to Kate. She took after her father's side. She was petite and dark skinned with large hazel eyes whose lids always seemed to be shaded with a light brown tint. She had Nana's faint, dark circles under her eyes that no amount of expensive creams or cover ups managed to erase.

Maryann was a beautician who was forced to drop out of high school and learn a trade so she could help send her brother to college. She had bigger dreams for Kate and her two other daughters, Maria and Theresa. It's not that Maryann hated being a beautician; she hated not having a choice. Maryann wanted her girls to see how far life could take them, to be iconoclasts. But from the moment Kate learned to walk, she clung to her parents like flypaper.

The Marino family lived in a small suburban community built in the 1950s when everybody liked Ike. They were starter homes for most people of her parents' generation, but it was to become the Marino's permanent home. Each house was a modest three-bedroom, one-and-a-half baths, brick split level with white asbestos siding. They were identical images, soldiered side-by-side along freshly paved roads, and distinguished only by their shutters, which were painted in various colors but accented with the same three white blocks on each side. The architectural detail was extended to the scrollwork on the aluminum screen doors. Their house was built on the side of a hill, which was great for sledding in the winter, but not so great when Kate's father tried to back their Pontiac Bonneville up the driveway after a snow storm.

The local Catholic school didn't offer kindergarten so Kate was enrolled at the public school a mile away while her elder sister Marie was already in the second grade at Our Lady of Perpetual Help. Kate lasted two weeks at Richardson Elementary. Her parents pulled her out on the grounds that being away from her mother made her sick to her stomach. She spent the rest of the school year coloring with her kid sister, Theresa. But as the clock ticked down toward the oncoming autumn, Kate's unstructured days of helping her mother and watching soap operas with Nana came to an end. She was to follow in her sister's footsteps and go to the parochial school. Her parents drove past the building the day before school began to get her used to the idea.

"Honey, that's where you'll be going," her mom said.

"It'll be fun, Kate, you'll see," her dad chimed in.

Kate's stomach felt like a walnut tree was growing inside of it. The two-story brick school looked like a World War II bunker she had seen in her mom's stack of old pictures. The steel gray doors bordered the north and south end of the school and all of the windows were covered with blackout shades. Kate didn't sleep at all the night before her first day and had no appetite the next morning even though her mother got up early to fry bacon and scramble eggs – her favorite breakfast. As the kitchen clock moved closer to eight, she took her sister's hand and walked to the bus stop. When the large, yellow, flat-front bus screeched to a stop, Kate burst into tears.

"Don't be a crybaby, Kate. You've got to go. It's not that bad," Marie said. They rode together in silence and when they got off the bus, they were told to line up according to grade level. She held onto her sister's hand.

"Let go, Kate. I've got to get to my line."

"I want to go home, Re," Kate said.

"You can't. Just do what the nuns say and you'll be fine."

Sister Mary Samuel stood at the front of the line for Class 1A. The nun's black and tan habit had a clipped, short cape and a skirt that nearly touched the ground. Her shoes were like the black wing tips her father wore to Sunday Mass except with a one-inch heel. Not that Sister Mary Samuel needed height. She was a giant. Kate couldn't tell if she was old or young. There weren't lines around her face like Nana, but she wore glasses with silver wire rims. The bell rang and they walked silently into the classroom. Seven rows of ten seats were lined up side by side.

"Everyone take a seat immediately. We have a lot to do today." Kate's classmates hung their sweaters and jackets in the cloak room along the back wall and placed their lunch boxes on the shelves. They each took their desks while Kate stood in the doorway.

"Did you hear me, young lady? Take a seat."

"I can't," Kate whispered.

"What do you mean you can't? Be seated or I'll call your mother."

That's exactly what Kate wanted to hear. She wanted someone to call her mother and get her out of there. She was hot in her woolen, navy blue jumper. The white cotton shirt had short sleeves, and the Peter Pan collar had a clip-on tie that suffocated her.

"Are you being disrespectful, child?"

"No. I just want my mother."

"Take your seat," she repeated as if Kate hadn't told her exactly what she wanted to do and where she wanted to be. When Kate still didn't move, Sister Mary Samuel grabbed her by the elbow and jerked her into the room. Kate felt an eruption begin deep inside of her. As she was pushed toward her desk, a stream of vomit shot from her mouth like a fire hose, making a thick paste on Sister's shiny black pumps. Sister Mary Samuel jumped back two feet. She told the class to sit quietly, took Kate roughly by the hand, and led her to the janitor's door at the end of the hallway. Billows of cigarette smoke poured from the room.

"First one this year, Sister?"

"I'm afraid so, Tom. Would you mind taking the bucket to my classroom? It's everywhere." The cloud of cigarette smoke made Kate nauseous again and round two came up outside the maintenance man's cubbyhole.

"What's wrong with your parents?" Sister said. "Why do they send their kids to school sick?"

"I'm not sick," Kate said.

"If the nurse says you're sick, you're sick."

The nurse declared Kate perfectly healthy and sent her back to class after changing her into one of the extra uniforms they kept for emergencies. Day two was a repeat of day one, so were days three and four. Kate rarely went home wearing her own uniform. She was the shortest student in the first grade, so whatever spare jumper was found usually had to be pinned up around her waist.

During those interludes when Kate actually managed to hold it together, she learned to read quickly and discovered math was like doing the puzzles she loved. Mother Superior told Kate that

God had blessed her with a wonderful mind. She was picking up things faster than any of her classmates. She should be happy.

But Kate wasn't happy. She adjusted to sitting up straight as an arrow with her hands folded on her desk and replying, "Yes, Sister," and "No, Sister," comforted by the oversized black and white clock that hung above the steel-trimmed doorway. By noon, it told Kate she was halfway home. Since Kate was a picky eater, her mother usually packed her the same thing every day in her lunch box: a bologna sandwich, potato chips, and a pack of Tastykake peanut butter Kandy Kakes. Still Kate had to force herself to eat until one day she thought she couldn't finish her dessert. It was impossible to swallow another bite of those "peanut butter and chocolate enrobed cakes," but she did. She ate every last crumb. She knew better.

After lunch, the jet-black, one-inch, lace-up pumps moved down her aisle. Sister's heels punctuated each step like the metal on a tap-dancer's shoe. Rosary beads swayed side to side, softly lashing at students as she passed. She was on her daily mission, forging her way toward the hallway and the oversized garbage pail. She pulled up her billowing sleeves and began rummaging through the can. She came back clutching a crumpled brown bag in her bony hand.

"Who threw away a perfectly good tuna fish sandwich?" No one answered. "Who wasted God's precious food?"

Kate sat up straighter in her chair. She ate her sandwich – all of it. It wasn't her. The snack cake came back up into her throat and she swallowed it for the second time.

"Jesus knows who did it," Sister said. "If someone doesn't tell me who didn't finish their lunch, you will all be kept after school!"

Kate's eyes darted toward the clock. After school? But she was halfway home. She couldn't miss her bus. Her mother didn't have a car. Her father took it to work. She'd be stuck there. She'd be with Sister Mary Samuel till dinnertime or worse. She was sorry somebody wasted Jesus' precious food, but she was sure

Jesus didn't want a kid to eat tuna fish if he hated it. Kate got very warm. Her clip on bow tie was like a garrote around her neck. She looked up at Sister still holding that messy bag with pieces of wet lettuce and apple core staining its sides. Kate's uniform suddenly felt like it was made of elastic, cutting off her circulation and that snack cake wasn't where it was supposed to be. She was losing the battle. Swallow. Swallow. She did once, twice, harder. On the third swallow, the snack cake exploded from her six-year-old lips along with undigested bologna and potato chips.

"Was it you?" Sister Mary Samuel said. Kate shook her head. She just threw up her entire lunch and there wasn't one speck of tuna in it.

"Robert, tell Mr. Borkowski to bring the metal bucket – again." She ignored the chunks of vomit running down Kate's uniform. Silence fell over the classroom. Robert double-timed it up the aisle but stopped at the doorway and let loose worse than Kate. And then it happened, the vomit chain reaction. After Robert, Elisa McCann released a disgusting combination of peanut butter and jelly.

"That's enough! Elisa, close your mouth. Kate, go to Mother Superior's office immediately!" After Robert and Elisa, Sharon Gleason hurled, and then Jimmy Carr lost what looked like turkey roll. Lisa Miller glanced at Jimmy and she gave it up like nothing had left her stomach since her first bottle of baby formula. Frank Collins couldn't hold back. Chunks of his egg salad went flying across his desk.

"Stop it all of you!" Sister said. "Michelle, Joan, Richard!" It was too late. The Niagara Falls of indigestion poured onto the floor. Mr. Borkowski was going to need a bigger bucket. The acrid smell of partially digested food filled the room and wafted up and down the corridor. It was so bad that to this day, no one can remember who actually vomited first. Sister Mary Samuel never found out who wasted Jesus' precious food and the only one who was kept after school was the janitor who had to clean up the mess. The story became a small legend at Our Lady of Perpetual Help.

Kate learned something very important on that day of all vomiting. She learned she wasn't alone. The other kids were as afraid of Sister as she was; they were just better at hiding it. No one made fun of Kate after that day. Girls soon came up to her on the playground. She was no longer the sad little girl who brought out the big metal bucket. She had slowly become one of them.

Kate also discovered her salvation during those early school years. Even before she knew how to write, she created stories in her head each night before she fell off to sleep. She'd often replay the day's events and recreate her own version where she was more popular and bolder, even leading the class in a revolt against Sister. As soon as she mastered printing, then the Palmer method of handwriting, the stories took form. She'd write them down in a black marble copybook and tuck it away in her nightstand. Mother Superior was right when she told Kate she was very smart. Year after year, Kate won the annual English, Vocabulary, and Phonics award.

Kate's confidence grew. The sharp pangs of missing her parents and the panic attacks that came with them were as random as a high frequency that came and went without warning. Her last memorable moment of humiliation occurred in the sixth grade. It was also her first and only sex education lesson at Our Lady of Perpetual Help. Her teacher was a kind, single woman in her late thirties. She had short-cropped blond hair and wore shirtwaist dresses with collar pins. One day it would be a butterfly, the next a shiny jewel, or some days just the classic circle pin. Miss Braxton never yelled or slammed the pointer against the chalkboard. She seldom gave out demerits and never once went through the garbage can after lunch. If her tests were too hard, she'd give a retest.

Each classroom had a huge crucifix hanging prominently in the front, right behind the teacher's desk so you could concentrate on the suffering of Christ during the Morning Prayer, Grace, and the Afternoon Prayer. One day, on an uneventful Thursday afternoon, Kate looked at the crucifix just as she did on every other school day. She scanned the crown of thorns, down to the wound that pierced His side and then her eyes stopped cold. For the first time in her eleven-year-old life, she looked at Jesus hanging on that cross and noticed that the same nuns who harped about the length of their uniforms didn't seem to notice or care about a low-hung, ceramic loin cloth on an almost life-sized image of the Son of God.

Miss Braxton had just finished a lesson on the rotation of the earth on its axis when the thought flew through Kate's brain before she could filter it or say a quick ejaculation to cast out the devil. An ejaculation was a short prayer. You'd think the church would have come up with a better name, but when the devil tempted you, you were supposed to mutter, "Jesus, Mary and Joseph" or "Jesus, I love you." The only ejaculation Kate could think of at that moment had nothing to do with the Holy Family. And then the mortal sin exploded in Kate's consciousness. The crucifix grew larger in her eyes. It took over the entire wall from top to bottom. It surrounded Miss Braxton, threatening to fall onto her head and kill her on the spot. Kate closed her eyes. She opened them and refocused. She stared at the nail wounds in His hands and feet, but her sin played on a loop in her brain. The thought. The impurity. The worst image a Catholic girl could conjure. The image that Jesus was equipped with the one thing her Ken doll was not.

She squeezed her eyes tightly shut and prayed she'd go blind like that guy in the bible before Jesus rubbed mud in his eyes. She wondered if that's where the saying, "Here's mud in your eye," came from. Her brain was overheating, but when she opened her eyes she wasn't blind. That gargantuan crucifix was still looming over Miss Braxton.

Miniscule tears escaped from the corners of her eyes. Hell was now her only option. She thought of her sisters and parents in Heaven one day eating grapes, laughing, and listening to a naked baby angel play the harp while she burned, choking on soot and ash with Hitler and Stalin. Her eyes soon poured out their salty lava. Poor, kind, and helpful Miss Braxton looked confused at why studying the earth's rotation would reduce one of her students to tears.

She quickly assigned silent reading in the science textbook and called Kate out into the hallway. Nothing good ever came from Kate being brought out to the hallway, but she loved Miss Braxton because she hated teaching the Seven Deadly Sins. Kate remembered how gentle she was when they got to gluttony because Nancy Wisnecki was the chunkiest girl in their class. She explained how it was almost impossible for any of them to come close to committing even one of those mortal sins. Now Kate had done much worse.

Miss Braxton spoke to her gently. "What's wrong, Kate? Did something happen? Did one of the children say something to you?"

"No, Miss Braxton."

"Well, it has to be something. No one cries without a reason." Miss Braxton wouldn't let it go. She stroked Kate's arm and tried to console her. Miss Braxton told her to look back into the classroom at the Cross.

"Kate, whatever you are suffering it can't be worse than what Jesus suffered when they stripped off his clothes and lashed at his skin with leather whips." Now she brought whips into it? Kate's shoulders heaved in heavier sobs. She felt dizzy and her legs were like rubber bands. Miss Braxton caught her before she hit the floor. She carried Kate to the nurse's office and they called her father at work to come and take her home. The nurse suggested it was an anxiety attack. Children are known to have them. Of course Kate was anxious; she knew she was damned to Hell. She missed school the next day and never told a living soul what really upset her that afternoon.

Two years later, she graduated with the highest grade point average in the history of Our Lady of Perpetual Help. Maryann didn't worry about Kate anymore. She saw joy on her face every time she opened a new book or went on forever at dinner about her latest story idea. She went out with other girls instead of staying home on weekends. When Kate moved on to the same parochial high school as Marie, she was surrounded by a group of her own friends and the Marinos opened their door to all of them.

The girls had names like Maggie and Jill and Sharon. Kate wanted to be like them and eat the soft and squishy "American" bread and cold cut sandwiches, but Kate's parents refused to keep anything in the house that didn't have a crust that could crack a tooth. Kate's father was the one who defined them as a typical suburban, white-collar family. He was the first one in his family to graduate college. He had been a math whiz his whole life and after a long stint as an auto mechanic, he took advantage of the GI bill and went to college before Kate was born. He was an aerospace engineer at a time when John Kennedy and the rest of America were determined to put a man on the moon.

Tony took his daughters out every night to look at the stars. He'd tell them what kind of force it took for a rocket to break out of the earth's gravitational pull. He knew the make and model of every jet plane that flew overhead. He tried to explain the importance of hydraulics and aerodynamics, drag and resistance, but it was the sound of his voice, not the words, that kept Kate spellbound. He built an office off the garage and Kate would drift in and out to watch him manipulate his slide rule at the drafting board, scribbling numbers and letters that looked like a foreign language.

If she or her sisters gave their mother a hard time, Maryann would warn, "Wait till your father gets home." But waiting for her father to come home was one of Kate's favorite pastimes because she was in charge of his evening cocktail. The ritual began right after school. She'd put a double Old Fashioned glass in the freezer. It had to be just the right temperature. After he handed out hugs and kisses, he'd give her a nod and she'd head to the kitchen. Tony settled into his favorite chair and gave Kate a serious look when she returned and handed him the frosted glass with the warm, caramel-colored liquid. He'd take a small sip, and then break into a smile.

"Best one yet, Sweetheart." Kate swelled with pride. "So how are my favorite girls today? School good?" They'd take turns filling him in on their day while their mother was upstairs finishing her makeup. If Kate's ritual was making his nightly drink, Maryann's was making sure she looked pretty when her husband walked through the door. Every evening before Tony came home, she changed her clothes and freshened her makeup. Maryann carefully applied eye shadow, mascara, lipstick, and pancake powder before coming downstairs to welcome her husband home.

Even years later, Kate was still touched by the memory. As hard as she tried, she couldn't remember the last time she put on lipstick for Michael.

5

Michael James McAllister escaped from the Midwest faster than Dorothy's house flew her from the drab farmlands of Kansas into the colorful Land of Oz. He left to escape his parents' emotional repression. He left to escape the long, harsh winters. Most of all he left to escape the prying eyes of small-town neighbors who always meant well when they had a good story to tell about another neighbor, and that neighbor on any given day could be you.

Elna, Indiana was a farming hamlet about fifteen miles south of Lake Michigan. The McAllister farm was a mile and a half out of town. Town being a four-way stop sign with the bank, the grocery store, the pharmacy, and the gas station on each corner. It was beautiful in its simplicity. Everything you needed was on those four corners. Those that didn't farm inhabited the half dozen streets and cul de sacs around County Highway 56. But once you left the intersection, the landscape was painted with large, lush, green fields, red barns, and towering, blue silos with windmills on top. Michael's father had inherited the farm from his father and hoped that one day his sons would take over and carry on as he did. Michael was six when he started milking and following his father out to the fields. He didn't mind waking at dawn and cleaning out stalls. There was always something to be repaired, machinery to be fixed, or loose boards to secure on a building. Every morning before school and every afternoon after he got home, he had a list of chores to be done. He was fifteen when he first approached his father about working off the farm and trying something new. After a few months of making an argument about earning money for college, his father finally agreed – as long as Michael made himself available early mornings and weekends to help out.

Michael knew even then he wanted to see the world past Elna. His older brother, Dick, was almost a full partner in the farm, so he had little guilt when he announced he planned to attend college in the east. His mother had hoped he would go to a small state satellite campus close to home like most of his friends, but said she wouldn't "fight" him. She would give him his freedom so he could get it out of his system before coming back home for good.

Although Michael had grown six inches his senior year and put on twelve pounds, he was still too lean for the basketball coach to take him seriously. His athletic friends had the one thing he lacked, swagger, so Michael used his greatest asset to move up in the high school food chain – his popularity. His secret was simple, be nice to teachers, classmates, and the entire school staff. He joined as many clubs as he could handle with his academic schedule. By senior year, he was elected student body president. That was the year he also won Barb Wipperman's heart.

Barb was a year younger and one of the prettiest girls in school with long, straight blond hair and deep-set blue eyes. She was co-captain of the cheerleading squad and served with Michael on the decorating committee for the Harvest Dance. The basketball team was playing away that Friday night so they had the gym to themselves to prepare. Michael kept the doors locked and covered the windows with black construction paper. He recruited a half dozen other kids to hang twisted orange and yellow streamers around the gym and cover the backboards with cardboard pumpkins. They wrapped the poles like haystacks. Everyone was sworn to secrecy. No one could see the "magic" until they walked through the doors the night of the dance. As president of the student body, Michael had a key to the gym so they could work as late as they needed. The teachers and administrators trusted Michael. They knew he was the kind of student who would never abuse that trust.

The night before the dance, most of the volunteers had drifted out of the gym and gone home by seven, but Barb volunteered to skip her driver's education lesson and help Michael finish. Time was running out. Michael had to set up the audio equipment. He was going without a date and had agreed to emcee while Jesse Steinerman, a former graduate who ran a DJ business on the side, was spinning records. He was sure Barb was going with Tim Tickner, the star forward on the basketball team. They were always in the hall together. Last week, Michael saw Tim lift her by the waist as she laughed and threw her arms around him.

"Watch those scissors. They're sharp." Barb was struggling with a yellow gourd. The art department had sketched them out and all they had to do was cut along the lines.

"I ruined it." She put the scissors down.

"No, it's fine. Here." Michael took it and finished cutting out the rounded tip.

"We'll never get this all done in time," Barb said.

"Sure we will. Thanks for staying tonight."

Michael's palms were sweating so hard they practically slid off the scissor handles. He put the gourd down. His head was pounding.

"I'm starving. Want to grab something to eat?"

"What about the rest of the decorations?"

"I'll come back and finish in the morning," Michael said.

"Okay, then sure. Why not?" It wasn't the enthusiasm Michael hoped for but it was a start. He locked up the gym and walked Barb to his dad's truck. He opened the passenger door and took her hand to help her up. They drove a few miles to a popular burger joint in the next town. The last thing Michael needed was to make Tim Tickner his enemy, but he wasn't thinking about anything except how pretty Barb looked sitting beside him on the ride to the restaurant. She told Michael that Tim was a pest and kept asking her out, but she knew he had already slept with at least two of her teammates on the cheerleading squad.

"Why don't you just tell him to get lost?"

"I'd love to, but it's a small group so I go along with it. Besides he's my man," she said. Michael looked confused.

"For that cheer. 'Tim, Tim, he's our man....'" They ordered food and talked about their classes and future plans. Barb loved accounting. Michael told her he wasn't sure what he'd study in college, but he was looking forward to living on his own. They were still talking when he checked his watch and saw it was after ten o'clock. He drove Barb home and walked her to the door.

"Barb, I know it's really last minute and I'm sure you're already going with somebody but if you're not, would you want to go to the Harvest Dance with me?"

"I thought you were emcee."

"I can get somebody else to cover. But it's cool, if you don't want to."

"No, I want to. I'd love to. I was just going with friends, but I'd really like to go with you, Michael."

He wanted to kiss her so badly but wasn't sure it was the right move. So he gave her a quick hug instead and left before she changed her mind. He took her to the dance the following night and by the end of the month they were officially going steady. That Christmas was as perfect as they were together. He gave her a silver locket and a photo album of pictures he'd taken of them so she could decide which one to put in the pendant. Then he wrapped up his school ring in its small box and placed it in a bigger box then nestled that one in an even bigger box. He wrapped six boxes in all and she had to open each one to get to the ring. His mother scolded him, saying the ring was expensive. What if they broke up and Barb didn't give it back? It was foolish to give away something that cost that much money to a girl he just started seeing. Michael ignored her advice and was proud to see Barb wearing the ring at school with white athletic tape wrapped around it so it fit her finger. Barb gave him a framed picture of herself and a cardboard gourd she'd kept as a souvenir from the Harvest Dance, the same one he'd help her cut out the night of their first unofficial date.

Right after Christmas, he and Barb started talking about having sex. Months later as Senior Prom rolled around, Michael was eager to make his big move. He didn't want to rush her, but reminded Barb that Senior Prom was the most romantic night of the year and he wanted to make it the best time of their lives. Michael had been borrowing his brother's porn magazines since he was twelve and saw things that were never covered in health class. He loved Barb and was ready to join that elite club he heard bragging about their conquests while strutting around in the locker room. Everything had to play out perfectly for his strategy to work, so Michael decided to approach his mother first and test the water with her.

"Ma, uh, some of the guys are staying over at Luke's after the prom."

"Does Luke's mother know?"

"Sure. It's cool. A bunch of us are going there, hanging out."

"And where are your dates hanging out?" She ran the peeler over the potatoes like it was an automatic weapon.

"With us." Edith McAllister had a way of looking at her son as if she knew every lewd and disgusting thought that ever ran through his mind.

"With you?"

"Yeah, we're staying up. Playing games, making breakfast together. That kind of thing. Luke's parents will be around the whole time."

"Luke's mother hasn't stayed up past eight o'clock since she was your age," Edith said.

"They promised they would. And you know Barb's mom; she's stricter than you. She wouldn't go for it if there was anything funny going on."

"So Ida Wipperman approves of you two being out together all night?"

"Yeah. She's fine with it."

It was time to play his ace, so Michael threw it out casually. "Why don't you call her?" Edith's peeler slipped and nicked her finger.

"You know I can't stand that woman. The only reason I say 'hi' to her in the Piggly Wiggly is because you're sweet on Barb. It's not the girl's fault her mother is a vicious gossip. Do you know she told Mrs. Koontz that Dick has anger issues? She needs to keep her eyes in her own backyard. That boy of hers is the one with a mean streak. I've seen it."

"You okay, mom? Need a band aid?"

"I'm fine. But I'll have to run this prom thing by your father."

It was done. His father would shrug and tell her to "let the boy have a little fun." Barb gave her mother the same story and told her to call Michael's mother if she had any questions. This would never happen because Ida Wipperman's opinion of Edith was equally as low as Edith's was of her. Dating a girl whose mother detested his own was working out perfectly for Michael. His virginity was as good as lost by the time Edith tossed the last spud into the pot.

Michael had to pay for his tickets, get his best suit cleaned, and buy flowers for Barb. His parents constantly reminded him of how much things cost. "Thou shalt not waste money," was their eleventh commandment. They agreed to help with his college tuition but "You better find a way to come up with that room and board, mister." Michael worked summers as a house painter, leaving Dick and his father to work on the farm. He had plenty saved. The week before prom, Michael drove the eighteen miles west into Elk City.

The Lakeside Motel had only twenty rooms and not a lake in sight. Its rusty metal stairs led to the second floor and all the dark green doors faced a cornfield. Stick-on gold numbers identified the rooms. It was old but it was clean and they let him pay cash in advance. After securing the motel room, Michael drove thirty miles in the opposite direction to buy a box of condoms from a store where he wouldn't run into anyone he knew.

It was early May and still cool when he walked Barb home from play practice one night. The subject of prom sex came up and Michael was careful not to pressure her. "Are you sure? Cause if you're not sure, we don't have to do it." Michael blew the words into Barb's ear.

"I want to."

"Really, 'cause I don't care. I don't," he lied.

"I guess I'm a little scared. But we'll just do it, okay?" Michael thought he saw tears.

"Barb, we can wait. We've got the rest of our lives."

"No, I said we would." Michael stopped walking. Barb looked straight ahead as he put his arms around her.

"We'll wait till we're both ready, okay? It's not a big deal. It isn't. I love you." He stopped and kissed her in front of the corner gas station. "Look, we'll go to prom and then head over to Luke's like we planned."

"You wouldn't mind?"

"Of course I don't mind." He made the words sound as sincere as he could. She leaned on her toes, reached up and kissed him.

"I love you too, Michael."

The next day he drove back to the motel and got a refund. For the first time in his young life Michael McAllister felt like a man.

He and Barb saw each other constantly until Michael left for college. They told each other that distance didn't matter. They could weather anything because there was no one they would ever love as much as they loved each other.

6

Kate and Michael both attended Montgomery State University in Montgomeryville, Pennsylvania. The school was less than twenty miles from Kate's home. Her father had been laid off after America got bored sending rockets to the moon. Money was tight and she heard her parents' muffled voices at night. Tony eventually found another job, but the pay was not as good and they were already struggling to help her sister Marie pay her college tuition. The family was getting by, but her mother went back to work in a beauty salon to make ends meet. Kate decided to commute to college and borrow the money to pay her own way.

Her dream was to become a writer and she knew she'd need money in the bank as she tried to figure out how to make a living at it. She calculated the amount she saved on room and board would be in the thousands.

"It's not right," Tony said.

"Why not? It's my education," Kate said.

"I'll get a second mortgage. It's not a problem."

"I'm not taking your money, Dad."

"We'll see."

"No, we won't. I'll live here. I'll eat your food. I'll even let you help me put gas in my car, but that's it."

"You're as stubborn as your mother."

"I've got it all figured out. I can do this. I want to do this."

Tony eventually agreed and took Kate to the bank to cosign for a student loan. Sitting in the metal chair beside him, she felt her father's shame about not being able to afford the cost of her education. The assistant bank manager looked at them through the glass wall of his office as he went over their paperwork. It was a simple process; a couple of signatures and a handshake later and Kate had enough money to enroll. She ignored friends and family who said she'd miss out on the real college experience by not living in a dorm with other coeds. Maybe they assumed she was still that frightened little girl afraid of leaving home, but they were wrong. Her old fears had been conquered by long weekends away with friends and their families, overnight field trips, and "sleep away" camps for kids who loved to write. This decision wasn't about her past. It was about her future.

When Michael McAllister walked into the same modern British literature class as Kate, she had just started her junior year. It was the last day before the drop/add period ended. He was tall, at least six foot two, with light brown hair and a mosaic of freckles across the bridge of his nose. He walked awkwardly around the room as if he were lost.

"Have a seat, young man," Dr. Sessa said. Michael found an empty spot one row over and two seats behind Kate's desk. Dr. Sessa intrigued Kate. She was one of those free spirits Kate knew she'd never become. Kate sat toward the front of the classroom, writing down everything the professor said. Dr. Sessa had long, dark hair with bold streaks of gray that betrayed her timeless look. She seemed like the kind of woman who didn't give a damn about what people thought of her. She was beautiful without a touch of makeup or nail polish. To the Marino women, gray hair was the silver flag of defeat. Her Nana was over eighty and sported cotton candy pink curls. "Never let age win, Cara," she told Kate. Kate was positive she had the only grandmother in the world with naturally pink hair.

On his first day, Michael shuffled past Kate without looking up at anyone. Over the next couple of classes, she refined her first impression of him. He was actually handsome. His eyes were pale blue and his shoulders wide with a narrow waist. He looked like a poor man's Christopher Reeve. Kate had been obsessed with the actor since she first saw him in that flowing red cape with the huge "S" on his chest as a love-struck thirteen-year-old.

After a couple of classes, Michael smiled at her before he took his seat or waited for her to exit the room in front of him. Dr. Sessa kept notes on a blackboard on the side wall, and Kate found herself looking back at them a lot more than necessary. Michael was usually staring straight ahead and rarely took notes. She noticed almost everything about him. Most likely her growing obsession with the new guy in class had something to do with her current dating drought. While sorority sisters and roommates went back to their dorms to firm up their plans, she went home to her life-sized poster of Christopher Reeve, complete with a generous package girded in tight red stretch pants. Kate rationalized it was okay to fixate on Superman since he wasn't Jesus and she wasn't eleven years old anymore.

Classrooms are like church. People pick a pew, or in this case a certain seat, and it becomes their place. They move to it like they are sleepwalking and nobody else sits there once it's pretty clear it's your place. Every Monday, Wednesday and Friday, she and Michael took the same seats in modern British literature. They didn't have any other classes together since she was an English major and he obviously wasn't. She watched him go into McCarthy Hall one day on her way to the library. McCarthy was an upper-class dormitory and he was surrounded by a bunch of guys. She even saw him at the Student Union, where Kate often went for lunch or to study between classes. He was buried in a textbook and didn't look up as she walked past him. He seemed quiet. Her mother had always warned her, "Look out for the quiet ones." Kate wasn't sure what that meant but she knew if they ever met, her mother would peg Michael as one of those 'quiet ones.'

Montgomery State's campus had a beautiful quad. Six stone and ivy buildings outlined its perimeter. Kate's favorite building was Old Main with its indigenous green stone mined not far from campus. The quad's worn, wooden benches were often packed with students. Kate usually set up camp at the quad when the weather cooperated or at the library when it didn't. Sharon, one of the old high school gang, had a room in Ramsey Hall. Kate would drop in there once in a while for lunch, but their schedules were completely different that semester. Sharon was a music major and spent most of her time in the practice studio.

She and Sharon had become close in the eleventh grade when they confessed to having a secret crush on the Salmons – the boys, not the fish. Luckily they both liked different ones. Sharon got over Jimmy Salmon pretty quickly, and now had a serious college boyfriend – his twin brother, Tom, the one Kate had her eyes on a few years earlier. Kate wasn't jealous. Every time she looked at Tom now, she saw the fish, not the boy. He had a downturned mouth and narrow eyes. Tom and Sharon were pretty serious, so Kate's visits to her room became less frequent.

If she had problems connecting with other students, at least she'd graduate with a manageable loan. It was a trade Kate was willing to make. Fall came early that year and the trees boasted colors in shades that defied the jumbo Crayola box she once shared with her sisters. On a brisk October morning Kate ran across the quad, tugging her wool jacket around her neck, juggling books and her purse. She promised Sharon she'd meet her in the dining hall.

"Hey!" She heard a guy's voice call out. She kept moving. "Kate, right?" She stopped and looked in the direction of the voice. "Hey, it's cancelled. Lit class this afternoon." She recognized the voice, but didn't want to make eye contact. Her hair was a mess. She was the first one in the bathroom that morning, but the knocking started five minutes later.

"Hey, Marilyn Monroe, I've got to get to work." The rule was her father never waited. So there was no blow-drying her hair, just a quick spray of perfume and a mad dash down Route 204 toward campus.

"Want to grab some coffee?" Michael was right in front of her, wearing laced work boots and jeans that were a little loose at the ankle, but not too loose. She could have written a thesis on how he looked from the knees down because she still hadn't looked at his face.

"Okay, yeah, thanks – I mean for telling me about class."

"Want to get some coffee?" he repeated.

If she didn't look up soon, he'd think she was one of those people they let on campus from the mental hospital one town over. The ones the state gave the university money to admit so they could readjust into society. She slowly lifted her chin. Michael smiled and the cool October air felt twenty degrees warmer.

Kate forgot all about meeting Sharon. She'd been stood up so many times for quickies with Tom Salmon; Kate didn't think she'd be too mad. She and Michael walked to one of the new places on Marshall Street. Montgomeryville was going through revitalization. More stores and restaurants had opened up than ever before in the history of the town. Café Monty was between Stitches, a store that sold thread and sewing supplies, and Hare Raising, a small pet store. A bell clinked as they walked in. The cafe was lit by the large storefront window and low-wattage track lights. The walls were exposed brick that met the faded maple floors. The butcher-block counter held shiny stainless steel grinders and coffee makers. Michael asked what she wanted. Kate kept it simple, just regular coffee with cream.

He went to the counter and ordered. The waitress knew him by name and asked if he wanted the usual. She was flirting with Michael, but he didn't seem to notice. Kate wasn't sure what was happening. But since she had nowhere to go now that class was cancelled and needed to stay on campus for a lab later that afternoon, she couldn't think of one good reason why she'd turn down his offer.

If heaven had a smell, Café Monty was it. The air was filled with that moment when you open a fresh can of coffee, multiplied by an infinite number. The small shop had its own high from the assortment of exotic beans. Michael moved to the pastry case as she got them a table.

Kate took in every detail as if it were a journal entry. She glanced back at Michael chatting with the cashier as he paid. Kate wasn't sure if this was his idea of killing time or was it possible he was even slightly interested in her?

Students were huddled around small circular tables. Some were studying, but most looked like they were on vacation instead of facing midterms. That's what it's like to live on campus, she thought. No one cares if you're drinking coffee instead of going to class. The empty table she found was by the front window. It had a view of beautiful, old Victorian houses with matching pear trees planted in front of each one. Most were owned by the fraternities and sororities. A few guys tossed a football. The poor kid who caught a pass was brought down by an ankle tackle that flipped him straight into the air and back down, flat on his back. His friends heckled him till he got up, doing a pretty good impression of her Grandpa Joe getting out of his chair on a bad day.

"I hope you like it. It's my favorite blend." Michael put the steaming mug in front of her along with one piece of pound cake.

"How much do I owe you?" she asked.

"My treat. You can get it next time. Or, and this isn't a bribe or anything, but maybe you could help me with my paper on Auden." Kate quickly covered her disappointment. "You don't have to. Coffee's still on me." He smiled again, but it was a nervous smile.

"I chose Conrad," Kate said. "But I could write about Auden in my sleep." And in one of those split seconds that often chart the fate of a life, Kate decided she would dive into Auden if it meant spending more time with Michael.

"You wouldn't mind?" he asked.

"No." And Kate didn't mind. He was very honest about what he needed. Michael didn't seem like the kind of guy who used people. And even though she couldn't be absolutely sure that was true, Kate decided Michael McAllister was worth the risk.

"Thanks, Kate. I really appreciate it. I've got to pull my GPA up and this class is killing me." That was the second time he'd said her name. They hadn't really introduced themselves, not on the quad or on the walk over to the coffee shop. Michael and Kate assumed, as most coeds do, that everyone knows everyone else. Introductions and names were formalities that usually weren't necessary.

"I'm sorry. I ask you for help and haven't even told you my name." Kate knew his name.

"I'm Michael McAllister and since Sessa calls on you at least twice each class, I've known yours since day one."

It was true. She was one of Dr. Sessa's favorites because Kate truly loved modern British literature and never looked bored during her lectures. Kate shook his hand.

"It's nice to meet you, Michael. I can be in the library around four tomorrow, if that works for you," Kate said.

"Sounds good." He smiled and cut the piece of cake in half and put it on her napkin. He waited for her to take a bite before he did. At first she wasn't sure she'd get it past the lump in her throat, but Michael started talking about his other classes and her anxiety eased. She learned he was also a junior. He talked about his favorite movies and the business courses he was taking. Kate confessed to having no interest in ever taking a business course. Michael laughed easily. Kate explained about living at home and wanting to be a writer. As they talked, she slowly began to relax and by their second helping of cake, Kate experienced a sensation she had never experienced with a stranger before that autumn afternoon. By the time they left Café Monty, Kate felt as at ease around Michael as she did in the safety of her own family.

They continued to meet for coffee, then study and write papers together in the afternoon. They'd often rendezvous in the library and once in a while in Michael's dorm room. His roommate left school mid-semester and no one in campus housing had reassigned it, so it was quiet and private.

The first time she entered Room 412 she noticed a picture of a pretty blond girl on his desk. Michael explained he had a steady girlfriend back home in Indiana. Her name was Barb and they'd been dating since high school. He had hoped she would come to Montgomery State, but he wasn't sure that was going to happen. Michael smiled when he talked about Barb and that made the rules very clear to Kate.

Eventually they discovered they were both crazy about James Taylor and Pink Floyd. Michael wasn't a reader and the only books in his room were textbooks, but she got him to appreciate Joseph Conrad. Michael said he was afraid of Kate's dark side. He said any girl who loved <u>The Heart of Darkness</u> had to be a little off. She laughed and told him she could never be a friend with someone who didn't love it, so he agreed to read it again.

The subject of Barb rarely came up in their conversations, but in those moments when Kate felt there was even the slightest chance there could be something more between them, the picture of the pretty blond girl quickly brought Kate crashing back down to reality.

7

Kate brought Michael home that first semester right before winter break. He'd been complaining he hadn't had a home-cooked meal in months. He had aced the midterm thanks to her help, and they were already studying for the final. She gave him a rundown of all the players he would meet at the Marino family's traditional Sunday dinner: the various aunts, uncles and cousins, including Aunt Millie and her daughter, Anna. Aunt Millie's husband had died in the Vietnam War. Her aunt had a scattering of pictures and wallet-sized photos of him in uniform proudly displayed all around her house, but Kate overheard her parents talking in their room one night about the "bastard" walking out on Millie while she was pregnant. Kate never told them she knew the truth. She didn't like her cousin Anna, but she couldn't think of any reason to let her know her dad didn't want her. Grandpa Joe would be parked in front of the television watching the Eagles game with his glasses perched loosely on his nose. The others would move through the house like fish in a stream, probably gliding past

Michael with feigned nonchalance like he was a curious object in their way. Eventually everyone would crowd around the table, making enough noise to be heard back on campus.

She warned Michael it would be chaotic, but he didn't seem intimidated. He walked a couple of blocks to a grocery store early in the day to buy her mother a small bouquet of flowers. He didn't have a car on campus because he planned to pick up his Torino over winter break, so Kate drove to school to bring him back to her house. When she saw him standing in front of McCarthy Hall with his fall bouquet, she slowed down. It was happening more and more; familiar warmth filled her and she felt she could do anything and be anything as long as she shared it with Michael. He got into the car and Kate beat back the urge to lean over and kiss him. Michael noticed her curious expression.

"What's wrong? You said your mom likes flowers," he said.

"She does. It's nice Michael. She'll love them." Kate glanced over at Michael, taking in his unfaded jeans, button-down shirt and a sweater she'd never seen him wear to class.

They drove most of the way in silence, each nervous in that way you don't want the other person to know in case it makes them even more nervous. Michael was looking forward to putting faces to all the names and stories Kate had told him. He never had a girl who was just his friend and he liked it. He had been seeing Kate at least two or three times a week for a couple of months, and he secretly hoped they could continue next semester. He almost told Barb about Kate when he called home last weekend but he wasn't sure he could explain it in a way she would understand. Kate found herself taking more time to get ready that morning – and every morning when she was meeting Michael. But she had one rule: she would never drop in on him. Their time together was always scheduled.

Her mother had noticed the change in Kate a few weeks earlier.

"Are you wearing mascara?"

"A little," Kate said.

"To school?"

"What's wrong with a little make-up? It's no big deal, Ma."

"I didn't say it was a big deal, and watch your mouth. You're not too old for the wooden spoon."

"Sorry, I'm late."

"I thought class wasn't till noon."

"I have study group," Kate said. She was off to meet Michael so they could go over notes for their next class. Kate had bought some new lipsticks and was experimenting with her hair. Her large green eyes were a challenge and her hair did whatever it wanted depending on the weather and humidity. She longed for the poker-straight locks of so many of the girls on campus. She'd have to sleep with three-inch rollers on top of her head to even come close. Most nights she was too tired to care, but she pulled the rollers out of the closet the week before and could now whip them on top of her head in a few minutes. She took her time in front of the make-up mirror but no matter what she tried, Kate wasn't happy with the results. She did what she could with her olive complexion and Roman nose. But on most mornings, Kate would look at her reflection and wish her mother's fair skin and bright eyes from those beautiful old photos were staring back at her.

They pulled into her neighborhood. The street in front of the house was already lined with Buicks, Chevys and Fords. The dining room window was open. Nana must have over-browned the garlic again.

The Marino family surrounded Michael from the moment he and Kate walked through the front door. Kate didn't try to control the stampede. He was on his own. Michael smiled and shook hands. Her mother waited at the center of the throng.

"You must be Michael!" Kate saw his hand begin to extend, but Maryann pulled him into a bear hug. "We're so happy you're here."

"Thank you for having me, Mrs. Marino." He handed her the small bouquet of flowers. "These are for you." Her mother was touched by the gesture.

"That was very sweet, honey. Thank you." She kissed his cheek and Michael blushed at being called "honey" by this woman he just met. He was very dear with Nana and told her the next time he'd bring her flowers too.

"Don't spoil them," her father said as he entered the cramped entryway. Tony put his arm around Michael's shoulder and extended his hand, but his eyes were straining to see the television in the family room. Michael shook his hand quickly.

"Nice to meet you, Michael."

"You too, sir."

"Come with me." Maryann beamed as her husband led the boy to the family room to meet the men. Kate followed. The men were always in front of the television on Sundays and holidays while the women were in the kitchen, dining room, or anywhere else real work was being done.

"Have a seat. The Eagles are winning for a change. You from Philly?"

"No, sir; Indiana."

"Cut the 'sir.' Call me Tony." Michael nodded. Grandpa Joe examined the stranger in the room. Kate felt the tsunami of questions about to hit Michael so she jumped on the offensive. "Grandpa, this is Michael."

"Kate's friend," Maryann added on her daughter's heels.

"Come on, Mare, not during the game," Tony said.

"It's almost over and we have a guest," Maryann protested.

Grandpa Joe's lips spread apart, and the slight dip in his dentures warned everyone what was coming.

"What's your last name, Michael?"

"McAllister." The old man already knew the answer wouldn't end in a vowel. The clues had added up – the freckles, the sandy brown hair, the trim build.

Thinly veiled disdain spilled from his lips, *"Merigan."*

"Pop!"

Michael whispered to Kate, "What did he say?"

Maryann rescued the moment. "It's Italian for 'nice to meet you'."

"Nice to meet you too," Michael said.

"Mare, the game?" Maryann knew she was pushing the limits of her husband's patience.

"Fine. Dinner as soon as it's over."

"What can I do to help?" Michael said. No man in the Marino family had offered to help in the kitchen since one of her mother's distant cousins came to visit, and as her father once told Kate, he was "that way."

Maryann beamed. "Isn't that wonderful, Tony?"

"Yeah, yeah, it's great."

She put a gentle hand on Michael's arm. "Don't be silly. You sit here and enjoy the game with the men. Kate will help." Kate glanced back at Michael who gave her a half-smile and took a seat next to her father. Michael had just been made.

At dinner, everyone talked over everyone else as spaghetti gravy flicked off the perciatelli. Serving perciatelli was a cruel joke to play on Michael. Kate was hoping for a clean rigatoni or a simple penne, but perciatelli was her father's favorite pasta. It is a long, thick noodle with a very small hole in the center. Maryann placed Michael next to her. She assumed the role of teacher and he her student.

"Kate, would you pass the sauce please?" Michael said.

The table went silent. Anyone who has grown up in an Italian-American family knows there is no such thing as sauce. It's gravy. Be it brown, red or anything inbetween, it's always gravy. Saying "sauce" is the equivalent of saying you are better than us because you use a fancier word to ask for something we know is simple and honest, like us – and that something is "gravy." Michael looked confused, but his teacher stepped in.

"Honey, the boy needs gravy." And just like that, the talking continued. Kate looked on helplessly as Michael tried to twirl the noodles on his fork. Her mother was busy arguing with Nana about which grocery store had the best price on canned tomatoes. She took her eye off her prize pupil just long enough for him to pick up his knife and start cutting the perciatelli into bite-size pieces. Everyone pretended not to notice. They left him to enjoy his food peacefully.

"This is really good, Mrs. Marino. Kate told me you were a great cook, but this is incredible." Maryann smiled. She was pleased he was enjoying himself, but she knew as they all did that from that day forward, Michael McAllister would always be known as that *Merigan* boy who came to dinner and used a knife to cut his pasta.

Maryann had bought a special Italian rum cake for dessert. She served Michael first, bypassing Tony for the only time in Kate's memory. A look came over Michael. Kate was afraid all the rich food had made him sick, but then he smiled and looked up at her mother. Michael was happy he had come to dinner in this circle of strangers. After the espresso, he moved his chair back and started to help Kate's mother and aunts clear the table. Tony's eyes darted his way.

"Sit down, Mike. The ladies will do that."

It was the first time Michael looked uncomfortable but he followed orders. He and Tony went back to the family room with the other men and Kate didn't see him again until it was time to drive back to campus. Her mother sent him home with a large bag of leftovers and another round of hugs before he walked out the door.

Michael was quiet on the ride back to the university. Kate assumed he was on cultural overload. He looked out into the darkness. His voice was low. "Your family's really nice, Kate."

Even then Kate felt it was her job with Michael to fill the silence. "I'm sure your family's nice too." Michael didn't confirm or deny it. "Tell me about them. You've got a brother, right? What are they like?"

"There's not much to tell." He looked back out the window and didn't say more than goodbye when she dropped him off in front of his dorm. The ride unsettled Kate. She wasn't sure what had happened. The day went better than she expected, but all the way home she felt something had gone wrong. She couldn't pinpoint when or what had changed his mood, but from the moment they left her neighborhood, she saw a distant and moody side of Michael she hadn't seen before now.

When she walked through the door, her mother was still at the sink. Her father had driven Grandpa Joe home. Nana was already in bed and her sisters were in their room studying. Maryann was washing the last of the pasta pots. Kate picked up a towel and dried what had piled up on the drain board.

"Thanks for today, Ma. It was fun." Maryann was unusually cautious.

"Michael seems like a nice boy. Did he have a good time?"

"He said he did."

"Invite him back," her mother said.

"Maybe."

Kate waited for the question her mother had been dying to ask since she'd first told her about Michael. Maryann put on a nonchalant tone.

"Do you like him?" Kate was flushed and embarrassed. She liked him very much and in a way that he didn't like her. Except for a few shared smiles and their hands barely touching as they passed books back and forth across a library table, there was nothing to tell her mother because nothing had ever happened between them. Kate put her towel down and walked out.

"What did I say? Kate! Kate, get back here." Kate was already halfway up the stairs. She was too embarrassed to tell her mother she was falling for a guy who would never fall for her. She didn't want her family to resent Michael for hurting her because he hadn't. He was honest about having a girlfriend. Kate admired his devotion to Barb. She just wished he were devoted to her. Kate flopped down on her bed. She had her own room. Marie was the eldest but when Theresa was born, she insisted the baby be put in her room. The baby was now sixteen and Marie was still stuck with her. When Nana moved in, her father built a bedroom in the basement for Marie and Theresa, and Nana took over the room next to Kate's. Kate's bedroom needed a facelift, but facelifts cost money so it looked girlish with ballerina wallpaper and a French provincial twin bed.

"Hey, Beans, Mom said you were upset." Her father was in the doorway. He always called her Beans. The nickname came from Grandpa Joe's wife, who died when Kate was three. Kate was small and thin as a child and her grandmother called her *fagiolite*, which was Italian dialect for little string bean. After his mother died suddenly, Tony started calling her Beans.

"I'm not upset." He pulled her desk chair closer to the bed. "There's nothing to talk about, Dad, really."

"Okay, but if you change your mind..."

Kate finished his sentence. "You'll be in your office." Tony winked, then rose to leave, but turned back with a smile.

"Mike seems like a good kid."

"He is."

"But we've got to teach him how to eat pasta."

Tony closed the door softly and Kate immediately heard her mother's not-so-hushed questions.

"What did she say? Are they dating? Do they have any other classes together? What about his family? Did she say anything about his family?"

Kate had asked Michael about them less than an hour ago. She worried she had crossed an invisible line. He must have been on overload after meeting so many members of her family. Kate had forgotten there were limits to how much they shared. But Kate knew worrying about what you say is never good for any friendship.

They talked after class on Monday and agreed to meet in his dorm later that day. They each had another paper to write by the end of the term, and they sat around trying to pick a topic he'd actually enjoy. Michael seemed more careful around Kate. Something had changed between them. Kate waited for him to tell her what it was, but he never did. Time passed, they had more study sessions, and Michael was eventually himself again. Kate never found out what had troubled him that night. Michael was that rare species that didn't exist in her family – a private person. She was the open book in their friendship, and Michael read like a mystery with every page she turned.

8

The majority of Montgomery State University coeds were first-generation college students hungry to succeed. Professors indulged them with generous office hours and department chairs networked off campus to ensure jobs were waiting after graduation. Michael escaped modern British literature with a B.

He and Kate continued to study together that following spring even though they didn't share any classes. They would often quiz each other in their respective subjects. Kate was frustrated with her math requirement, so Michael gave her a hand with it. He usually found his way to the Marino house on weekends. He put his arm around Kate once while they were crossing the quad when a bike cut them off without warning. But Michael stayed true to Barb. She still wore his ring, and if he sometimes fantasized about Kate, he figured it was normal because his girlfriend was halfway across the country. Michael continued his weekly Sunday night phone calls home, but it was getting harder to make conversation without including Kate in it. Barb wrote him long letters about the summer plans she was making for the two of them.

Kate helped Michael pack up his room after their junior year ended that May. Barb's picture was still a fixture on his small desk, tucked in the corner of the room. Barb was wearing her cheerleading skirt and sweater, pom poms strategically placed off her hips. Her skin was fair and her perfectly straight blond hair fell to her shoulders. It was draped on either side of her sweater and came to a blunt edge right above the image of the school mascot, a tiger. She was pretty in all the ways Kate knew she never would be.

Michael looked up from packing and caught Kate glancing at the picture. "She was supposed to come here last year," he said.

"Why didn't she?"

"Lots of reasons."

Kate tried to convince herself the three of them would be great friends if Barb had only changed her mind and decided to come east to school like she had promised.

"Does she take classes or work?" This was the longest conversation they'd ever had on the subject of Barbara Jean Wipperman.

"She's taken a few classes, but works full time in Doc Brown's office. She's a receptionist. Maybe she'll start somewhere in the fall. Probably close to home."

"She'll figure it out," Kate said. That was the kind of half-assed spirit that kept her off any cheerleading squad.

Michael's parents let him take his car to campus that spring. He had bought himself a used Ford and made a case for needing one so he could work. True to his word, he stocked shelves at a local grocery store at night after classes.

He planned to leave for Indiana later that day and drive through the night. Kate couldn't imagine her parents letting her drive hundreds of miles by herself. And she was pretty sure she would never want to.

Michael was a slow and methodical packer. Everything he placed in a carton or suitcase was put at specific angles to maximize space, but his clothes were still in the dresser and the closet was a mountain of dirty laundry.

"You sure your folks don't mind storing a few things?"

"No, it's fine," Kate said.

"It's just the rug, TV, and my boom box. You can use it this summer. I have another one at home." Michael stuffed the dirty laundry into his brother's old Army duffel.

"Thanks," Kate said.

Kate felt living on campus was impractical with her house so close, but now as they peeled down the posters and folded the bedding, this small, painted cinder-block room felt like she was leaving a second home where Michael made her tea as they read quietly or listened to music.

"You don't have to drive all the way back to my place," she said. "I can take your stuff."

"No. We stick to the plan. I'll follow you home so I can say goodbye to your folks," he said. The room was almost empty. By tomorrow he'd be with his girlfriend. Michael never pretended there wasn't a Barb in his life, but Kate had pretended not to care and that kept things pleasant. She sat on the bare, stripped mattress.

"Are you okay?" Michael said.

"Yeah, fine, why?" Kate was silently hearing her mother's voice from countless conversations they've had since the first time she brought Michael home.

"What I don't get is how you can know this boy, what – almost a whole year – you go out to eat, to parties, the movies and nothing?"

"We're not going out. We just like being together."

"I like Michael, Katharine, you know that, but he's got a girlfriend. It's not right."

"For the millionth time, Mom, we're friends."

"Does that girl know he practically lives here on weekends?"

"If you don't want Michael around..."

"Of course I want him around. But how can another boy ask you out with him glued to your side? That's all I'm saying. And this girl, Barb, does she know about you?"

"Yeah, I guess," Kate said. But she wasn't sure.

"Unless he's – I don't want to say it."

"Say it, Mom."

"No, it's wrong."

"Ma – what?"

"Okay, maybe, you know, probably not, but do you think he's that way?"

"Gay? Michael's not gay."

"Cause sometimes they don't know till later. My cousin Frankie was forty with two kids. Next thing you know he leaves Sandy for the meat manager at the supermarket."

"I'm late for class." Kate brushed her mother's cheek with a hurried kiss and flew out the door. But now her classes were over for the semester and Michael was leaving her to go home to Barb.

"I hate this shirt. Maybe your mom wants it for a dust rag?" He tossed it at Kate and went back to sorting his laundry.

"Thanks." She threw it in with the stuff going to her house.

"I'll be back mid-August," he said. That's plenty of time for both of us to finish <u>Pet Sematary</u>."

"So, you enjoy reading now?" Kate said.

"No, but there's this girl who's always on me about it. She doesn't quit."

"Between work and catching up with friends, bet you don't crack it open," Kate said.

"Bet you a pizza I finish it first," he replied.

Kate rolled up the Springsteen and Mike Ditka posters, snapping rubber bands around them.

"You mind taking those too? I want them for my apartment next year," he said.

"No problem."

A few scattered pieces of clothing were still on the bed. He picked up one of his socks. He looked like he wasn't sure what to do with it. He held it a long time. Kate was rearranging things in the box she was taking with her.

"I'm breaking up with her, Kate. Barb and I aren't right anymore." Kate's face went warm and she worried Michael would see how long she had wanted to hear those words. "We've talked about the distance – a lot." He fixated on the sock. "It's been coming for a long time." Kate wondered if Barb knew it was coming or if Michael just hoped she did to lessen his guilt. "Say something," he said.

But for one of the few times in her life, Kate didn't know what to say. Michael put his laundry down and took her hand. He sat next to her on the bed. Kate didn't move as he leaned in and kissed her. Michael's lips were soft and caressing. She had thought about kissing him so many times but now that it was happening, none of her fantasies came close to how it felt. He pulled back slightly and whispered, "I love you, Kate."

Kate answered with her mouth on his. She kissed him gently at first and then like a starving woman. Michael's hands moved down her body, their lips never separated. His fingers reached under her t-shirt and touched her breasts, setting off a chain reaction that ignited every nerve in Kate's body. He stopped to lift the shirt over her head and deftly unclasped her bra. He tossed them on the floor beside the bed and smiled as he looked down at Kate. She gave him a nervous grin as he removed his shirt. She had fanaticized about his broad shoulders and chest, and now she reached up and stroked his muscles that were firm and unyielding. He lowered himself onto her and circled her nipples with his tongue. He tickled each tip, lapping at them and sucking them gently until her breath quickened. He unzipped her jeans and reached beneath her panties, caressing the tender folds of her skin. His long body stretched across her and he moved up to kiss her earlobes, her neck, and then the area between her breasts, lingering to explore them again with his mouth. His small tender kisses blazed a path down her abdomen and stopped as he reached her panties. As if in one fluid motion he removed her jeans and they were tossed at the foot of the bed. The throbbing between her legs left her dizzy when Michael's fingers continued to stroke her. Kate took hold of Michael's jeans and tugged at them, and soon they were both lying naked. A few seconds passed when neither of them moved nor spoke. Michael broke the silence.

"Are you sure?" Kate was surer in this moment than she had been of anything in her young life. They kissed again, and now Kate pulled Michael toward her. Her hands explored his body and pleasured him with the same supple movements he had shown her. When Michel finally entered her carefully, Kate felt a sharp, stabbing pain. He stopped.

"No, don't. It's okay," she said. He waited a moment then moved further inside of her. She kissed him and wrapped her legs around his waist while Michael's fingers moved tenderly across her clitoris and when he was completely inside of her, the flash of pain was replaced by waves of pleasure that made Kate moan softly. She was breathing so quickly she felt lightheaded and out of control, until her body undulated in quick rhythms, faster and faster until they were released with an explosive rush. When they were done, she rested in his arms. He laid his hand low on her abdomen. Neither spoke for a long time.

Kate wondered if any girl had ever felt what she was feeling. She decided it was impossible, because this was her passion, and Michael's passion. It could never be the same for anyone else. And that's when she understood the simple truth that everyone's story is different and everyone's love is different. She would never accept that Michael or she could feel this way with anyone else. There may be others, but nothing would come close to what they felt on that hot afternoon in his empty room. And no matter how slow and tender Michael was, it was obvious he knew what he was doing and she didn't. She stayed in his arms a long time.

"Are you okay?" He got a towel to help her clean up. Kate's head was buzzing with questions. "Will my mother be able to tell? Will it always hurt? And why does he have condoms in his room?" But none of those things really mattered to Kate. Michael said he loved her.

Michael was in love without knowing the day, or the hour, or the minute he actually fell in love. It all blended together and grew during the time they had shared over books and coffee and long walks on campus. It happened in the little moments when he opened his dorm room door and hoped it was her, or looked at an empty chair in a classroom and wished Kate were sitting across from him.

Unlike Michael, Kate knew the exact day and time she fell in love with him. And it happened only a couple of weeks after they began studying together. She broke the news she had to cancel an evening study session.

"What's going on?" he asked.

"It's my birthday."

"Why didn't you tell me?" She shrugged.

"I've got a couple dozen relatives coming over to celebrate."

"Really?" He looked confused.

"You know, relatives? People related to you," Kate said.

"I've got relatives, but I'm not sure they'd come over just because it's my birthday," Michael said.

"You're kidding," she said.

"They all have their own kids."

"Yeah, but they love you too."

"Sure, I guess."

That's when Kate feared her family would be like Estonia to him. Beyond knowing it's an actual country, most people have no knowledge of the intimate details of their customs, how they live, work, and play. Those things are known only to other Estonians.

Kate wasn't sure Michael could ever feel comfortable in the middle of the foreign country she called home.

Her family had played cards late into the night on her birthday and she stayed up to help her mother straighten the house after her party.

"Did you have a good time?"

"It was great. Thanks, Ma."

"Twenty now. Nana was married when she was eighteen. Had me a year later."

"That's just crazy."

"You could have invited some friends," she said.

"It's a school night. I'd have to drive them back."

"How's that boy? The one you're helping in English?" she asked.

"Fine. Nice."

"Maybe you want to bring him around."

"I don't think so," Kate said. "But maybe."

Kate was tired the morning after her twentieth birthday party. She was late and everything was going wrong. Her father had to jump-start her car and she barely made it to class on time. Michael was panicked about next week's exam and begged her to squeeze in a quick study session even though it was Friday. She agreed to meet him at four. When Kate finally made her way to Michael's dorm it was already four-thirty. The usual Friday night parties had started early. The smell of tapped beer and cigarettes hung over everything. Michael's door was the only one closed on his wing. He probably gave up on her and went to a party at one of the frat houses. Kate decided to shove a note under the door, go home and sleep till Sunday. But there was already a note taped to his door. "Come in, it's open." When she entered, the room was lit by the glow of twenty candles on top of a small layer cake. Michael had watched her crossing the quad and was ready to surprise her when she got there. There was a balloon bouquet on his desk. He handed her a card that read, "To the girl who saved me from the most boring class of

my life. Happy Birthday, Kate. Your grateful pupil, Michael."
He handed her the balloons, and that's when Kate fell in love
with a boy who was in love with someone else. They ate cake,
read some poetry for class the next week and talked nonstop
until she left.

Seven months later, Kate was in that same room after making
love with Michael for the first time. He had gone down the hall to
the bathroom. Kate was wrapped in his velour robe. She glanced
over at the desk and saw Barb's picture looking back at her with
accusing eyes. Kate felt a wave of shame and embarrassment. On
that afternoon, somewhere in her rush of uncontrolled passion
for Michael, Kate had just become the "other" woman.

Part II

Penetration & Intrusion

9

Kate sat at her desk calmly. Since finding Marilyn Campbell's business card, she had trouble focusing on her next column. She made a list of possible topics. "Secrets" were an overdone choice, but seemed perfect in light of her dilemma. So far she had always managed to put a fresh spin on whatever she'd written, but she also knew the harder she tried to think of something original, the faster her creativity would shut down and leave her in the abyss. The only thing that lived in that place was the chronic fear that her success up till now had been a fluke. One day she'd be discovered and her fans would abandon her in record numbers, the magazine would drop her feature, and she'd be forced to find a real job. No amount of gushing fan mail had managed to erase her fear of the abyss.

Kate had started out at a small weekly advertiser, *Inside Burbs*, where she gushed over the latest offerings at a shoe store or grocery market. The editor thought she had promise and eventually she was a regular contributor. She'd written about anything they assigned and gotten paid next to nothing.

A few months later, she mustered the nerve to approach Philadelphia's largest newspaper and sent Esther Rosen, the Life Style editor, a sample of her work. Esther never got back to her. Kate decided she'd write columns on whatever interested her and keep sending them off to Esther, the formidable head of the most popular section of the paper. Esther was something of a local celebrity. She chaired important charities, her face graced the society page, and she was a personal friend of the mayor. She became Kate's mark. She sent a new sample of her work every two weeks, a column about local traditions, current events, important and not-so-important national issues, whatever interested her at the time. There was never a rejection letter, never a response. Kate didn't know if her pieces were read or tossed in the trash, but she refused to go away.

Something had changed in Kate. She had gone from the passive schoolgirl who escaped in the stories she wrote, to a young woman ready to fight for her words. Kate saw Esther as no worse than the nuns who had once bullied her. If she survived them, she was determined to survive Esther Rosen.

She called to schedule a meeting with Esther, but her secretary explained she was too busy to take the call. Kate once read that you can throw a letter away but you can't throw a person away. She tested that theory and took the train into Philadelphia to make her first appearance at Esther's office. That's when she met Violet Evans.

From the moment she introduced herself, Kate could tell Violet ran the office. She was a sweet and soft-spoken African American woman who possessed the type of serenity that lowered pulses. Kate estimated Violet was probably fifteen years or so older than she was. Violet rang Esther to tell her that Katharine Marino was here to see her. Violet made her name sound important. Kate couldn't hear what Esther said, but when Violet hung up, she smiled and told her that Ms. Rosen was tied up and was sorry she couldn't take the time to see her. Kate was pretty sure the word "sorry" never came up in the conversation. Kate pulled her latest article from her briefcase.

"Could I leave this with you? I'd like Ms. Rosen to read it when she has time."

"Of course," Violet said. "I'll make a copy, and leave one on her desk."

"Thank you." Violet went off to the copy machine. Kate noticed a picture of a handsome boy, just a few years younger than herself on her desk. Violet quickly returned Kate's original and pulled a paper clip from her desk drawer. Kate spotted an issue of the *National Enquirer* tucked away in the drawer along with an impressive variety of candy bars. She guessed Esther Rosen wouldn't be happy with her assistant's taste in scandal rags. Kate left that afternoon feeling she finally had a chance, but she never heard from Esther.

Starting that day, Kate kept the same schedule. She went downtown every other Wednesday with a new column and dropped it off personally. She'd bring Violet some homemade pastries and the latest edition of *Star Magazine* or the *Enquirer*. Esther passed through the area once in a while, but she never acknowledged Kate or her work. She looked past her, onto the next item on her busy agenda. She treated Kate like an out-of-place ottoman she tried not to trip over when she flew in and out of her office. But Violet never wavered. She was always warm and welcoming. She treated Kate with respect.

"Come on over here and show me what you've got today." Violet would look it over, laughing out loud or giving a "uh-uh, that's right" and then in a whisper confide, "Much better than some of the deadbeats they got around here. You keep at it." She always made that second copy and told Kate she'd put it on Esther's desk and Kate believed she did. This went on for almost a year. Kate researched and wrote furiously to meet her self-imposed deadlines. Her bi-monthly train trips into the city to drop off a column had almost become a full-time job. If Tony and Maryann thought she was wasting her time, they never said so. Her parents had perfected the art of total and unconditional support for their girls. They were unique in their circle of friends, most of whom expected their own kids to earn a paycheck straight from the podium on graduation day. Kate's father appreciated the long road. Tony knew what it meant to love what you're doing so much that you would literally do it for free. He wanted his daughters to have that same feeling.

Kate's family was loud and in each other's business. They could be exasperating. Their house was too small for all the people who came and went and the latest drama could amp the volume to unbearable levels, but the one thing that set her family and her parents apart was their absolute faith in each other. Tony and Maryann believed in their daughters, so they believed in themselves. Marie was a teacher and, much to Tony's delight, Theresa was planning on a degree in mathematics. In those early years when she had no car, no money, and no idea if her constant harassment of Esther Rosen would ever pay off, Kate was creatively her happiest. Years later, she discovered every single thing she'd ever written stashed away in the back of her mother's closet. Kate found them one day when she packed up Maryann's clothes, but that's a day she doesn't like to think about.

Her professional courtship of Esther Rosen seemed like a lifetime ago and thinking about Marilyn Campbell's business card made her head hurt and her stomach grumble. Kate went back to the kitchen and pulled out the leftover eggplant parmigiana. This was a morning for comfort food. Kate made hers exactly the way her mother did. Three cheeses with lots of extra sauce. She called it "sauce" now, further proof to her father that she had sold out. She and Michael made a comfortable living. His market research firm employed over twenty people with clients that ranged from small start-ups to Fortune 500 companies. Kate's column was syndicated nationally in a prominent news magazine and she squeezed in a few speaking engagements a year for several thousand dollars an appearance. She polished off the eggplant and decided her column would have to wait. She thought of calling her sisters to discuss her quandary, but they would go off the deep end and bring Marilyn Campbell down like a suspected terrorist. Even Marilyn didn't deserve the collective wrath of the Marino sisters.

Kate tried to give the morning a positive spin. She always loved a juicy story and now she had one brewing on her desk. She fantasized about Michael missing the card and being thrown into a panic, emptying drawers and shaking his pants inside out with a wild look in his eye. Michael, careful in everything he did around the house and in the office, meticulous in almost every detail except obviously emptying his pockets, never liked loose ends or any kind of mess, and if there is one thing a suspected mistress can become it's a big mess. Just ask Tiger Woods. But Kate was getting ahead of herself and too quick to assume the worst of a man she'd lived with for over two decades. It was the card's fault. It resurrected old insecurities that Kate thought she had buried long ago. Now they were bubbling to the surface along with the haunting feeling that something wasn't right in her marriage. Maybe it hadn't been right for a long time. Months of emotional isolation from Michael and her simmering discontent seemed understandable because of Michael's travel and her constant deadlines. Wasn't it true most couples their age seldom spoke about anything but the house and the kids? Kate wasn't upset when their getaway to Bermuda was canceled because one of Michael's business trips had to be rescheduled. It just became too complicated to rearrange their entire lives to make sure Bermuda happened.

But Kate knew that in marriages, isolation comes in pairs. Passing each other in the house without acknowledgment or silently staring at the television before falling asleep became a pattern, that became a habit, and was now a lifestyle. The changes came slowly and unnoticed, disguised as mature love wrapped in a happy marriage. Kate hadn't realized how much she missed passion in her life until she opened that tiny brown envelope. She worried that Michael missed it too and had gone to look for it somewhere else. She grabbed her gym bag and decided it was time to work off the eggplant parm and get her head in a better place. She called her trainer from the car. Luckily Justin had an hour open.

She threw the bag in the backseat and lazily pulled out of the driveway. Kate loved driving, and it didn't matter where or for how long. Behind the wheel, her life was suspended between here and there. She wasn't at a specific place where she had to do a specific task. She rarely answered her cell phone while driving unless it was the kids. Music was kept low and if she was hit by a burst of inspiration, she'd pull over and jot down her ideas on her phone's Notes App. Until an hour ago, Kate's life, like her marriage, was on cruise control, but now she had no idea how it would play out. She made a left onto Meadowbrook Boulevard, struck by the beauty of the poplar trees that lined it. Shades of gold created a warm canopy over the narrow road as Kate made her way to the gym.

It was years ago when Kate was lying in bed on a lazy Saturday morning as bright and crisp as this, gazing at the huge maple outside her window, when she heard her mother squealing from the kitchen.

"Kate! Katharine Elena Marino get down here this instant!" Kate thought Nana had died in her sleep or one of her sisters had a car accident. She threw on a sweatshirt and flew down the stairs.

"Ma, what's wrong?"

Her mother's face was buried behind the morning paper.

"Is it Nana?" Maryann lowered the paper and smiled.

"You did it, baby. You wore that Esther Rosen down. Look, you're famous." She handed Kate the paper and there it was. Her first column with a byline had finally been published. "I have to call your Aunt Millie. She won't believe it." But the phone was already ringing and it rang all day. Every single person even remotely related to the Marinos called to congratulate Maryann and Tony.

Her check arrived a few days later with a personal note from Esther Rosen. Kate almost fell over when she saw the amount. Esther called and they met to discuss ideas Kate had for future columns. Violet had a bouquet of flowers waiting for her when she stepped off the elevator. Esther never mentioned the year she ignored Kate. She was too busy promoting her hottest new find and Kate was savvy enough not to make waves. The topic of her first column was, "Where Did All the Good Men Go?"

10

Kate found a parking spot right in front of the gym. There was plenty of time to squeeze in her workout before Michael left for Dallas. Kate thought he was doing research for a drug company, but she wasn't sure. Lately it seemed all of the products he worked on were for depression. She had suggested to Michael they just call them happy pills; it covered all the angles. Who wouldn't want to take one of those? Kate wished she had her own private stash right now.

She was alone in the personal training studio. Her arms rowed, her feet peddled and her mind raced on the elliptical machine. Up and down, round and round. She tried to purge her pre-holiday anxiety. It would all get done. One mile down, fifteen pounds of potatoes to be peeled. It would all get done. Three huge casseroles of string beans almandine. It would all get done. She moved with the words. In five minutes, Justin would put her through her paces and exhaust her to the point where her brain would be numb. She had tried meditation and yoga, but failed to reach inner peace.

She'd started with imagining a white cloud drifting across a pale blue sky and ended up obsessing over paint colors for the living room and did Jake have a clean gym uniform?

The workout studio was different. She moved, lifted, and sprinted, doing shoulder presses and lunges until it evaporated the to-do lists, work demands, and constant worries that camped in her mind. Kate's trainer was young enough to be her son, if she had foolishly gotten pregnant in college, which to her parents' delight, she did not. Justin was twenty-five, with the wisdom of someone twice his age, if you bought into the theory that age actually brings wisdom. Kate found most people became less wise with age. They drank more and took the people they loved most for granted. Couples she and Michael had known for years had thrown away some pretty good marriages and families for the chance to "finally have 'me' time." Her best friend Sharon's husband left because he couldn't handle the constant pressures of parenthood. He screwed around with his secretary and now had a new baby. He'll never retire if he wants to put that kid through college. Karma – Kate thought. Maybe she'd revisit mediation after all.

Justin's two tours of duty in Iraq beat the bullshit out of him. He told the truth and not what people wanted to hear. Kate's energy was low. It was either the eggplant or Marilyn Campbell.

"Why are you a wimp today?"

"What, fifteen pound weights are wimpy?"

"For you, yeah. Your head is not in the game, Kate. Get it there."

"Do you have a girlfriend, Justin?"

"Sure, why?"

"Do you trust her?"

"As much as I trust anybody."

"What does that mean?" Kate really wanted to know.

"It means you trust yourself first – your instincts, your strengths, your weaknesses. If you know what you trust in yourself, you'll see if you trust it in others. The real question is, 'have they earned your trust?' Now give me a set of walking lunges. Let's go." It all sounded so sane and reasonable when Justin said it. But Kate had no idea if she even followed his logic. Trust had become a word she took for granted in her marriage.

She got serious about her workout and finished with five of the best push-ups she'd ever done. Kate hadn't thought of the woman behind the business card in over an hour. She toyed with telling Justin about Marilyn to get his opinion on what she should do. It would be safe since he didn't know any of the players, except for her and what she had told him about Michael. She held back and decided it was too soon. She knew that words, spoken or written, made things real and she wasn't ready for any of this to be real. Kate made an appointment to come back in a couple of days. Justin wanted her to eat more protein since her weight was inching up again. She promised to try but Tuesday was pasta night.

She reached for her jacket and noticed triceps. They had definite form. Her time with Justin was paying off. Kate had a conference call in an hour and still wasn't sure how she'd explain to her editor she had great arms but not a single idea on a topic for her column. She zipped up her fleece against the cool November wind.

"Have a good one, Kate." Justin was already on the computer, ticking off how many sessions he had left for the day. Kate's head was down as she held the door for his next client.

"I'm here for my complimentary first session." The door was already half closed. "Marilyn Campbell?"

Kate's head spun around. Did she say Marilyn or Carolyn? Was it Campbell or Castor? Her mind had already shifted to the canned yams on sale at the grocery store, so she wasn't paying attention. She looked in through the glass storefront, but Justin's massive shoulders shielded the woman. The light was all wrong. Kate couldn't make out any details, except for a familiar smell lingering in the air.

Kate resisted the urge to rush back in and check Justin's workout schedule. The odds were lottery-sized that it would be <u>the</u> Marilyn Campbell. Even if it were, what would she say? "It's a pleasure to meet you. I found your business card in my husband's pants?" She was stressed and hearing things. She would casually mention the new client to Justin at her next session and find out what he knew about her. It would be bad enough if Marilyn Campbell had moved in on Michael, now she wanted Justin too?

Kate made a quick pit stop at the grocery store next to the gym and grabbed eight cans of yams before the store ran out. Canned yams were every Thanksgiving hostess' dirty little secret, playing the role of the homemade specialty while the truth was buried in the recycling bin in the garage. She'd doctor them with brown sugar and butter, but her sisters were on to her, and thought a canned yam was sacrilegious, even though Thanksgiving isn't a religious holiday. Theresa always offered to make them from scratch, but Kate held firm to her devotion to canned yams. People only took one or two anyway, and they'd have to heave a lot more onto their plates to motivate her to peel those filthy things. She loaded up the cart and decided to leave the rest of the shopping for Michael. At the very least, a large can of yams makes a convenient weapon if the Marilyn Campbell conversation got out of hand.

She took a quick shower and settled in at her computer to Google Marilyn. Her first hit was the advertising agency Lewis, Kramer, DiMayo & Campbell. She clicked on their website and there was a smiling picture of the four of them, a tall attractive blond in the center of three older men. She tried to enlarge the picture but it wouldn't budge. She scrolled through the entire website but it was short on pictures and long on accomplishments. Marilyn's profile had the company logo and a headshot. She scrolled down the page. There was professional experience, client testimonials, and a list of awards. Kate scrolled back up to the photo. Marilyn was strikingly beautiful. Kate's magazine had recently updated the photo that accompanied her column. She wished they hadn't but her publisher was insistent. Her old image was a dozen years old and it was time.

A dozen years ago, Kate was still holding Jake's hands as he tiptoed between her legs eager to walk on his own. Unlike Laura, who was practically conceived by mental telepathy, Jake was an entirely different story.

Laura was a cautious child who spoke early and often and didn't take a step until she was sure she wouldn't fall. She was patient and mature, eating politely in restaurants from the time she could sit up in a high chair. She said "please" and "thank you" and didn't believe in making a mess. All-in-all it was as if they had ordered the dark-haired, blue-eyed beauty with the all-inclusive good manners and pleasant, no-mess personality from a catalog. Michael was as smitten with her as Kate. He worked more from home, and was so thrilled with fatherhood he took it as a sign they were destined to have more. Destiny had other plans. Soon after Laura's first birthday, Kate and Michael decided to try again. They wanted their kids to be close in age, but no amount of good thoughts, positive thinking, sex, prayer, or fertility pills helped. It was as if conceiving Laura had been a fluke. After three years of trying, Kate still wasn't pregnant. The doctor called it secondary infertility. Kate and Michael thought it sounded more like a made up condition than a real medical problem.

"It's my fault," Kate said. They had just made love and both were tense, already worried about the outcome.

"None of this is your fault."

"I said I never wanted kids."

"You were twenty."

"God remembers."

"God's got other things on His mind, like war and starvation..."

"Don't piss me off, okay?"

"I'm just saying you were young. You didn't know how great you'd be at it, Kate. And you are." Calm, patient, methodical Michael tried to convince her that guilt wouldn't solve anything. She had to let it go. That was easy for him to say, he wasn't Catholic.

The more time went by, the more Michael lost patience with Kate's anxiety and the constant pressure of trying to conceive. The shame that this was somehow his failure ate away at him. They had a bitter argument one night when she accused him of not wanting another child. He stormed out of the house. After that, sex became on demand, scheduled, and routine. Many nights Michael retreated to his office drained by conversations that revolved around wanting to be pregnant, getting pregnant, body temperature, and maximizing ovulation. Months passed without having sex just for the fun of it.

Kate avoided taking Laura to the playground. Seeing other mothers juggling toddlers and infants, those with multiples of children living in that swirling world of confusion stung because Kate feared that would never be her world. She was worn out and tired. Thinking about what she couldn't have eventually sapped most of the good out of the life she did have. Her cycle became more erratic. One month she was a week late. Then two weeks turned into three, that became a month. She finally bought a home pregnancy test, not sure she could stand to look at the results. Kate sat on the bathroom floor and cried when the stick turned pink. It was positive; she was finally pregnant again. She and Michael celebrated quietly and told their parents and siblings. She started on her prenatal vitamins and had a due date. After a couple of weeks, Kate had an ultrasound to check implantation. Everything was going smoothly. The following month, they told Laura she was going to be a big sister and the month after that, Kate had a routine check up. Life had returned to normal and she and Michael found joy again. During her next visit, the doctor put the probe on her midsection to hear the baby's rapid-fire heartbeat. Dr. Rodgers' smile faded. She moved the probe around in a circular motion. Michael squeezed Kate's hand tightly, but Kate felt like someone had driven a nail through her heart. Dr. Rodgers suggested a quick ultrasound. Michael whispered in Kate's ear that everything was fine. It was just a precaution. Kate didn't speak as the cold jelly was lathered across her skin. The muted images, the abstract and unformed steaks of gray and white that were her baby appeared on the screen. She heard the doctor murmur, "unviable." Tears escaped Kate's eyes and ran into her ears as she lay perfectly still on the table. Three days later, Kate went in for an outpatient procedure to have the fetus removed. She was home in just a few hours. An entire future of dreams she had for a child she'd never know was gone on a random and rainy morning. Her sisters came over with meals and took Laura back to their house for sleepovers. They called Michael's mother to tell her what had happened.

"Just thank God for what you have," Edith said. "Should I come out?" They thanked her for her offer but told her they were fine. Edith's practical approach to life's problems conflicted with Kate's raw emotional outbursts, but this was how Michael's mother gave comfort. Translating Edith had become easier over the years. She was telling Kate to enjoy Laura and not to mourn what wasn't meant to be. But Kate still didn't understand why phrases like, "I'm sorry" and "I love you" were so difficult for Edith.

Work saved Kate in those days. Her creativity was fueled by anything that was happening outside of her womb. She wrote constantly and the instant an idea hit her, she'd dive into the research and have another column ready to go as soon as her editor gave his approval. She eventually became more engaged in the world around her and was nominated for an award for her piece on the battle for universal health care. Kate went back to enjoying wine and eating fast food. She broke the cycle of anticipation and devastation. It had pulled her and Michael down into a dark place that made them angry at each other and unable to be the parents their little girl needed. She returned to her three mugs of regular coffee in the morning without an ounce of guilt. She was relieved to be done with it.

And then, one morning Kate recognized an unusual sensation she had only experienced twice before in her life. She casually drove to the pharmacy without telling Michael and for the second time in a year, Kate was pregnant. She had prayed for a miracle and now it had been granted without fertility treatments or ovulation kits. She dismissed Michael's explanation that, "Sometimes, things just happen."

But miracles obviously come with a price. Kate was sick from day one and grateful for every nauseous morning. Her world had balance: life, work, and family. She exercised, drank plenty of milk and, once the nausea subsided, she felt better than she had when she carried Laura.

Kate was asleep when the mild cramping started. She woke Michael up immediately. She was spotting. They called the doctor and went to see her first thing in the morning. She assured Kate everything seemed fine, but recommended a new procedure to assess risk that could be done months before she'd be able to have an amniocentesis. It would rule out any chromosomal abnormalities and possible complications with the baby. There was a one in a hundred chance it could cause a miscarriage. Kate was torn between wanting a guarantee that her baby was healthy and the fear of losing her miracle. Michael pointed out that if they had a ninety-nine percent chance of winning the lottery, they'd play more often, so she agreed to have the procedure.

Once again, Kate found herself flat on her back with bright lights blinding her; powerless to control the outcome or have any say in what would happen next. It was slightly more uncomfortable than a routine gynecological exam but was over very quickly. Kate didn't spot afterward and she never had another cramp. She went home and put her feet up to wait for the results that the doctor warned would take days. She closed her eyes and channeled every self-help book she had read for various columns over the years. All we have is the moment. And in the moment all is well. The past can't be changed and the future doesn't exist. She had tried her entire life to embrace calmness and dispel fear, but that was someone else's life. Hers was spent hoping for guarantees that she knew did not exist, but it didn't keep her from praying for them.

"It's perfectly normal to be scared. You've had a miscarriage and then the spotting," Michael said.

"I know, I know."

"Remember what the doctor said. No one is expecting a problem."

"We didn't expect a problem the last time."

Michael gave up arguing with her and went downstairs as she drifted off to sleep. An hour later, he shook her awake. His face was close to hers.

"Kate, Kate – wake up."

"What's wrong? Is it Laura?"

"Laura's fine."

"Did the doctor call?"

"No, it's not about the baby." Michael paused in that way that never brings good news. "Honey, it's Grandpa Joe. He's had a stroke." Michael didn't move. Why wasn't he moving?

"We have to get to the hospital. What time is it?" she asked. But Michael didn't budge.

"The paramedics tried, but it was too late. I'm sorry, honey, he's gone."

Gone where – was Kate's first thought. She had talked to him the night before and he wished her luck. He said he couldn't wait to be a great-grandfather again. He was old, but the kind of old that was still interested in the world. He didn't retreat into complaints about his chronic aches and pains. If he didn't feel well, a couple of glasses of wine usually cured it. Kate had to get out of bed. She had to go to her father. He would need her. Later that day, they met at the house to make the arrangements. Kate sensed the words Tony wanted to say, so she relieved him of the burden and asked if she could speak at Grandpa Joe's funeral.

"It's okay, Dad. I feel fine. I want to, please?"

"No, you have enough on your mind."

"It'll take my mind off of the baby." Kate wasn't being noble. She couldn't think of anything worse than shutting herself away from her family in her grief to watch the clock and wait for her phone to ring. Her father had tears of gratitude and held her tightly.

The next day, Kate and her sisters sifted through the debris of Joe Marino's life. They went through his box of papers. Her grandfather saved everything. His naturalization documents, his passport with King Victor Emmanuel on the cover. The only thing they obviously weren't so rigid about in the old country was naming their children. They sorted through his lockbox and found out Grandpa Joe, wasn't a "Joe" at all. His first name was actually John. John Joseph Marino. There was no birth certificate, no record of schooling, but his passport was issued as John, and his wedding certificate listed him as Joseph. They were apparently interchangeable. For every piece of paper they found with one name on it, like his first mortgage, they'd find another, like his will, with the other name. So Grandpa Joe, or John, left a little mystery behind along with four thousand dollars in a savings account and a twenty thousand dollar savings bond to pay for his funeral. Tony and his brothers would inherit what was left. Kate tucked away the name confusion maze for a future column.

The morning of the funeral was a gorgeous spring day. The bright sunshine evaporated the dew before they stepped out of the house. Long, black Cadillac limousines took Kate and her family to the church. Kate didn't recognize some of the mourners that had no connection to her or the family but who cried tears of grief as if they were saying goodbye to a loved one. Many were younger than she expected. After the Mass, a man who looked like he was in his late thirties came up to her in the narthex. His suit had a worn sheen and the soles of his shoes were paper-thin. He hugged her and began to sob. He introduced himself as Paul Scorzetti. His grandfather and Grandpa Joe had been close friends when they lived in South Philly. Paul told Kate her grandfather had picked up his mortgage payment when he was laid off last year. He talked about how Joe never forgot the old neighborhood. Groceries would appear on someone's doorstep when there was an illness. If someone were struggling financially, their child's tuition to the local Catholic school would be mysteriously paid. There were a half-dozen Grandpa Joe stories from people she'd never met before and would never see again.

After the burial and the luncheon, Kate went home and headed for their bedroom to get out of her shoes and off her feet. Laura was with a friend so Kate decided to pick up a book. She looked at the pages, but couldn't concentrate on the words. The twin demons of fear and anxiety that she recognized from childhood had returned. They frightened her with unspoken words like "what if." "What if there's something wrong with this baby?" "What if her friend wasn't watching Laura and she ran into a busy street?" "What if?" "What if?" "What if?" Michael lay on the bed next to her and gently rubbed her back. He recognized Kate's struggle with the demons over the years and knew it was his job to cast them out.

"Do you want to talk?" She shook her head. "I'll drive over and get Laura. You rest."

"Thanks."

"Kate, why don't I call the doctor, see if they got any results." She turned over and faced him.

"It's Friday. Nobody'll be there," she said.

"It won't hurt to try."

The phone number with the post-test precaution sheet was on her nightstand. Michael walked around the bed and dialed. He got the recorded message. "We're sorry. The office of Doctors

McNabb, Rodgers, and Thompson is closed for the day. Our normal office hours are Monday through Friday, nine to four-thirty. If this is an emergency, hang up and dial 911 immediately. If not, please call back or leave a detailed message at the tone." Michael hung up. "Sorry, honey, they're gone for the day."

She closed her eyes as if the simple motion would rid her of the terrifying thoughts that left no room in her mind for anything positive or good to exist. Michael put her book on the nightstand and spooned her body into his. They didn't speak. Kate was sure the demons never visited Michael.

She fixated on a small crack in the ceiling. She imagined it spreading into a spider web of chipped paint and rotting plaster. The intricate pattern would fan out from the small imperfection into a maze of slow-moving destruction, eventually overtaking the entire area above the bed, moving outward toward the borders of the ceiling, down the walls, crumbling and crumbling. Thousands of spider webs moving faster along the plaster till it turned to dust and smothered her.

She didn't react to the phone at first. Michael reached over her and picked it up. "Hello?" He sat up. "Oh, hi, no, it's her husband. Sure, of course, just a sec." He covered the mouthpiece. "Kate, it's Dr. Rodgers. She wants to talk to you." Kate hesitated before taking the phone.

"Hello?"

"Hi, Kate. The lab called me after hours with your results." The air left the room. She was alone with the crumbling plaster and a rush of silent ejaculate prayers left over from Our Lady of Perpetual Help that gave her the strength to fight the demons as a child. Dr. Rodgers broke the silence.

"Congratulations, you're having a healthy baby boy."

"Thank you, Jesus. Thank you, Jesus. Thank you, Jesus," she repeated silently in her head.

"Kate, what's going on?" Michael whispered.

"Kate? Are you there?" Dr. Rodgers' voice was rushed.

"You're sure? It's a boy?" she said.

Michael leaned in closer.

"The X and Y are lined up. Kate, I've got to run, but everything points to a perfectly healthy baby. I'll fill you in on all the results when I see you next week. Go out and celebrate. This is good news. Bye." Michael took the phone. He was crying.

"It's a boy," she said. "He's okay. He's okay." Michael held her close. "How about John Joseph McAllister," she said. She cried tears of joy and relief.

"How about we call him Jake for short," Michael said.

"Jake for short," she agreed. Michael kissed her softly and for the first time in over a week, the demons faded away and the cracks in the ceiling disappeared.

11

"What's this doing here?" Michael called out from Kate's office. Her family was always passing through looking for something they had dumped there – mail, keys, school bulletins. A few months ago, when Kate threatened to gather all of it up, drive over to Michael's office and dump it on his desk, he got defensive.

"That makes no sense," Michael said.

"It makes perfect sense. This is my place of work. It may be in our home, but it's still where I work."

"It's the mail, Kate."

"No, it's junk, Michael. Everybody's junk. The junk nobody else has time to deal with. Estimates, field trip notices, school projects. This is where it all comes to die."

"All right. We'll find another spot for that stuff."

"Where?"

"Jesus, Kate. I don't know. A spot."

But they never found a spot, and her desk continued to disappear under the constant avalanche. She walked into her office. Michael's carry-on bag was packed and in the doorway.

"What's what, doing where?"

This." He was holding the business card. Kate feigned nonchalance.

"The dry cleaner found it in one of your suits. It was stapled to the bag. I didn't want to forget to give it to you. I wasn't sure if it was important."

"Thanks." He pocketed the card. "Let's go grab a bite. I'm starving." Michael willed his heart rate to slow down. He was careful to keep his speech even.

"Now?"

"Why not? We'll have lunch together before I have to leave for the airport."

"But Jake..."

"...Is in school. You'll be home before the bus." Michael hadn't suggested they do anything together, let alone in the middle of the day, for a very long time.

"I would like some time with my wife. Please?"

"I have to change." Kate saw the physical changes come over her husband. He wanted to end this conversation.

"Kate, you look fine."

"I don't look fine. I look like somebody's mother. I'll be down when I look like somebody's wife."

Kate walked out and ducked behind the doorframe. She peeked back into her office. Michael took out the business card. He looked at it, then flipped it over and reread Marilyn's message. He rubbed his hands over his face and sat down on the small loveseat to wait for Kate.

Ristorante Primavera was a fixture in Valley Forge. Beyond the three thousand acres of national park was a quaint town. Good economy or bad economy, Primavera served up pasta and brick-oven pizza to its loyal customers. She and Michael knew

Umberto, the owner, Antonio, the maitre' d, and DeWitt, their favorite waiter. They sat in their usual section. This is where they celebrated birthdays, anniversaries, and good report cards. They gazed out the window from their table that overlooked town square with its large bronze statue of General "Mad" Anthony Wayne perched on his horse.

Neither mentioned Marilyn's card. Instead they discussed Jake's grades and Kate's frustration with her latest column. Michael called for DeWitt and ordered a bottle of wine.

"In the middle of the day?" Kate said.

"Why not?" DeWitt went off to get a 2004 Chianti as Michael glanced at the menu.

"You'll figure the column out, hon. You always do."

Kate was sure Michael had stopped reading her columns long ago. They seldom sparked a reaction in him. Years earlier she got into an argument with his mother when Edith mentioned Laura was watching too much television. Kate had then let it fly in a column about boundaries and parenting in general. Her sarcasm got the better of her. The subject was in-laws, a hot button that started off objectively but got very personal as Kate went on. Her editor loved the edgy tone and pushed it further than Kate intended.

Michael found out about it when his mother called in a fury. Kate apologized, but damage had been done. Kate made the column a turning point in her relationship with Edith and Carl. She was embarrassed by the tone she set and decided she'd work harder to appreciate them for who they were rather than be angry for who they would never be. And if Kate wasn't the ideal mate for their son, she was stunned by the joy they found in their grandchildren. They laughed and played games with Laura and Jake. There was no end to their patience in explaining a complicated card game and when Jake finally beat Carl at cribbage, the laughter could be heard throughout the house. After many years, Kate made it a habit to never end a conversation without saying she loved them. It wasn't the love she knew growing up, but it was true and faithful. And if nothing else, it was light-years away from where they started.

She and Michael had been together over eight months when she made her first visit to the McAllister farmhouse. He wanted her to go home with him the day after Christmas. Michael stayed in Pennsylvania after the fall term ended and spent the holiday with the Marinos. Their plan was to drive back to Indiana on the twenty-sixth. Thinking about it now, Kate was sure it had hurt his mother when he didn't go home. She knew how she'd feel if Laura decided to share her Christmas with another family. But they were young and in love and being apart was out of the question.

Kate didn't want to go to Indiana, but she owed it to Michael for spending Christmas with her family. She bought gifts for his parents and his brother and sister-in-law. They left very early in the morning. The drive out was uneventful except for a flash blizzard in Ohio. The squall passed quickly and they made it to the farm later that night.

The farmhouse was bathed in moonlight. Michael's description didn't do justice to the stark white clapboards and wrap-around porch. The bold red door set off the white house against the white snow. The porch floor was painted gray. It was freezing and the McAllisters had their exterior holiday lights on. Kate felt like she had stepped into a Christmas card. It had been cold and rainy in Philadelphia, but the McAllister home looked magical. Michael put his arm around her as they walked up the porch steps. Everything seemed warm and inviting. And then she walked through the door.

Mr. and Mrs. McAllister were watching television and got up to greet them. The floors were covered with large braided rugs, and a wallpaper mural of a woman waving from a bridge covered an entire wall. Edith extended her hand.

"Nice to meet you, Kate." Kate shook her hand, and then did the same with her husband Carl. Edith explained that tomorrow the extended family was coming over for their official Christmas dinner. It had just been the two of them and Dick and his wife on the actual holiday. A wave of guilt washed over Kate. Carl quickly excused himself to go to bed, explaining he had to get up early for the morning milking. Edith asked if they were hungry. Kate helped her put sandwich meats out as Michael brought their bags in from the car.

When the dishes were washed and put away, they went to collect their suitcases from their resting place by the front door. Weeks before their visit, Kate told Michael she wouldn't be comfortable staying in the same room with him, but he insisted his parents would be fine with it. Michael promised to talk to them just to be sure, so she had nothing to worry about. He'd handle it.

Edith took Kate's bag. "I have Dick's old room all ready for you."

Michael finally spoke, "Mom, I think we'll share my room." This was obviously news to Edith.

"Michael," Edith said.

"We'll stay in my room, Mom."

Kate broke the stalemate. "No, we won't, Michael. Dick's room will be fine." But it was out there. Edith knew they were having sex and she glanced at Kate, and then leveled Michael with a sharp look.

"Your brother's room is fine." Kate repeated.

"I want us together," Michael said, but Kate stood her ground. Edith still had her bag and Kate followed her to the back hallway without saying another word to Michael. She and Edith exchanged an awkward, "goodnight." Kate slipped on her pajamas quickly and got into bed. The room was painted a deep tan. It had two twin beds and a dresser. There was a quilt at the foot of the bed and she pulled it up to her chin to stay warm. Kate was angry and confused. Ice had formed on the windowpanes and the wind rattled them when it gusted loudly across the fields, its force severed and made stronger by the house as if it was angry because the building stood in its way. Kate waited, but Michael never came to talk about what had just happened. She was suddenly as homesick as she had been back in her early school days. She missed the sounds of home. She missed her father hugging them goodnight and the new stereo playing the Goodyear Tire Christmas Album featuring Andy Williams and Johnny Mathis. She missed the way her mother would sing along to "It's the Most Wonderful Time of the Year." Just yesterday, her aunts, uncles, and cousins were jammed into their small dining room with the table that spilled out into the living room almost reaching the front door. The house echoed with their voices. "The turkey is overdone." "No, it's perfect." "I can't eat another bite." "Where are the figs and nuts?" Presents were passed around. Maryann bragged about the candlesticks Michael gave her. She placed them on the hutch so all the aunts could fawn over them.

Kate kept expecting Michael to show up in the frigid farmhouse bedroom and apologize for putting her through that scene with his mother. She wanted him to explain why he hadn't talked to his parents after he promised Kate he would. Shivering under the weight of the homemade covers, Kate realized it was the first time since they'd met that Michael had lied to her.

The next afternoon his Uncle Roy, Aunt May, Uncle Peter and Aunt Janine and their two daughters, along with Michael's brother Dick and his wife Karen came for dinner. After talking about the weather and the drive out, things grew quiet. They sat down to dinner at noon and Kate noticed Michael's Uncle Roy followed her movements as if she were an exhibit at the zoo. Michael was busy catching up on the local gossip and talking Bears football with his brother. By the time food was served, Kate was taking long breaths trying to quell the nausea she recognized from so many years ago when she was alone and scared in a new place. Michael's father said grace. When he finished, Kate made the sign of the cross. Old habit. Uncle Roy pointed a bony finger at her from across the table.

"Look, she makes the sign of the cross." He might as well have said, "Look, she sucks the blood out of little children."

Edith jumped in and explained. "It's just that we don't have any Catholics in Elna, Kate, or any of your kind of people really. We're simply not used to it." Kate stared at her plate, not sure how to even respond. Michael was helping himself to a third portion of red cabbage.

"I hope you like it," Edith said. "Michael mentioned you eat pork. You do eat pork?" Kate nodded. It was a good thing she ate pork because Edith dressed it up so many ways during their visit it was mind-boggling: pork chops, pork steaks, pork loaves, pork tenderloin. She looked over at Michael, who was busy filling his plate. Later that night she tried to talk to him about how uncomfortable she had felt.

"Jesus, it's just the way they are, Kate. Not everybody's like your family." He grew more silent over the next couple of days. She remembered the ride back to school after his first dinner at her house when she asked about his family. She had seen his mood change as he retreated into himself. But this was worse. This silence was heavy enough to push her farther and farther away from him.

Kate was cold during that visit. Cold when she woke up, cold during the day, and definitely cold in her room at night. Carl bragged that his fireplace insert could heat the entire house. "No need to keep that thermostat over fifty-five. Our last power bill was thirty dollars – thirty dollars! You don't get those kind of bills back east, I'll tell you." He pounded the table for emphasis but there was little warmth in that house. It was weighted down by a shared and chronic pessimism as they found fault with everything from the economy to local politics, from the weather to the prices of things they dreamed of buying but were certain they never would. Hardship was worn like a badge in Elna. It took years for Kate to understand that being at the mercy of nature, crop survival, and the fluctuations in supply and demand had made optimism a trap. A strong year of good crops and profits could be ruined in one afternoon by a tornado or washed away after a week of torrential rain. Years of working from pre-dawn to late in the evening had worn Michael's parents down. If they didn't have time to indulge in expressing themselves, it wasn't because they didn't love their son; it was because filling his head with romantic ideas about life wouldn't help him when things went wrong. And something always went wrong.

At the end of the week, Michael and Kate headed back east. She couldn't wait to be home again and except for a quick flurry of pictures at their college graduation, it was over five years before Kate saw Michael's parents again.

Now as Kate observed her husband over the lunch table, she was as desperate to draw more conversation out of him as she had been on that first visit to Indiana.

"How do you think he'll do?"

"Who?" Michael asked.

"Jake. In high school next year."

"Fine. Why?"

"He seems too young."

"He's not. He's ready." Michael checked his watch.

"So what's up in Dallas?"

"Not much. An HIV drug." Michael sopped up his large roll with olive oil sprinkled with salt, pepper, and Romano cheese. A drop of oil bounced off his tie.

"Son of a bitch." Michael dipped his napkin in water and blotted it against his tie.

"Did you pack an extra?" Kate asked.

"Two." He gave up on the tie. "I meet with the client tonight. Research tomorrow and Thursday, back on Friday." Kate set her timetable. She had two full days to figure out if a tornado was heading her way.

Kate polished off the smoked salmon in a blush sauce. She had ordered a half portion; trying to adhere to whatever calorie limit she set for herself that day. Michael poured her another glass of Chianti.

"How's your pasta?" Not that he seemed interested.

"Fine. I picked up the yams for Thanksgiving," she said.

"I told you I'd do it. We've got plenty of time."

"Not really," Kate said.

"What do we need?"

"It's goddamn Thanksgiving, Michael. What do you think we're serving?"

He put his fork down and glared at her. "What the hell's your problem?"

"I'm sorry." Kate retreated to safer ground. "I'm stuck on my column. Jake's tanked his last two math tests and I can't wait to see Laura.". "I talked to her this morning. She sounds great," he said.

"You did? "

"She called while I was at the office. She's happy. Her classes are going well."

Michael's tone suggested there was nothing his calm presence couldn't process and smooth over whenever Kate's hysteria resurfaced. When they were younger, she adored listening to his soft voice as he held her and whispered that they were stronger than anything life threw at them. But now they were long past working toward that bigger house and the ongoing and never-ending responsibility of small children. It was close to being just the two of them across the table again, but this time without the rush of youth and expectation. It had been replaced by an unsettling loneliness that had grown slowly between them, and it was as if neither could figure out if they should cast it out or welcome it into their lives as the way of their future.

When the kids were younger Kate practically lived in her car, driving Laura to lacrosse, piano, and voice lessons. Jake still had soccer and needed rides to golf practice and swimming, but her calendar was no longer the maze of which child was doing what where. There were long stretches then when the only conversation with her husband was over a quick kiss on his way in or out the door or a late-night phone call from airports between cities. There was just enough time to get the essentials said. "Did the plumber fix the sink?" "Did the bills get paid?" When he was home, it took days to fold him back into their daily routine. The only person who kept Kate sane and the loneliness at bay back then, just as she did now, was Violet Evans.

12

Kate always had two snapshots of Violet in her mind. The first image was of the kind woman with a soft voice that she met at the newspaper. Everything about Violet was soft then, as if she had deflected or absorbed life's harshest blows and learned how to live outside or above them. The second time they met, Violet was tired.

Twenty-five years of working with Esther Rosen had its share of highs and lows, but the last year had been lower than Violet could have ever imagined. She was still deeply loyal to Esther, who fought for every raise and promotion she'd been given at the paper. It was Esther who encouraged Violet to go to night school and get an associate degree in business. And when Violet's son, Greg, needed a letter of recommendation to the University of Pennsylvania, it was Esther Rosen, Class of '59, who wrote it.

Greg was born smart, reading by the time he was three. His teachers sent home letters praising him from elementary school right through Masterman High School. He graduated at the top of his class with near-perfect SAT scores. Greg was set on going to Penn, but the thought of the Ivy League was in that same bucket of dreams where Violet kept her trip to Fiji – a beautiful but impossible fantasy. They'd gone back and forth about it dozens of times in their small condo.

"I'm just saying there's lots of good schools, baby."

"Penn is right for me."

"They don't take but a handful of kids."

"My counselor thinks I've got a shot."

"Your counselor doesn't pay the tuition."

This wasn't the message Violet wanted to send her son. She raised him to work hard and reach farther than she had, but now those dreams were at her doorstep and Violet still had a mortgage. She'd have to refinance and was looking at years of digging out of that kind of debt.

"I'll get a scholarship," he said.

"You're awful sure of yourself."

"It's my mom's fault. She taught me to be sure of myself. We'll be okay," he said. "We always are."

Greg was right. They had been more than "okay" since Eddie left and she'd find a way to make it "okay" now.

Violet met Edward Charles Evans in the halls of South Street High. He was hard to miss at six-foot-five and sporting a jacket with letters from three varsity sports. There was talk he'd get a full ride to a Division One school. Coaches from around the country showed up at his baseball and basketball games. Violet was a year younger than Eddie. He was the boy all the girls wanted and their mothers didn't. But Eddie was kind to everyone. He never bragged after a big game. No matter how well he'd done, he smiled and made small talk up and down the row of lockers and even though Violet once smiled back at him, she doubted he knew her name.

One winter day, she took her usual route home, crossing 13th and Dewey streets, around the park toward her house on Rose Hill. She spotted Eddie at the corner with his entourage of athletes and friends from the neighborhood. She slipped over to the other side of the intersection. The crowd went mute when Eddie broke from the center and headed toward Violet. One of his friends called out.

"Hey, Eddie – man, what are you doing?"

"You ditching us for that?" Eddie glared back at them and stepped in front of her.

"Can I walk you the rest of the way?"

"I'm fine. Thanks though," Violet said.

"Hey, Eddie, you playin' with jailbait and Georgetown'll dump your ass."

"Don't listen to those assholes. I'm Eddie Evans," he said.

"If they're such assholes, why are they your friends?"

Violet was staring at his beautiful brown eyes.

"And you're Violet Martin." She was stunned he knew who she was.

"How do you know my name?"

"I see you at school. You take all those tough classes and you practically live up in the art studio. You're on the quiet side, but definitely not shy. And you're not going out with anyone. See, Eddie Evans does his homework."

"Does Eddie Evans always talk about himself in the third person?"

"You would too if they wrote all those newspaper articles about you every week." He laughed easily at himself and Violet made sure she stayed with him step for step. Eddie noticed Violet because she was a challenge and Eddie liked challenges.

"What's your favorite subject?" she asked. Eddie stopped cold. Most people asked about his favorite sport.

"The one I pass."

"What did your friends mean about Georgetown?"

"I got a verbal to play."

"It's a great school," Violet said.

"You planning on college?"

"I take the SATs in a couple of weeks." They stopped in front of her house. Her neighborhood was either "up and coming" or "forgotten" depending on the latest political spin coming out of the mayor's office. The streets and sidewalks were soldiered by row houses that vied for their touch of originality. Last spring, Violet's dad had painted their exterior a pale blue to look like the sky. Even if she wanted to ask Eddie in, her parents weren't home, and they had rules, strict rules.

"So are you free Friday night? I've got a game," Eddie said. Violet hesitated. "It's a yes or no thing, girl. Not a debate."

"I'll have to check with my parents. I watch my brother and sister."

"Bring them."

"I'll ask," she said.

"Why don't I come by tomorrow and ask with you?" Eddie turned and walked back toward Dewey Street before she could object, and the following afternoon he met her at her locker.

"You were serious?"

"Yes, I was serious. I've got practice in an hour. Let's do this," he said.

"Okay, my mom should be home."

They left school and crossed through McKaig Park, avoiding most of the kids who were stopping in the mom-and-pop convenience stores on the corners. It was a mild winter's day and Violet kicked at the weeds peeking through the cracks in the asphalt path that snaked its way through the park. They came out of the gate on the south side, a block from Violet's house. The cheesesteak shops vented their grills and the smell of fried onions wafted over the entire block. The window boxes that lined the houses and porch rails were empty, waiting for the first sign of spring to be filled with pansies and crocuses.

They talked about her paintings and the small art studio her father had created for her in the basement. Eddie told her he'd moved from Cleveland when he was thirteen. His father had passed away and his mother wanted to be closer to family. His dad used to coach his youth football team, but he liked basketball better and hoped to break their school scoring record. Violet hesitated on the porch. She turned the key and entered, dropping her things in the hallway.

"Mom, I'm home."

"In the kitchen, baby." She walked Eddie to the back of the house. Her mother couldn't believe this was the Eddie Evans everybody talked about. He accepted the iced tea she offered and explained he had practice but wanted to get her permission to have Violet come to his game on Friday. He was quick to include her younger brother and sister. Her mother said she'd have to discuss it with her husband, but she didn't see a problem with the kids going to the game. Eddie shook her hand politely and left. After that first game, Violet never missed another.

She was there when the Villanova basketball coach came to Eddie's house to talk him out of going to Georgetown. She was happy because the campus was closer to home and they'd still get to see each other on weekends, but Georgetown didn't stop wooing him. Syracuse and Michigan also came to visit. Violet was sure he would get tired of her once he was living on a big campus with girls who were older and more experienced.

Eddie eventually kept his commitment to Georgetown. That summer before he left they were together whenever they weren't working. Violet waitressed at a small restaurant and Eddie made deliveries for McMurray's pharmacy. Every Friday night, he had a regular pick-up game with his buddies at the neighborhood park and Violet would meet him there so they could go out afterward. One night, Andre Wilson came down hard on Eddie as he drove for the basket. Eddie dropped to the ground in excruciating pain.

He tore his ACL and there was damage to the kneecap when he landed on the asphalt court.

Georgetown agreed to honor his scholarship while he endured surgery and physical therapy. They gave him a year to rehab. Once he was off the crutches, Eddie worked nonstop with the therapists until he left for Georgetown the following fall. Violet enrolled in art classes at Philadelphia Community College and agreed to take the train to Washington as often as she could. Eddie practiced with the team all through his first semester, but he'd lost a step and his rhythm was off. Georgetown had recruited another prospect while Eddie sat out his first year. He played a total of seven minutes that first season and eventually lost his scholarship. His coach suggested he try a junior college and see where it took him. Instead, Eddie came home and got a job working for the Philadelphia Streets Department on the night shift. He tried to stay positive.

"Lots of guys go this route. I'll be back on top, Vi. I know people who can get me where I need to be. But I want a little life without basketball before I jump back in." Violet believed in Eddie and felt selfish at how happy she was because he was home again.

The following fall, Eddie decided that with money getting tight, he could earn more working double shifts with the Department of Public Works. He saw Violet's disappointment.

"It's not forever. I can always do school at night."

"Or borrow the money and go back full time," Violet said.

"I can barely live on what I make now. How am I going to pay off a loan?"

"I'll get a job too. I'll help," she said. He kissed her.

"And who's going to help you? You're way smarter than me. You belong in college more than I do."

Violet was transferring full-time to Drexel University as an art therapy major starting in the winter term. She was awarded a grant, but also worked at a department store to pay the rest of her tuition. Eddie rented a tiny apartment in North Philadelphia.

Violet helped him spruce it up. Her parents had donated an old bed and some furniture from the basement. Violet spent most of her time there. They were happy, but six weeks before winter term started, Violet found out she was pregnant.

They snuck off to City Hall right before Christmas and got married. They didn't tell her parents or Eddie's mother, not wanting to argue with them, or worse, see the hurt and disappointment on their faces. Violet's parents liked Eddie. They'd get used to it. They went back to his place for their honeymoon. Violet's mother cried when they told her. Her father shook Eddie's hand, but didn't talk much the rest of the afternoon. Violet tried to convince them that nothing had really changed. Drexel had a lot of married women on campus and she was still planning to get her degree.

Gregory Edward Evans was born the following August. He was named after Violet's father and her husband. He was a beautiful baby who inherited Eddie's smile and sparkling light brown eyes. They moved to a bigger apartment once Eddie was promoted to crew supervisor. They couldn't afford sitters and Violet didn't want to rely on her mother, so she deferred the fall semester at Drexel and the one after that. She got work at a temp agency to make ends meet. Greg stayed with Eddie during the day until Violet rushed home from work so Eddie could catch a few hours sleep before he headed out on the graveyard shift. They were happy and they were making it work until Eddie lost his job during a round of city budget cuts.

The agency sent Violet on a constant stream of receptionist jobs. She was bored and over qualified until she landed at the city's largest newspaper. She was assigned to work for the Life Style editor, a quirky and difficult woman named Esther Rosen. For no discernable reason, Esther was immediately fond of Violet. She was the first temp who wasn't intimidated by her brashness and lasted more than three days without storming off in a torrent of tears. Esther demanded human resources hire Violet full time as her assistant.

Eddie had no luck finding work and relied on his old friends dropping by to lift his spirits. Violet often came home exhausted, and found them talking about the good times over a few beers and countless hands of poker.

It was bitterly cold that January. Greg was eighteen months old. It had been dark and snowing for over an hour by the time Violet climbed the stairs to their third-floor apartment. She opened the door and saw the dirty breakfast dishes still in the sink. The air was heavy with stale cigarette smoke. Greg's clean laundry she had folded that morning had spilled out of the basket and onto the floor.

"Eddie?" Violet looked through the tiny apartment. "Eddie?" She flew to the phone and quickly dialed his mother.

"Joyce, it's Violet. Are Eddie and the baby there?"

"He called 'bout two hours ago Vi, sounded like he'd had a few. I told him I'd come by but he hung up."

"I've got to go." Violet grabbed her purse. It wouldn't be the first time she had to go looking for him at one of his favorite bars, sitting on a stool with Greg on his lap, laughing with the guys from his old crew. She was fumbling for her keys and trying to remember where she found him the last time when she heard a sound coming from the bedroom closet. She threw open the door and found Greg on the floor. A cup of milk had spilled and dried down his front. His diaper hadn't been changed in hours. He was exhausted from crying. She took him in her arms and saturated him with her own tears. She bathed and fed him then cleaned the apartment. Violet was sitting in a chair reading when Eddie came home a little after midnight. He tried his key but Violet already had the super change the locks. He banged on the door, still drunk.

"Goddamn it, Vi. Open the door." He slammed his fist against it over and over again. Greg woke up from the noise and started crying. "It's me, dammit, open up!"

"I don't want you here, Eddie."

"This is my house! Open the goddamn door or I'll kick the fucker in!" Eddie went from cursing to crying about how sorry he was he left the baby. Violet remained calm and called the police while Eddie begged from the hallway for one more chance. He'd get a job. He'd do better. She finally opened the door when the police identified themselves. Eddie tried to push his way in, but they grabbed him and took him to his mother's place to sleep it off. Eddie never came home again. He saw Greg a few times after that night, but Violet never left him alone with her son again.

Now that same little boy had his heart set on the University of Pennsylvania. He interviewed with one of the deans who felt Greg was a perfect fit for Penn, but Esther Rosen pried the door open rest of the way. She wrote a glowing recommendation letter and set up interviews with faculty members she'd kept in touch with over the years. She was Greg's champion.

Greg never forgot Esther's kindness and remembered her at every birthday and holiday. He stayed at Penn and got his masters in bioresearch and worked for the university while completing his doctorate.

By that time, a larger media outlet had bought out *The Philadelphia Journal*. After a few months of meetings about improving layouts and editorial guidelines, Violet noticed a change in Esther. They brought in a new management team with ideas on how to win young readers. Esther was a purist. Readers were readers and if the material was good, she could care less about their age or demographics. She didn't believe in catering to advertisers or think twice about the dire predictions and growing financial woes of the print media. She made noise about their constant budget meetings. She wanted to be left alone to do her job, but with declining circulation nobody was in the mood to tolerate noise.

Esther was the old guard. Her new bosses were ignoring her and her opinion didn't hold the same weight. She became a figurehead, the queen who went from ruling an empire to cutting ribbons at library openings. That's when the drinking began.

Judith Donato

Esther's once-rigid schedule became erratic. Violet came in one morning and found her asleep in her office. Violet had little patience for alcohol since Eddie left, but she cleaned Esther up and drove her back to her condo in Rittenhouse Square. She made her drink black coffee and tried to be the supportive friend Esther had always been to her. But they were never truly friends. Violet worked for Esther and Esther had found in Violet something that passed for friendship. Esther had many acquaintances and business associates but true friendships eluded her. And the truth of who and what she and Violet were to each other came out one ugly Friday afternoon in the middle of the newsroom.

Esther was going over copy with a writer. She raised her voice. She'd just come back from a late lunch and Violet knew what that meant. Violet walked over to the writer's desk and spoke softly.

"Esther, why don't you take a break? It's been a long week for all of us."

"I'm fine, Violet. Get back to work."

"You're fighting that cold. Let's get you home." Esther's bloodshot eyes turned on her.

"Get back to your desk." Violet smelled the alcohol on her breath. The copywriter looked up at Violet, hoping she'd tell him what to do. He was new on the job and terrified of Esther.

"I'll get you a cab, and some of those cold pills from my desk," Violet said.

"Don't you dare condescend to me, not after all I've done for you."

"Esther, please."

"If it wasn't for me, you'd still be a temp in some garbage dump of a secretarial pool. I hired you. Me. They fought me, but I hired you." Violet knew it was the booze talking but it didn't take the sting out of Esther's words.

"Nobody wants to hear our ancient history. Come on now."

Violet tried to take her arm.

"Get your hand off me." Esther's hand flew up, striking Violet hard across the face.

112

Violet stepped back and saw a large dried stain from lunch on Esther's Dior jacket. She pointed her finger in Violet's face.

"You've got a short memory, Violet Evans."

"We'll talk in your office," Violet said.

"I'll talk wherever I damn well please." Esther stood center stage. All eyes were on her and she lifted her head with a patrician air. She struggled to articulate the words, clearly and loudly. "If it wasn't for me, her boy would be working the press room. Ask her about that. Ask her how I got him from the 'hood' to the Ivy League." Esther turned, stumbled back to her office and slammed the door. The entire copy room was quiet. Violet walked to her desk while people averted their eyes. Printers started humming. Keyboards clicking. She quietly packed up every single personal item she kept in and on her desk, then walked out of the building. She never saw or heard from Esther Rosen again.

Three weeks later, Violet went to listen to Kate McAllister speak at Temple University's lecture series on women and contemporary journalism. It had been almost a decade since Kate had stalked Esther at the paper. Ten years since Violet would get the young woman a cup of coffee and read her articles before putting them on Esther's desk. Violet waited until the crowd thinned, then went up to Kate at the podium and gave her a tight squeeze.

"Look at you, all grown up and famous."

"Violet, it's great to see you, and I'm not so famous. How's Esther?"

"As cranky as ever."

"She never forgave me for leaving the paper. I tried calling her a few times," Kate said.

"Won't do any good." Violet looked away.

"How about you? Are you still at the paper?" Violet shook her head.

"I'm back temping. But with Greg off on his own and my house nearly paid off, I'm ready to cut back. Still, I like keeping busy," Violet said.

They went out for coffee and Kate explained her deadlines and working at home with a young daughter and another baby on the way. Kate told her it was still early but she had some tests done and everything was going well with the pregnancy. Violet congratulated her. Kate finally got around to mentioning she may need an assistant. Nothing high pressure, just someone to help her stay organized.

"Are you asking me to work for you?" Violet asked.

"I think I am." Kate wasn't sure Violet was interested. They exchanged numbers and met again over coffee a few weeks later.

By the following month, Violet had a key to Kate's house and had gotten things organized in no time. Files were actually labeled and the mail was sorted. Violet bought a shredder and tucked it away in the closet. Laura loved her and Violet was at the hospital along with Kate's sisters when Jake was born. She became a part of their family. Kate watched her read Mercer Mayer books with Jake and she was an artist with a needle and thread, sewing Halloween costumes and mending hems. A few loose seams threatened to turn what Laura proclaimed "only the greatest night of my life" into a nightmare. Junior prom was saved by Violet's quick hand. She kept mother and daughter calm as she told stories about Greg's prom and how his tuxedo pants were so long they would have fit LeBron James.

Violet never dated after she divorced Eddie. She had developed a unique philosophy on the opposite sex. "Better no man than the wrong man," she once told Kate. "Besides men are like martinis. Look around the next time you're out – all those drinks lined up on a bar are pretty to look at – the pink ones and green ones, you throw in a mango with that vodka. Hmmm – hard to resist. The first one goes down so smoothly you'd swear God poured it straight from heaven. You get all warm inside and your brain goes soft and tender. You're likely to fall in love with the damn thing or worse, fall in love with the guy offering to buy you the next one. So then you have another, and another until you're sick as a dog and never want to look at one ever again for the rest of your life." Over time, Kate knew better than to ask about her love life or worse, try and fix her up with anyone.

But Michael genuinely liked Violet and often coaxed her to stay and share a glass of wine with them after work. Violet was polite and they had no trouble making conversation, but Kate always sensed an undercurrent in Violet that ebbed when Michael wasn't around.

It became one of those things Kate didn't dare talk about because it could change the precarious dynamics in her household. She never wanted to be in the middle of tension between her treasured assistant and her husband. Kate feared she would defend one or the other and no good could ever come of that.

On the day she found Marilyn's business card, if Kate was being completely honest and had to make a choice between Violet and Michael, she was pretty sure she knew who'd get voted off her island.

13

Michael and Kate lingered over lunch, which was not like Michael, especially when he had a plane to catch. Kate took a couple of bites of her cheesecake, but preferred using whatever calories were left in the bank to finish her third glass of wine. She stared at Michael's hands. They were still smooth, without an age spot on them. He never wore jewelry, not even his wedding band, and his knuckles had the same small freckles she had noticed on the day they met. She reached across the table and linked her fingers through his.

"You okay?" he asked.

The question of the business card hadn't come up and she was feeling the effects of the Chianti.

"So who is she?"

Michael finished off his third profiterole. "A business contact." He knew exactly who she meant so he deflected her question with one of his own. Now wasn't the time to have the "Marilyn Campbell talk."

"What's going on with you? You've been acting weird all morning."

Kate studied her husband. She had once researched an article on lying. A famous psychiatrist claimed liars get defensive, then attack as a shame mechanism to deflect from their own bad feelings. Michael had just proven the theory by making the discussion about Kate.

"Thanks."

"Just not yourself," he said.

"Can we just get the check, Michael? I have to get back to work." They drove home in silence. Kate was tired from the wine. When Michael dropped her off, he reached over and kissed her softly.

"See you on Friday. I'll call tonight if it's not too late," he said.

"Sounds good." He pulled out of the driveway. Kate did a few loads of wash before Jake got home from school, but no amount of sorting and folding could keep her mind off the fact that Michael never directly answered her question about Marilyn. He offered no real explanation and Kate didn't want to start an argument at Primavera and risk getting banned from their favorite restaurant. Losing Michael and the smoked salmon farfalle in one day would be too much.

Kate felt as if she had stepped into a dark cave without so much as a wet match to light her way. She tried to second-guess her gnawing feeling about the business card. Maybe this woman wasn't a problem at all and Michael was right. She was just "a business contact." Maybe it was all an invented drama to fill the enormous silence that had settled over her marriage and her life. Her suspicions could be nothing more than a by-product of perimenopausal paranoia, leaving her feeling unloved and unappreciated. Or was she fading in her husband's eyes and becoming a transparent image that had no real form or use to him?

She raced through the dirty laundry, looking for a way out of that cave. She finished the last piece and placed it in the plastic basket. She left it in the laundry room. Everything around her suddenly seemed heavier and more difficult. She decided to lug it upstairs later or maybe not at all.

Life seemed much simpler back in the old bungalow they bought soon after they were married. Everything was on one floor and the rooms and people in them could be reached in a few quick steps. They owned less than an acre, but their gardens were a river of yellows, reds, purples and pinks that wound around the house and were scattered throughout the yard. Michael inherited his father's love for growing and nurturing the land. He spent hours planting and pruning. He sketched out flowerbeds, did research on what grows in different amounts of sunlight. His plan rivaled a professional landscape architect's design. They spent Saturday afternoons strolling through nurseries picking out plants and flowers. Kate was content to walk behind Michael and pull the overflowing flatbed cart. She barely knew a weed from a fern, so it was the perfect arrangement. They spent long afternoons together and the results were gorgeous. Michael worked tirelessly that first spring.

In June, the local garden club awarded them "Yard of the Month" even though they refused to join the club on the principle that judging their neighbors was no way to make new friends. In warm weather, they'd linger over morning coffee on the small brick patio admiring the backyard. Michael's landscape was part of his proud tradition. He knew about soil and fertilizing and organic pest control. He could work almost any piece of machinery; from the very small tiller they bought, to the mini-backhoe he rented to clear out an area of dead stumps.

Edith and Carl came out to see their new house that summer. Michael's meticulous watering schedule kept everything bright and vibrant. He greeted his parents in the driveway and pur-posely took them through the freshly painted white arbor with brilliant roses cresting over its arch. They stepped into the back yard. The lawn was emerald green outlined in dark brown root mulch that covered the beds and nurtured the vibrant annuals and perennials. He'd sent them pictures of what the neglected yard had looked like when they first moved in so they'd have a "before" shot. Carl and Edith were silent taking in the landscape.

"Looks a lot different from those pictures, doesn't it?" Michael asked.

"I'll say," Edith said. Kate was in the kitchen. She wanted Michael to have this moment with them. The window was wide open as she made a pot of coffee. Sixteen hours cooped up in a car with each other didn't do much for Carl and Edith's moods, so she always softened their arrival with a hot mug of coffee and sweet Danish.

"You should have seen Kate's face when I ordered fifteen yards of mulch," Michael said.

"Spread it all yourself, did you?" Carl asked.

"Every last yard."

"You missed a patch of weeds back there. They'll kill off those flowers if you're not careful," Carl said. Kate's chest tightened. Michael had prepared a huge presentation for work that week, and had come home and collapsed. He barely got the lawn cut before his parents had pulled into the driveway. Michael was quiet when he and his parents entered through the sliding back doors. Kate poured coffee and put out the Danish, screaming inside, "Do you realize how hard he's worked? Do you get that he wanted a kind word, not a compliment, just a kind word?" But she didn't say any of those things and neither did Michael.

From the moment his own children were born, Michael was determined to nurture the positives in everything they did. When Jake struggled to keep up with his friends in baseball, Michael drove him to the batting cages and applauded his great hand/eye coordination. He calmed Laura through her first "C" in AP European history. Now and then things snuck out of his mouth he'd regret, but he was always quick to apologize and find a way to make it up to them.

Kate had changed her mind about putting the clean laundry away when Michael called to say he boarded the plane. He felt bad about how they left things at lunch.

"Are you delayed?" she asked.

"No, they're just about to close the door. The weather looks clear from here to Dallas."

"That's good." A spontaneous lunch out and an unexpected phone call had rekindled her suspicions.

"Before I forget, did you talk to Jake about that new golf coach?" she asked. "He has to step it up if he's going to try out for the high school team."

"There's plenty of time," Michael said.

"Not really. Tons of kids sign up for that indoor place over the winter," she said. "If he doesn't keep up, he won't have a chance."

"I'll handle it, okay?"

"We should start him earlier than we did last year." What she meant was "than you did." Michael decided he'd handle Jake's golf lessons and play with him more often, but they rarely got out on the course together.

"Are you there?" Kate asked.

"Why don't you call the guy? His number is in that mess of a drawer in the kitchen. I've got to go." He hung up. She had provoked him. She wanted him to feel bad about not following up with Jake's coach, and not telling her about Marilyn Campbell. She wanted to refocus his attention back on his family and away from work and women who wore expensive perfume. He heard the criticism in her voice and hung up without saying goodbye. In that moment, she had become his father and Jake's golf lessons had become that old patch of weeds.

14

It was well after midnight and Marilyn Campbell couldn't sleep. She hadn't heard from Michael McAllister in three days. She threw back the covers and surfed for something on the Home Channel. Watching people argue over countertops or paint colors was her equivalent of taking an Ambien. The narrator's voice went on with that sugary-sweet false enthusiasm. "Shirley and Paul are looking for their dream home, but will budget be a problem?" Marilyn was starting to drowse when her cell phone erupted into "Ode To Joy." It was "his" ring. She lunged for her smartphone in the tangle of sheets, duvet, and throws. By the time she fished it out of the folds of Egyptian cotton, it had gone to voicemail. She tried calling him back, but he didn't pick up. He hadn't left a message. They had so much to talk about, why didn't Michael at least leave a damn message?

Now Marilyn was wide-awake. There weren't enough home shows on the air to put her to sleep. She reached over and hoisted her briefcase onto the bed and switched on the bedside lamp.

At least she could be productive. Since she had been made a partner in the firm, there had been no time to sit back and celebrate.

She scanned the third-quarter sales reports on the cereal brand that plagued her. Reinventing her grandparents' favorite oat flakes was no small job. She didn't touch the stuff. Diet was her religion and product labels her bible. Marilyn measured everything she ate. Not an ounce, calorie or gram of protein went unaccounted. Her obsession with what she put in her body began right after college, when she decided she'd never eat anything that sat under a heat lamp for a living.

Marilyn's earliest memory was wearing a beautiful white cotton dress with a bright red bow at the waist and being tossed in the air by her father while he exclaimed, "Who's the prettiest little girl in the world?" By age five she had been paraded to the offices of the local talent scouts, ending up on the cover of a small catalog for children's clothing. She and her mother, Phyllis, took the train into New York once a week until young Marilyn eventually got an agent to represent her. He immediately lined up a photographer and had a battery of photos taken to pass around to editors and casting people. Marilyn loved the attention and was eager to please. She became the darling of casting agencies and was a perfect angel when she sat through make-up and hair for a photo shoot. After six months of auditions and interviews, she landed on the cover of *Parents Magazine*. That began a surge of layouts and print ads. Her mother allowed her to skip kindergarten. Her father had argued against it, but her mother won, claiming Marilyn was a very smart child and didn't need to waste her time cutting and pasting with less attractive children.

The extra money helped her family move out of their apartment into a two-story house with aluminum siding and a modest yard with a large, pink playhouse for Marilyn. Her big break came several months later when her agent called with incredible news. Marilyn was cast in a television commercial for a national ice cream brand. Millions would soon recognize her face. Phyllis surprised her daughter with a new bike, bought with Marilyn's money. She reasoned that without her, Marilyn would just be another faceless student among a sea of faceless and underachieving students at the local public school. She made a note to look into an exclusive private girls' school for her daughter. Marilyn was the center of everything good and fun in their home. She had gotten a new dress and her hair tinted just a half-shade lighter a few days before the commercial. And if her parents were quiet around her, it probably meant they had the same flutters in their tummies she had. Her mother let her mark off the days on the calendar until the ice cream commercial with a bright red marker.

There was one more red X to cross off the calendar when she heard a scary noise from her parents' bedroom. Her father was shouting. There was a loud sound like the time she broke her mother's favorite vase. She was playing with a doll when her father ran past her in the living room and out the front door. When her mother came out, she looked like she had a really bad cold.

"Can we mark the day, Mommy?" she asked.

"Later, okay? Mommy's tired." Phyllis took a pill and went back to her bedroom. Later, Marilyn ate some cookies and marked the day by herself as she went around the house turning off the lights. She got ready for bed, brushed her teeth, said her prayers and went right to sleep. They had an early train to catch. She knew this because her mother had repeated it over and over again. Marilyn woke up when she heard her parents' bedroom door slam. It was still dark, so she didn't know if she should get out of bed. Maybe her mother was getting up extra early for the commercial. She heard a man's voice. Daddy was home. She ran to the hallway. He had a suitcase.

"Daddy, are we going on a trip?"

"Go back to bed!"

"Don't talk to her that way," Phyllis said.

"This is still my house and I'll talk any way I damn well please," he said.

"Don't be mad, Daddy," Marilyn cried.

"I said bed!"

"We'd still be in that shithole if it wasn't for her," her mother said.

"You'll be back there soon enough." And then he left. Her mother ran after him, grabbing his arm. He shook her off roughly and she fell back, screaming after him. Her father took their car. Marilyn's mother didn't get up the next morning and they missed their train. They never made it to the commercial, and her agent was very angry when he called. Her mother begged him to reschedule, but they found another little girl at the last minute. Marilyn wanted to get her pictures taken again, but her mother was too sad to take her to the city. She was too sad to do anything, so Marilyn tried to keep the house from getting messy and learned how to steep the tea that helped with her mother's headaches.

Her father came home again after the night he left with his suitcase. Her parents didn't yell, but Marilyn heard the word "divorce" for the first time in her life. He took her out for ice cream of all things and said he'd found a job in Georgia. She saw him the morning he left for his new life in the south and at least once a year after that when he came to visit his parents. Her mother managed to get Marilyn to the school bus stop in the mornings, but was still in her room when Marilyn let herself back in with her own key every afternoon. After almost three months, some of Phyllis' girlfriends came to talk to her. Not long after that, her mother stopped sleeping all day and found a job as a secretary at their church. The pay was just enough to cover the late child support checks. They moved out of their house to an apartment the church owned.

Marilyn resented the insincere smiles of the other parishioners. Her mother said they were jealous of her because she was much prettier than their own daughters. But Marilyn knew they saw her as a charity the church had adopted. They were spared having their names on the "giving tree" at Christmas. Instead they handed her mother a small bonus and grocery store script for a free turkey every year. Phyllis accepted with embarrassing humility. Marilyn begged her mother to get another job, to stop taking anything they offered. But Phyllis had become comfortable in the role of the wounded woman providing for her child. She embraced defeat too easily and Marilyn resented her surrendering what little pride she had left. Phyllis began to date again. None of the men had much to offer in Marilyn's eyes. Most were lonely – divorced or widowed – but no matter how bad their lives were, Marilyn sensed they felt superior to her and her mother. So Marilyn distanced herself from Phyllis, spending as much time as she could with her friends and their families. She wanted little or nothing do with the small and desperate life that Phyllis had made.

Marilyn graduated from high school at the top of her class and was awarded a scholarship to Bryn Mawr College. Her friends thought she was crazy to go to an all-girls school, but Marilyn loved the tight-knit environment and the feeling of empowerment that was available to every girl, if they were smart enough to grab it. On that beautiful Gothic campus, she learned self-reliance, a lesson that had escaped her mother. Marilyn was a high achiever in a world of high achievers. Their mandate of strength and intellect, independence and service sent her off to grad school determined to be one of the small circle of women invited back to lecture on campus. She'd wait. The call would come.

She toyed with the idea of dying her blond hair. The round of dumb blond jokes infuriated her. In the end, she decided to keep it and shatter the stereotype. If anyone was foolish enough to tell one in her presence, she was armed with a heavy dose of sarcasm and could verbally annihilate them thanks to her days as captain of the debate team. Being beautiful was a convenient asset when charming a maitre d' into getting a table at a trendy spot and if the vice president of the company that interviewed her for a job wanted to discuss her resume further over drinks, it would be foolish to say "no." But the evening ended when the tab was paid.

She used her five-foot-nine frame to her advantage. When the time called for it, she'd slip on three inches of Jimmy Choo insurance to meet members of the old boys' club eye to eye. It was even better if they had to look up at her. She learned early that even the most successful executives feared failure, and if they believed that someone had the game wired, they'd follow them like lemmings. Marilyn was determined to be that someone.

It had taken her five years of grunt work at several less successful firms to float her name around the small business circle that drove the Philadelphia ad scene. Her smartest move was a detour to New York and a low profile job at Ogilvy. She answered phones and arranged meetings for a senior vice president. She gave herself a year in the cramped two-bedroom apartment she shared with three other girls on East 37th. She made herself indispensible to her boss. It paid off when he asked her to attend The American Association of Advertising Agencies meeting in Los Angeles.

Marilyn was the only assistant invited to the dance. She was there to make sure he was on time and ready. She polished his speech and was his first line of defense if his wife got wind that he was travelling with his mistress from accounting. On the second day of the conference she spotted Stephen Lewis of Lewis, Kramer & DiMayo from across the ballroom. Marilyn knew every name, face, and title of the top players in Philadelphia advertising. His agency was a marquee shop. They struck up a conversation and Mr. Lewis promptly insisted she call him Stephen. Later, after a martini or two, he invited her to come in and talk to the people at his firm. After a round of interviews with the other partners and top management, she was hired as a junior associate and moved back to Philadelphia.

She was handed small, local accounts at first. Boutiques, accessory lines, up-and-coming anythings were her specialty.

Marilyn believed in creating opportunity, and when a nondescript manilla folder of some nothing of an account nobody else wanted fell onto her desk, she wasn't insulted. She threw herself into the brand until her coworkers were envious they hadn't thought of the potential in the product before she did.

A year after she started at the firm, she was handed a problem client. The folder didn't have a project number or even a proper label. The name, "Our Brands," was scribbled in a hurried hand. This ancient company with no ad budget and a product that had years of promise and little else going for it, felt like an orphan with no hope of ever getting adopted. It was a perfect match.

Marilyn sat down with the board or directors of the family-owned company and insisted a name change was their first priority. It wasn't an easy fight. The name was the brainchild of the CEO's grandmother, who had founded the business with her husband almost fifty years earlier. They manufactured and distributed cookware. The irony of the assignment wasn't lost on Marilyn, who hadn't picked up a pot or a pan as a matter of principle. She didn't cook because she wasn't good at it and Marilyn never did anything that resulted in less than excellence. Our Brands never became a big player on the national stage. Jim Carson didn't want to break his grandmother's heart by changing the company's name just when they were starting to show a slim profit after many lean years. Jim was a loyal and kind man. Marilyn charmed him into bringing her to the senior assisted living community to visit the Carson matriarch the following month.

Golden Summerhill had a palatial lobby with a deep mahogany winding staircase. But Marilyn noticed no one was actually going up and down the stairs. For all its beauty and rich cherry wainscoting, signs of limited life were all around her. Jim chatted on about how long it took to find such a quality village, how the meals were all five star, and the exercise room was Olympic caliber. No amount of hype could remove the bile Marilyn felt rise in her stomach from the moment the large sliding glass doors opened automatically in front of her. People in wheelchairs or with walkers could not open huge glass doors. And she'd be willing to bet the treadmill in the Olympic-caliber gym seldom went over two miles an hour, even on a good day.

It wasn't fear that made her unable to look at the bent-over figures that passed by her on the way to the elevator. Marilyn simply refused to believe that she would lose a step no matter how old she got. She was addicted to exercise, ate a controlled diet, and had the will of a drill sergeant. She wouldn't go down easy. She wouldn't go down at all.

They walked along a narrow corridor lined with fox hunting lithographs. All the doors were stark white with small black, wrought iron knockers in the shape of pineapples. Jim rapped softly when they reached Apartment 655.

They heard a gentle voice from the other side. "I'm coming."

"It might take her a while," Jim confided.

Marilyn was in no hurry. She had thought of nothing but this meeting for days. The woman who opened the door was striking. Like Marilyn, this was someone who didn't believe in the inevitable. Eleanor Carson was in her early eighties but could have passed for a woman twenty years younger. She had just the right amount of work done. Marilyn guessed she had a brow lift and some injectables every four to six months. She was wearing a deep tan Chanel suit and held out her hand.

"Ms. Campbell, my grandson warned me you were a beauty."

"It's a pleasure to meet you, Mrs. Carson."

"Eleanor, please. Come in, dear." Jim kissed his grandmother. Eleanor had the air of old money. Marilyn had tried, but she couldn't trace the Carson fortune. Most of the holdings were privately held in a family trust. There were a number of other businesses run by various family members and she added them to her list of future prospects.

Eleanor had prepared chamomile tea. Jim served as Marilyn scanned the room. She assumed most of the furnishings came from Eleanor's old house. They showed signs of age, but were still elegant. Scalamandre silks covered the chairs and a modest Picasso line drawing hung over the sofa. There was the usual amount of casual conversation and as so often happened to Marilyn, things turned her way on the most unlikely coincidence. Marilyn sipped her tea slowly as Eleanor spoke to her grandson.

"I'm sorry to change the subject Marilyn, but Jim, did the trust cut the check for this year's scholarship?"

"Last week, Grandmother." Marilyn was intrigued.

"I didn't know your company funded education," Marilyn said.

"It doesn't," Jim said. Marilyn risked stepping in where she didn't belong, but Eleanor spoke up.

"It's not the business, dear. Every year I personally provide a scholarship for a needy, incoming student at my alma mater, Bryn Mawr College." That was it, the hook. Marilyn had her. They spoke about the cloisters, Lantern Night, May Day, and what it means to be a true Mawrter. And wasn't it a great coincidence they shared an interest in antiquity and the pagan gods? By the time Marilyn put her teacup down for the final time, "Our Brands" had morphed into "Edesian Cookware" – named after the Roman goddess and her mythical feasts. Eleanor loved the idea. What woman wouldn't want to use something that sounded that sexy? Exactly, Marilyn argued. Introduce the lure of food and romance with an exciting redesign and new color palate to take the dull right out of the chore and the entire brand. Marilyn soon pitched a variety of vibrant and innovative designs. She reshaped the marketing plan and soon Edesian had opened over thirty niche stores nationwide that catered to the idea of moving the kitchen one step closer to the bedroom. Their profits tripled and they branched out into a line of elegant, if slightly naughty, accessories, aprons and hot pads.

The partners in Lewis, Kramer & DiMayo promoted Marilyn to vice president. They celebrated at Pod, a trendy Center City restaurant, and Stephen suggested they bring in an outside market research firm to track the new product pipeline for Edesian and other clients. As usual, Marilyn had done her homework and would have a recommendation to them first thing in the morning. She had her eye on a small to medium-size company called McAllister Research Group. They had done product positioning for an impressive client list. She set up a meeting with Michael McAllister for the end of that week.

Teaming with McAllister was a huge success. Edesian Cookware eventually expanded into the outdoor market and padded its product line with grills and patio furniture, all geared toward relaxation and fun. Marilyn was promoted to partner in the firm.

Her relationship with Michael had been strictly professional, but the dynamic between them changed dramatically over this past year and they were at a new and exciting place. She was flush thinking about it.

Marilyn threw the cereal file onto the floor and checked her voicemail again as if a message from Michael would magically appear. It didn't. She would wait till morning. Instead of turning off her light to go back to sleep, she threw off her covers and made her way down to the twenty-four hour gym in her building. Thinking about Michael had made sleep impossible. She needed to work off all that excess energy.

15

Michael's career in market research began right after college. He loved figuring out why people purchased Brand A instead of Brand B. Were purchases impulsive, emotional, or steeped in the latest overkill from the Internet? He opted out of his corporate job to start his own firm when Kate was pregnant with Jake. Her column was being syndicated and they could afford to live on one salary until he got things up and running. When McAllister Research Group was born, he was cautious and never took on an employee unless he had enough work to keep them busy six months out. He eventually went from retail work to establishing his firm with some of the largest pharmaceutical and consumer product companies in the world. There were twenty-three employees on the payroll now.

Michael hated being on the road, but he hated being alone even more. He never embraced solitude. It was one of the reasons he fell in love with Kate. No one had ever filled the silence in his life like Katharine Marino. His assistant, Colleen, usually traveled with him to take notes and keep things moving smoothly, but Michael didn't want her coming to Dallas. He needed to protect his privacy on this trip.

He rushed from his hotel to make sure everything was in order for his meeting with the client. He used Wilkinson Focus Group's facility when he was in Dallas. Michael was confident his respondents, or more accurately the patients who used his clients' medications, would be greeted with refreshments and current issues of magazines. Wilkinson practically guaranteed they'd be in good humor before he held them captive and grilled them about how they were faring on their current pharmaceutical regimen.

Michael was usually in the back room with the client while one of his employees handled the interviews. He rarely moderated anymore or had face time with consumers, but every once in a while he personally moderated a group to remind himself that ultimately his business was about people. This was an important contract and future projects were on the line. He wanted to give the client his personal attention, but it would be a rough couple of days. He'd be talking to patients about HIV meds, and they came in all varieties depending on how they reacted to their diagnosis and treatment. Some put their dreams on hold; others refused to put anything on hold and were suddenly skydivers and deep-sea fisherman. The toughest ones to interview were those who still saw it as a death sentence. He didn't create the drugs, he didn't formulate them, or make any promises, but they saw Michael as someone offering hope and it weighed on him.

He arrived through the back entrance so he could check out the patients through the two-way mirror that faced the waiting room. He thought of giving Kate a quick call. He had tried earlier on both the house phone and her cell and gotten no response.

He still had a mountain of grocery shopping he was supposed to do for the holiday, but his heart wasn't in it this year. His parents were coming out to stay for the week. Michael stiffened just thinking about their visit. His father had grown increasingly uncomfortable in Michael's home. As Michael and Kate's success grew, Carl had become uneasy with their lifestyle. So little tied Michael to his father anymore except for a long-standing affection for the Chicago Bears and a fondness for Belgian beer. He decided to wait before trying to reach Kate again. Michael was always at his best when he focused on only one thing at a time.

There was another two-way mirror on the far side of the room. The client and ad agency people would file in and watch him work through that one. They were late, as usual. Michael paused and glanced at his faint reflection in the two-way mirror. His reddish-brown hair had a few steaks of gray, but he was lucky, most of his contemporaries were either balding or on their way to the "salt and pepper" stage. His good genetics kept him fit and looking younger than his forty-six years. Kate teased him about being vain, but it wasn't vanity, he liked being active. He played squash, tennis, and golf regularly, sometimes with Jake. Kate had battled her weight since Jake was born and it was only in the last three months she'd started weight training and dropped a few pounds. Michael noticed the difference, but hadn't told her. He didn't want her to feel self conscious about it.

There was a lot he neglected to say to Kate in the past year as their relationship slowly got lost under the pile of Laura's college applications and Jake's sports schedule. The anxiety of waiting for acceptance letters to roll in had them sniping at each other. Things didn't improve after Laura left. Change always made Kate sad and since Laura was living at college, Kate hadn't been able to shake the feeling that the best times in their life were behind them. Michael shared her fear but it had always been up to him to keep Kate from falling apart. He didn't dare let on that the morning they drove the 140 miles to Vassar, was one of the worst of his life.

When they took off for Poughkeepsie, their SUV was bursting with Laura's bedding, clothes, computer, and television – all of the conveniences of home that could fit into a dorm room. Michael tried to lift the mood by talking about plans for Parents' Weekend. Eventually Laura and Jake watched a Disney movie on her laptop. It was a flashback to their annual trips to the Outer Banks when the kids were little. They would cruise down Route 13 through Delaware, Maryland and Virginia while "The Little Mermaid" or "Beauty and the Beast" underscored the ride. Kate fought tears the entire trip to Vassar. Both kids were too old for Disney but they insisted on bringing "The Lion King." When they burst into a "The Circle of Life" duet, even Michael had a hard time holding it together.

The college sent a letter advocating a drop-and-run policy. "A warm and affectionate hug after you've helped your student arrange their room and a quick good-bye is best." Michael refused to do something as big as launch his daughter into adulthood with a quick "good-bye" and not look back. He booked a room at a small inn not far from campus. Michael's cell phone rang soon after they checked in.

"I hate it here. I want to come home." Laura's voice broke.

"Honey, you've only been there a few hours," he said. Kate was immediately at his shoulder.

"What's wrong? Tell her we'll come get her." Michael held up his hand.

"Get out of your room," Michael said. "Knock on a couple of doors. I'm sure other kids feel the same way."

"Okay, I'll try. Thanks, Daddy."

"And if you want to call back later, we'll be here. I love you."

"Love you too." Michael hung up.

"Why didn't you let me talk to her?" Kate asked.

"She'll be fine," he said. They didn't hear from Laura the rest of that night. Kate was silent on the way back from Poughkeepsie.

"Laura will be okay. We'll get used to this, all of us will." Jake was deaf to the entire conversation. His music was turned up and they could hear the muffled heavy metal pounding into his eardrums.

Kate stared out the passenger window. She didn't see the New York countryside; she saw what Michael saw – the two of them, living alone in that big, empty house one day.

Michael's client had arrived. He needed to go to the back room and make small talk about sports and the stock market. But they were running late and his first respondent was due any minute. He'd wait until there was a break in the schedule. He thought about trying to reach Kate again, but his phone rang before he got the chance. The caller ID spread across his screen like a headline. Marilyn Campbell. He had tried to reach her late last night. He looked back toward the two-way mirror, then turned away and answered.

"Michael McAllister."

"I know who it is, I called you," she said. "Sorry I missed you last night."

"We're about to start here."

"I get in very late tonight."

"I'm not sure what time I'll wrap up here."

"I'll wait. And, Michael, don't eat. I'd much rather share room service."

She hung up quickly. This is not how he wanted to start his day. He had gotten rid of Marilyn's business card right after Kate gave it to him. He knew she had read it, but he dodged her question. He couldn't tell her about Marilyn with the holidays so close and Laura due home next week. Kate was obviously suspicious and their awkward lunch made it worse. He felt like Marilyn was sitting between them the entire time, and was sure Kate must have felt the same way. That's why she drank so much wine. Michael needed to tell her the truth, but not today, and not over the phone. And then, distraction being a man's best friend, right behind his dog, Michael's first HIV patient walked in.

"Mr. McAllister? I'm Kevin Todd." The young man extended his hand. Michael recognized the bruises from Kaposi's sarcoma. Kevin's grip was strong and firm.

"Nice to meet you, Kevin. Please, have a seat." Michael took out his notes. "Do you mind if I record our interview?"

"Not at all."

Michael glanced up at the man's face and the hollows in his cheeks. He saw the evidence of end-stage disease. The profile said Kevin was thirty-eight, but he looked twenty years older than Michael.

16

Violet came in to work early Wednesday morning. It was her first day back from visiting her sister in Memphis. Kate was amused at how easily the Southern drawl had slipped into her voice.

"What'd I all miss 'round here?"

Kate wanted to tell her about the business card and the loneliness and how she'd hurt Michael's feelings, but she knew Violet quietly mistrusted most men. The only one she had complete faith in was her son Greg.

Kate had gone over their credit card statements the night before and poked around in their home email account, finding nothing interesting except for the ridiculous amount Michael paid for his orthotics. She had searched his Internet history and saw he ordered a few business books on Amazon. His corporate card receipts went straight to his accountant so she didn't have access to those. Maybe a well-disguised mistress could be considered a business expense if they worked in a related field.

Violet produced a brightly wrapped box from her briefcase.

"Vi, what is that?"

"Nothing, just a remembrance." Violet always said that when she bought a gift for Kate or one of the kids. Kate unwrapped the package. It was an Elvis bobblehead from Graceland.

"Violet, I love it! But I thought you wouldn't be caught dead at Graceland."

"Cindy kept on me. Not like she hasn't been there a hundred times. I went to shut her up."

Kate had told Violet years ago that she and Michael's first dance at their wedding was to "I Can't Help Falling in Love With You." They weren't crazy about the song, but the band could play it and their other choices were "Hit Me With Your Best Shot" or "Love Shack." Kate hugged Violet and displayed the bobblehead prominently on her desk, wondering how she'd gone from that first dance to living with "Suspicious Minds." She mentioned Michael's trip to Dallas and Violet nodded.

"I don't know how that man does it. Never in the same city one day to the next."

Kate liked to think she and Michael weren't reduced to the obvious facts of their lives: she wrote, he traveled, and they both worked more hours than were good for them. Every once in a while, she asked Michael his opinion on a column idea or he'd share his frustrations with his latest project. He had yanked off his tie as he walked through the door a couple of weeks ago and was on a roll about an asthma device.

"The ad agency is making deep into six figures to come up with a new color and they give me black? Christ, I like being different and creative too, but I can't believe people want to pump their lungs full of medicine from a device the same color as a funeral suit." He stormed off to the kitchen to get a beer. Violet's voice cut through the memory.

"So where do you want the King?" Violet asked.

"What? Oh, right here so I can adore him." Violet broke into a smile.

"You need more coffee, if you want to stare at this thing all day," she said. "I'll be right back." Violet went to the kitchen.

Elvis was blocking Jake's picture, so Kate moved Elvis to the right. She looked at her smiling boy who desperately needed a haircut. She remembered their annual picture day argument.

"My hair's fine, Mom. Who cares? It's for a stupid school picture." Jake didn't know there was no such thing as a stupid school picture, and that she kept each one in the drawer in her nightstand, from preschool to this one. A slate-blue background illustrated the history of their lives from toothless, to braces, up to Laura's high school portrait holding the small plastic red rose against her shoulder.

She had gotten into the habit of driving Jake to school this year. He hated the bus, so she indulged him in the morning. He was her baby and since one had already left the nest, she wasn't ready to think of the day she'd drop him off to live another life in another place.

"You never drove me," Laura said to her over the phone one day. "He's perfectly capable. of walking to the bus stop like other kids. I did."

"Why is this an issue?" Kate asked.

"You're spoiling him, Mom. He knows how to get to you."

"I drive your brother to school because I obviously love him more than I love you," Kate said.

"Thanks." Kate heard Laura snapping baby carrots between her perfectly straight teeth, bought and paid for by the same woman who obviously loved her little brother more. Laura wouldn't let the subject die.

"I guess you'll want me to drive the little prince over winter break?"

"That would be nice. You two could bond over which one I love more."

"Not even a question. Gotta go, mom." Her daughter hung up, ending the conversation on her terms – again. It was either a sign of her age or a hint of the woman she'd eventually become. Kate hoped it was an age thing.

Laura would be home in a few days, just in time to set the Thanksgiving table. She was getting a ride from Will Tiernan's parents. Will and Laura had gone to preschool, elementary and high school together and both ended up at Vassar. He'd had a crush on Laura for years. They dated a couple of times, but she declared him too boring to take seriously.

"He's a mathlete," she said, as if it carried a prison sentence.

"Since when is being smart a disease?"

"I'm just not into him, okay?" Kate liked Will. He was sweet and considerate. She called Nancy Tiernan and offered to drive the kids back on Sunday. Kate secretly hoped Will would drop in on them over the weekend. Maybe she'd find a way to make that happen.

Kate was alone with her computer when the little email envelope icon popped up. It was from Laura. It was always like that. They thought of each other and the phone would ring or they'd text each other. The subject line read, "What's the body count?" Kate gave her the latest headcount for Thanksgiving dinner. Laura would complain about the work but she was always a big help. She ran errands and pitched in with dishes. She loved being with the extended family and holding her brother's hand when they said grace. Kate saw the four of them, she, Michael, Laura and Jake, as a fortress no one could breach, at least she had until yesterday. She opened the file for her next column. She'd written a couple of loose paragraphs, but was off her normal pace when Violet entered with two mugs of coffee.

"Thanks," Kate said. "I'm up to twenty-seven for Thanksgiving. Are you and Greg still good?"

"You sure? It's a lot with his kids now."

"In or out, Vi?"

"In. I'll do three mashed potato casseroles and I ordered four pies from Tess's Bakery."

"Marie's getting the desserts."

"Marie can get something else. I'll call her later, and drink that before it gets cold."

Kate took a long sip of her coffee.

"Michael get off okay?"

"Yeah, fine. We even went out to lunch first."

"Did I miss your anniversary?"

"We need an excuse to go out?" Violet's silence answered her question.

"How long's his trip this time?"

"Till Friday."

"So what do you have this week?" Violet opened the folder where Kate kept ideas for future columns.

"Did you book our tickets to Seattle?" Kate asked. She had a speaking engagement in a couple of weeks.

"Last night. I emailed you the confirms," Violet said.

"I didn't see it."

"Where's your head this morning?"

"Violet, do you think Michael's a good husband?"

"Now that's a trap. The kind that gets a woman fired every time."

"I'd never fire you. Just tell me what you think," Kate said.

"I think I'll sip my coffee till you tell me what's really going on with you today."

"Maybe I should write about traps," Kate said.

"What kind?"

"The human kind. How people feel when they're in one. Do they even know it or do they confuse the trap for purpose and meaning?"

"I like it so far," Violet said.

"Too many times they imagine they can't change things they don't like about their life. Most of the time they don't even try because they're afraid of what's on the other side of that change and that's the ultimate trap."

"Go on," Violet prompted.

"It could work. I don't know."

"It's a start," Violet said. "Look at all those people in Washington – the biggest rattrap of all. Are they happy or is power the crack pipe in their lives?" A rare silence set in between them.

"What?" Kate asked. Violet was staring at her.

"Think I don't know this game?"

"What game?" Kate asked.

"You're trying really hard not to talk to me this morning. If you hate Elvis, say so. Won't hurt my feelings."

And because she had never been able to keep anything from Violet for very long, the words came.

"I don't hate Elvis. I hate that I'm blocked. I hate that I don't know what to write. I hate that it's taken me two days to even look at that computer before I even have an idea, and it's not a very good one. And on top of it, I'm feeding a small army next week. And I love that small army." Tears rolled down her cheeks. Violet let her be. "And if turkey wasn't the only thing served on Thanksgiving, I'd be panicking over what to cook. Michael can wait till the last minute to shop. He's a man. He has that luxury. He'll go to the store and his work is done. He doesn't get how much other crap there is to do. I ordered tables and linens in September, Violet! Two frigging months ago, and there's organizing who brings what and the mountain of serving dishes to pull out and dust off, and the silver to be polished. I want to find something fun that doesn't involve me stuffing a dead bird. But I don't know what that is or even where to look for it. I'm so tired, Vi. Nothing feels new anymore and I'm selfish and shallow because I have no reason to feel this goddamn tired."

Violet handed her tissues. The doorbell chimed.

"If that's the goddamn dry cleaner again. Tell them I've got nothing." Kate blew her nose, hard. "Nothing!"

"Dry your eyes. I'll be right back."

Violet went off to the center hall. Kate tried to stop crying but she was so sad. She looked at the bobblehead. Instead of Elvis, she saw Michael's head bobbing up and down on that stainless steel spring. She grabbed Elvis and wrapped her hand around his jet-black sideburns that grew down the sides of his too-pink face. She was about to give it a fast snap of his imaginary neck when she was stopped by a strange voice coming from the hallway.

"Hi, I'm Marilyn Campbell. I'm here to see Kate McAllister."

17

Laura McAllister knew something was going on with her parents. She had been noticing little things for months. It wasn't the usual dreading-the-empty-nest syndrome. They still had Jake, two careers, a dog and a house to run. The weirdness had set in a while ago and had gotten worse. Something in her mother's voice the last few times Laura talked to her over the phone had a new variety of weirdness, fresh out of the can, with a rancid smell to it. She hadn't seen see sparks flying between her mom and dad for a long time, and that was fine with her. Laura didn't need to know what they did at night. From the sound of the television in their room, it was a regular dose of news or sports. The muffled sound of their voices engaged in any kind of conversation had stopped seeping through the walls a while ago. She forgot the last time she had fallen asleep to the sound of it. But Laura was grateful she didn't have to deal with the bullshit many of her friends did, like packing up every other weekend when it was time with your dad or having to make sure you had "fun" on those one-night-a-week court-mandated outings.

She had emailed and played phone tag with her mom the last couple of days. Her dad was less maintenance. She had reached him at the office yesterday morning before he left on one of his trips. Laura saw herself in the full-length mirror behind her door. She had none of the McAllister height. She topped out at five-foot-three and had dark brown hair that fell to her shoulders. It had a wave of its own and she usually wore it in a throwback ponytail. Her first semester was going too quickly and the workload was incredible. Her grades were holding steady, but she was juggling new friends, a new place and whatever independence living off your folks but sort of on your own brought you. Finals started in two weeks. Her professors would turn up the heat after Thanksgiving break and she wanted to meet with most of them to make sure she was prepared.

Her parents told her for years not to be so hard on herself, but their half-hearted congratulations when a sure "A" had morphed into a high "B" didn't go unnoticed. Their mantra was "We just expect you to give your best effort." But what Laura heard was "As long as that best effort results in perfection."

Her phone chimed. Another text from Will Tiernan. How many times could he ask the same thing in a different way? She agreed to ride home with him next week because she knew her mom would be a crazed getting ready for Thanksgiving. His parents were cool. They were quiet and seemed to like having her around, but Will had it bad for her and it made Laura nuts. He was cute, but not in a way Laura looked at twice. His jaw was square, high cheekbones framed his shaggy, straight blond hair. He had pretty eyes. She'd give him that. Not blue, not green, but something in-between. Her fingers responded furiously. "Cant meet 4 dinner, have study group. See u Wed." You'd think that would be a clue. Not for Will Tiernan. Seconds later his reply flashed across her phone screen. "No prob, lunch 2morrow?"

Laura gave up. "Fine. Noon. Vassar Express." She didn't have time for a leftover high school crush. It was hard enough meeting new guys and with Will hanging around, people would assume they were together, which was never going to happen. Her roommate, Deidre, was practically living in her boyfriend's room so on most nights Laura happily had the room to herself.

She and Deidre Holmes exchanged emails and phone calls over the summer about matching bedding and throw rugs, and who'd bring what to campus. They officially met at orientation but Laura hadn't seen much of her since. Laurence Layman, in an ironic nod to his sexual prowess, also met Deidre at one of the freshmen activities. They went back to his room right after, and except for the occasional drop-ins for books or a change of clothes, Deidre was a phantom roomie. She was from California and was already complaining about the cold weather. Laura didn't particularly like Deidre but she liked having the room to herself and as long as she didn't bring Larry back to their place, it was the perfect arrangement.

She kept up with old friends on Facebook and Skype. They were scattered all over, but most had stayed in the Northeast for college. She was lonely for her old friends, but didn't tell her mother because her loneliness would become her mother's loneliness, and her sadness would become her mother's sadness. It was always that way. Her mother was a "fixer" and Laura didn't want Kate fixing her life anymore. Laura couldn't wait to get home and see her friends. They would all be together again. The old gang planned an informal reunion on Friday night in Laura's basement. Everybody who had gone with her to the Jersey shore for Senior Week was coming.

But the main reason Laura was eager to get home was to figure out what was going on with her folks. She was afraid something was wrong, something she hadn't seen before and serious enough to have her thinking about it more than she'd like to be, especially with all the work that had to get done. She pushed the thought out of her mind and sent her brother Jake a quick text. "See you in a few days, jerk. Luv ya." He'd ignore it. She'd send another one later, giving him shit about not texting back. Laura remembered how hard he tried not to cry when they dropped her off; instead he stared at the ground and was the first to jump back into the car. He was taller than her already and his voice hit so many notes on the scale when he spoke, she had to keep herself from laughing.

Laura's brain overheated like her mother's when she was stressed and if she didn't slow it down, nothing would get done. Thoughts of Jake, her mom, her parents, the holiday, Will – had to be put on hold or her history paper would never get written. She booted up her computer. She'd deal with whatever shitstorm was brewing at home next week.

18

Kate's eyes were swollen and a smear of wet mucus covered her upper lip. She was wearing three-day-old sweats and Ugg slippers. Marilyn Campbell was just a few feet away. She couldn't let that woman see her like this. If Marilyn was involved with Michael, Kate wanted to be intimidating and brusque, too busy for this intruder. She wanted to appear nonchalant and dismissive and her office to look like it was a monument to her success. There were some awards scattered on the walls and some she never bothered to frame. She had fan letters that said she had changed lives. They were in a box or a drawer somewhere, not displayed where someone would know that she mattered to others, that she touched lives. Violet had gone out of town at the worst possible time. The chaos of unshelved books, papers, a month's worth of bills that needed to be paid, and that last load of laundry she planned to fold when she took a break surrounded Kate. With Marilyn Campbell a few feet away, her miserable life was exposed in a heap of crumpled bed sheets.

"Maybe I can help you. I'm Ms. McAllister's assistant."

"God bless, Vi," Kate thought. Her centurion at the gate had met the enemy and would defeat her. Maybe Kate would go to the mall later and buy Violet that Coach bag she had her eye on two weeks ago.

Marilyn's voice was uneven and high. Kate expected smoky and seductive, like Kathleen Turner in her prime. It wasn't unpleasant, but she wouldn't want to listen to it all day, every day. Kate could tell Marilyn tried to control it, but it got away from her.

Violet was cold and uninviting. "I'm sorry, Ms.... Ms...."

"Campbell," Marilyn said.

"Ms. Campbell, I apologize but Kate's on a tight deadline. She's busy working and I can't disturb her when she's in the middle of a column."

"Of course. I wouldn't want to bother her. I was close by and wanted to drop something off for Mr. McAllister, actually." She had a huge envelope, five times the average size, and bulging at every edge.

Kate reasoned that the concept of overnight express or a messenger service must be foreign to a woman who still uses a business card to hit on a man. Kate inched toward the doorway and got a brief peek at Marilyn before ducking back into her office. The instant snapshot she took in her mind made Kate ready to concede in her present condition. Marilyn looked flawless with a tall, trim build and shimmering blond hair layered stylishly to her shoulders. Kate never considered Michael or any man a prize worth lowering herself to a catfight. She had loved and lived with him for over twenty years, and until this week she thought of her husband as one of the unsung heroes of good men who were fair to coworkers and true to themselves. He was one who loved his family and was faithful to his wife. And if he wasn't the life of the party, he was the guy you wanted to be with when the party was over.

"Michael's out of town," Violet said. "But I'll be sure to give this to him when he gets back." Violet took the envelope. It was almost weightless.

"I appreciate it. And tell Mrs. McAllister I'm sorry I missed her. Maybe another time."

"I'll tell her. Thank you, Ms. Campbell."

"Please, call me Marilyn." Violet didn't respond. "Violet, isn't it?" Violet didn't remember telling Marilyn her name.

"That's right. Bye now." Kate heard the front door close and let out a long breath as Violet appeared in the doorway with Marilyn's delivery.

"So who is that woman and why are you hiding from her?"

"Are you looking at me?" Kate aksed.

"You've looked worse. How do you know her?"

"I don't," Kate said. "I know of her."

"Through Michael?"

"Yes and no," Kate said.

"She doesn't look like the kind of woman who wastes her time delivering envelopes."

"Thanks for not letting her in."

"I don't trust anyone in three-inch heels unless she's at a wedding or her ex-husband's funeral."

Kate pointed to the envelope. "What is that?"

Violet shrugged. "I don't know. It's as light as air." Kate stared at her nearly blank screen and typed a few random words as if that would distract her from the envelope. Violet placed a box of tissues by her keyboard and started sorting the mail, putting the envelope down on the loveseat. Kate's fingers stopped typing. She snapped a tissue from the box.

"I think Michael is having an affair." Her tears fell again, but she wasn't sobbing. Kate was sad. Sad for the times she rolled over in bed when Michael reached out for her, for all the times she harped at him when the garbage cans didn't make it to the street on trash night, for when she accused him of checking out on her and the kids when he was overworked and tired. She moved to the loveseat and told Violet about the business card and how she and Michael had drifted apart. About how much she missed Laura and how everything was changing and how Jake didn't even like being around her without his dad in the house. She cried because life had stopped surprising her in a good way. Her "firsts" were over, first baby, first house, first days of school, and don't even mention the first day of college because that was the kind of first that made her feel obsolete. Her life was behind her, and she was left to hold the door while her kids walked out of it. Any "firsts" that remained ended in "oscopy" – first colonoscopy, first endoscopy. Violet sat close until Kate ran out of tears, then took her hand and spoke softly.

"Honey, you need to figure out if any of this is real or is it just too damn quiet around here and this is your way of making some lively noise." Kate knew Violet was right. She had asked herself the same thing. Kate had to find out if Marilyn Campbell was the enemy or a misconstrued annoyance. She'd start with that monstrous envelope.

"Let's open it," Kate said.

"Are you sure?" Kate nodded and examined the seal. It was tight and Marilyn had added an extra wide strip of packing tape to secure it.

"Whatever it is, she doesn't want anyone but Michael getting his hands on it," Violet said. Kate tore it open violently. Violet never saw such a look on her face.

"What is it?" Violet said. Kate didn't respond. Violet took the envelope from her and pulled out two colorful bras and matching lace panties. "This bitch is crazy." Violet said. Pieces of notepaper were attached to some of the underwear.

"Read them," Kate said.

"No."

"Read them, Vi." Violet twisted a piece of paper around the strap of a pink bra. "This is my favorite. You'll get a closer look at it on the road."

"Panties next," Kate said. Violet read it to herself. "Out loud." Violet hesitated then read it.

"These feel incredible to the touch." Violet ran her fingers over them. "She's right. They do." Kate examined one of the notes.

"It's the same handwriting. Same pen. Put them back," Kate said. "Tape up the damn envelope anyway you can. I don't care how it looks. Put it on the center hall table so he sees it when he gets home." Violet placed the lingerie back in the envelope and haphazardly resealed it. She cleared off a place on the center hall table and left it there before returning to Kate's office.

"Now what?" Violet asked.

"God, Vi, I don't know. Let's check The Cheating Husband's Handbook."

"Have you checked his email?"

"Just the home account. Nothing. His work computer is at the office and he's always around when he's using his phone or laptop."

"Can you log on to his work account?" Violet asked.

"Not from my computer. He has a private server or something." Kate's voice was flat. She showed no enthusiasm for playing detective.

"There could be other accounts too. Hotmail? Gmail? Maybe some we never heard of," Violet said.

"Michael doesn't have other accounts."

"You didn't think he'd have a woman send him her underwear." It was one thing for Kate to suspect Michael, but why was Violet so eager to go there? Did she pick up on something Kate had missed over the years?

"Greg's got an old friend, a professor at Penn now. He's a computer whiz."

"I'm not talking to a complete stranger about this, Vi, forget it."

"I'll call Greg, tell him we're doing research for a column."

"On spying?"

"Not spying, techno stuff, the loss of privacy, how to protect yourself from hackers and snoops. You can't write word one till you know what's going on under your own roof." Kate waited a few seconds to give the impression she thought the entire thing was a waste of time. It was a silent defense of Michael's honor. Then, as if resigned to it, only to mollify Violet, she acquiesced.

"Okay, call Greg. I'll grab a shower."

Violet headed to the phone as Kate left the room. She didn't want to hear Violet lie to her son about a phony column. She didn't want to be in this world. It was one thing to feel a distance from Michael because they knew everything about each other, but to think of him as a liar was unnatural. Still – at least it was a "first."

No matter what Kate learned, she'd have to tell Michael about it. That's how marriage works. The day would come where she'd have to let out all her suspicions and doubts about Marilyn Campbell and hope he'd understand why she hadn't pushed him further at lunch when he dodged her question about the business card. Not feeling comfortable asking, "Who is this woman and why is she writing you a personal note?" was proof of where they were and it scared her more than that damn card. And when Michael had a chance to give her a straight answer, he changed the subject, living in that world of non-confrontation that sustained them.

Spying on Michael made Kate feel small, but it was a compromise she was willing to make for the sake of her marriage and her family. That was the lie she chose to believe. Kate was never comfortable in the world of moral ambiguity, and since she had found that stupid card, she was having a hard time telling the good guys from the bad guys.

19

Violet dialed her son's office the second she heard Kate moving up the stairs. She was prepared for Greg's questions. She was used to deflecting them or steering him to another subject. She had done it for years, but never out of malice. Violet knew how to protect her son from an overdrawn bank account or a collection agency that demanded payment on one of Eddie's old debts. His secretary said he was on the other line. She could wait or leave a message. Violet opted to wait.

Greg had met the McAllisters years ago while working at the University of Pennsylvania writing his doctoral thesis. He had made a small name for himself at Penn when he delivered a paper on the compounds his team created while conducting clinical trial research. A friend's firm attended the conference and approached him soon after about taking a job in the private sector. It meant a move to Chicago, leaving his mother behind. Greg knew Violet would never leave Philadelphia. She loved the city and once a year toured the sights like she had never seen them before. She started at Independence Hall, crossed over to the Liberty Bell, then took a quick swing by Ben Franklin's print shop and finished up on her way through Betsy Ross' house and Elfreth's Alley. It had been a tough year for his mother. The paper was bought out. She didn't complain, but he knew she wasn't happy there.

Greg shared an apartment in University City with a friend from college, but the arrangement was getting old and he was ready for a place of his own. He was mulling over the offer from Chicago one night on his way back to his place. When he got home, his answering machine light was flashing.

"It's your mom, call me." He still hadn't told Violet about Chicago. He was putting it off until he made a decision, but the more he weighed his options, the more he knew it was the only choice for him. Greg called his mom back, but she didn't want to talk over the phone. He heard something in her voice and headed straight to her place. He took the subway to the old neighborhood. Violet had looked exhausted the last time he saw her. He assumed there was trouble at work. She said she was worried about Esther. But why did she have to see him in person? What could be so bad that she couldn't discuss it over the phone? He took the stairs two at a time in her building instead of waiting for the elevator. She had something simmering on the stove by the time he got there.

"I figured you'd be hungry." She greeted him with a kiss.

"What's going on, Mom?"

"Does something have to be going on 'cause I want to see my son?"

"No, but – okay, it can't be too bad if you're worried about my stomach." He moved to the refrigerator and got a beer. Violet stirred the pot of chili while Greg looked at her closely. She hadn't lost weight. She didn't look happy, but she wasn't worn out like the last time he saw her. The researcher in him ruled out about a dozen illnesses in that long glance as she carefully put the spoon back on the small plate by the stove.

"Talk to me, Mom."

"I didn't ask you to fly over here like my place was on fire."

"No, you said you didn't want to talk about it over the phone. What was I supposed to think?"

"Get your mother a beer."

"But it's not the weekend."

"I don't need an excuse to have a beer in my own home. I may start pouring it over my cereal in the morning."

Greg knew when not to push her. He got her a beer, knowing Violet would tell him when she was ready.

"When did you have time to make chili?"

"Last week. It was in the freezer."

"You've been cooking?"

"I cook for myself," Violet said.

"How full's the freezer?"

"Full enough." Violet cooked when she was stressed. He assumed if he opened the freezer, plastic containers would fly at him like rocket-propelled grenades. Violet ransacked a drawer for a bottle opener. The clatter of utensils played under the simmering of the chili on the stove.

"These aren't twist off?"

"Not tonight. Check it out – imported. I'm treating myself," she said. She took the cold bottles from him, flipped off the caps and poured two pilsners.

"Thanks." The aroma in the apartment brought back a flood of memories. He had studied at this same table every day after school. Violet would come in from the office with an armful of groceries. She'd chop and prepare their meal. He'd offer to help, but she'd tell him his job was to do his schoolwork. Her job was to feed him.

"Sit down, Mama." Violet was shaving carrots for the salad.

"In a sec. Don't be in such a hurry."

Nothing in the place had changed in years. A chair here or there had been reupholstered, but most everything looked like it did in his childhood. The dark wood tables were polished to

159

mirror-like perfection. The old sofa now boasted a rich tan fabric that played against the floral side chairs with red and yellow cabbage roses. The original wood floors were covered with rugs Violet had purchased at second hand stores. She called them treasures people wouldn't recognize if they turned to gold right in front of their eyes. The neighborhood had turned over when Greg was still in high school and their building went condo. Many of their old friends were forced out, but no one was forcing Violet Evans from her home. She had money in the bank, got her first mortgage and bought the place. After Greg, it was her greatest source of pride.

Violet pulled out the plates and silverware and placed them on the table. He stopped her gently and took her hand.

"Sit with me."

"I'm not done with supper."

"Sit with me, Mom." Violet hesitated for a moment, and then sat down next to him at the table. She had spent the last twenty-eight years not wanting to cause him a moment's worry and she wasn't about to start now.

"I just had a rough day at work is all," she said.

"How rough?"

"Esther's gone crazy. She was in one of her moods. I've told you how she's been since the buyout."

"What did she do?" he asked.

"Her mouth'll be the death of her."

"Did she get fired?"

"No." Violet drew a deep breath. "I quit."

His mother had never quit anything, especially when a good paycheck was involved. He knew Esther had been impossible for months, but Violet never told him it was so bad she'd actually leave the paper.

Greg's mind was having a fencing match with all the conflicting thoughts going back and forth, up and sideways, jabbing at his conscience. On one hand, this was the day he had been hoping would come. The day he could give Violet the same steel-like support she'd always given him. He wanted to tell her it would be all right, that he could help her out until she found something else. He could say it was time she finally slowed down and took it easy for a while. But his head was log-jammed with the minute details of the Chicago package. They shuffled around like a deck of cards: salary, bonus, vacation, and retirement plan. He knew every detail down to the decimal point, the number of personal days, sick days, and the flex-comp health plan. He had downloaded a picture of the condo building he was considering that overlooked Lake Michigan. Violet lifted her hand to Greg's cheek.

"Don't fret. I've got more money in the bank than I could ever spend. Next week, I'll call that temp agency in Northern Liberties and get back on the circuit."

He didn't have to check in with the people in Chicago for at least a week, but the decision had been made. He would accept the job and still find a way to help Violet. She'd want this for him. He couldn't stifle his career when he was on the verge of real success. Violet smiled, watching her son try to quiet his mind. She'd seen him do it his whole life. With Greg, there was never a simple answer. He was a boy – and now a man – who calculated all the variables.

Greg pressed Violet for details on what happened at the paper, but she refused to trouble him. She served dinner and they talked about his work at Penn, his current project, and his girlfriend Meredith. They'd been together over a year and a half. Violet liked her, and said so every chance she got. Greg was hoping Meredith would come out to Chicago and look at the place he found. He bought her an engagement ring and planned to give it to her on her birthday. He left his mother's condo that night keeping two life-changing secrets from her.

The next day, Greg sent official letters of acceptance to human resources and the vice president in charge of biomedical research at the company in Chicago. Violet sensed something was going on with her son, the way she always knew when he tried to hide a problem at school or with friends.

She trusted him to tell her in his own time. Greg was always grateful for that. During those years when it wasn't smart or cool to admit how much you loved your mother, Greg held it close, but it was Violet who got him through when he doubted he could cut it at his small charter high school and later at Penn. He could afford to doubt himself because Violet never doubted him.

He told Meredith about the interview right after he got the call. She went over the offer with him. She was teaching high school and neither wanted a long-distance relationship. They agreed Meredith would stay in Philadelphia till the end of the current school year, then get her Illinois certification and apply for a teaching job in Chicago. They were taking Violet out to dinner the following weekend to finally tell her their plans. They were meeting at Violet's in case she didn't feel up to going out once she learned Greg was moving to the Midwest. Greg bought a bottle of champagne. Even if Violet was unhappy about the announcement, she'd insist on celebrating and he wanted to be ready.

True to her word, Violet found work in less than a week after the Esther Rosen fiasco. She was temping at a dermatologist's office. Greg made a reservation at Violet's favorite Indian restaurant in Center City. Meredith held his hand as the elevator arrived on the third floor. They had gone over their plans with Meredith's family the night before and it was time Violet knew before it leaked out.

Greg gave a quick knock on the door, and then let himself in with his key. The apartment was spotless as usual.

"Mom, we're here."

"I'll be out in a sec. Get comfy." He and Meredith saw a bottle of champagne already chilling in the kitchen. Three glasses were out on a silver-plated tray that was only used at Christmas. She had some snacks arranged on his grandmother's china plate and cloth napkins.

"Cloth napkins?" Greg said. "How did she find out?" He'd been so careful. Meredith's folks had promised they wouldn't say a word to anyone until they told Violet.

"It had to be your mom," Greg said.

"It wasn't my mom."

"Then how does she know, Mer?"

"I don't know, but it looks like she's happy."

"My mother will always be happy for me, even when she's miserable." He put the bottle of champagne he brought in the refrigerator.

"What are you two whispering about?" Violet looked beautiful. Her café au lait skin was smooth and her dark brown eyes shone brilliantly. Greg was concerned when he met Meredith's family that race would be a problem. But it was his family that pushed back. Violet was used to their prejudice. When she was dating Eddie a few of his brothers made remarks about her being too light and whispered about her bleaching the line. Greg's uncles called Violet after they met Meredith and wondered what Greg was thinking.

"He's thinking he met a beautiful woman," she said. Her former brother-in-law, Len, suggested having a talk with him. Violet came back at him. "Nobody's talking to my son about anything. You understand me? I didn't work to send him to school so he'd end up listening to the same ignorant talk I heard my whole life." Len grunted, but held his tongue.

"So what are we celebrating?" Greg asked.

"You'll never guess who I ran into." Greg shrugged. "Kate McAllister."

"The columnist?" Meredith said.

"I knew her when she was just a child starting out," Violet said.

"She made her mark at the newspaper, then threw Esther over for national syndication," Greg said.

"She didn't throw Esther over. She had a chance to shine and she took it."

"Esther isn't a fan of people shining without her holding the spotlight," Greg said.

"Well, Kate tells me she's up to her ears in work. She has a little girl now and a baby on the way – a boy. It's amazing how they know so soon. She has a house out in the suburbs and might put together a collection of columns for a book. She needs an assistant. The job's mine if I want it."

"Wait – you – schlepping out to the suburbs every day?"

"Why not?"

"You haven't driven in years."

"That doesn't mean I don't know how," Violet said.

"Mom, you don't even own a car."

"I do now. They took away your Uncle Marvin's license last week. I bought his."

"Besides, I don't want you on the Schuylkill Expressway every day."

"Stop worrying, Gregory. I won't be on the expressway. I'm thinking of buying a place closer to Kate's."

"You'd leave the city?" Meredith looked as stunned as Greg.

"Why not?"

"Because you've never lived outside the city," Greg said. "You love it here."

"Maybe you're not the only one ready for some big changes. And Meredith, honey, thank your mother for the 'heads up' on the Chicago move."

"Mom, we were planning to tell you..."

"Tonight – I figured. I saved you the trouble." Violet gave Greg a big hug. "You know how cheap it is to fly to Chicago these days? I've been checking out the fares."

"You know we'll be back and forth a lot," he said.

"I know you'll try. I'm proud of you, sweetheart. I'm proud of both of you." She held him tightly and never mentioned how hard she cried after Meredith's mother broke the news to her.

Greg had always been grateful to Kate and fate and whatever else brought his mother to the McAllisters. They gave her a new extended family to love and spoil. He got to know them on his trips east and eventually he considered them family too.

When Greg picked up his phone line and Violet said Kate needed a favor, he was happy to help. Violet said they were researching a column about privacy and the Internet, but didn't give many details. Greg promised to get her to the right person and as soon as he hung up, he contacted an old friend at Penn. If anyone knew how to dig into someone's cyber-history it was Steve Yeardsley. Steve said privacy was a relic. Everyone's life was just a few clicks away on a keyboard. The trick is in knowing which keys to click.

20

Steve Yeardsley was true to his word. He emailed Greg his latest paper: "Penetration & Intrusion: An Analytical Guide to Protecting Against Legal but Unethical Trespassing Into Your Cyber World." Greg forwarded it to Violet. Violet printed off two copies as soon as it hit the inbox. She and Kate scanned them together. Michael would be home in two days. There wasn't much time. Kate flipped through the document.

"Are you getting any of this?" Kate asked. Violet hadn't looked up from her copy.

"Is it in English?" Violet responded.

"I'm not sure."

"Kate, let's just ask Michael about this woman."

"I tried. He never answered me. Put a copy of that paper in my briefcase and shred yours." Kate knew Michael's hot button was trust. If she was wrong about Marilyn and Kate accused him of an affair, it would blow open their peaceful void. But then Kate remembered how nonchalantly he pocketed that business card.

While she was busy protecting his feelings, he didn't seem too concerned with hers. Michael knew her trust issues better than anyone. It had caused more than one fight in their marriage and yet he had left her out there alone with her self-doubt and anxiety when he could have offered up a reasonable explanation. And if it had been anywhere near reasonable, Kate would have believed him because she always did. She glanced at the Elvis bobblehead. Insecurities killed Elvis, Kate thought. Insecurities are powerful beasts. She jotted a note – 'insecurities' – another column maybe?

It was insecurity that made Kate drag Michael back home for his ten-year high school reunion soon after they were married. Michael resisted at first, but Kate wanted to put faces to the names she'd heard and seen in his old yearbook. She'd gotten acquainted with a few of his friends at their wedding, but most of the "old crowd" didn't make the trip. Michael finally agreed to go. Her in-laws were excited to have them come home for a visit. Kate still struggled with not calling them "mom" and "dad" because she was raised in that tradition. She had brought up the subject with Edith soon after their engagement during a visit to the farm. Edith was in the kitchen massacring another sack of raw potatoes.

"Edith, I was wondering if you'd be comfortable if I called you 'Mom'?" Kate asked. Edith never looked up, but her voice was as pleasant as Kate ever remembered hearing it.

"No, I think Edith is just fine. Pass me that paring knife over there would you please?" That was the last time the subject came up.

At least on this trip, there would be no question about where Kate would be sleeping. Edith fixed up Richard's old bedroom with the twin beds since Michael's room was now her sewing room.

"I wasn't sure you'd want me to put them together," Edith said.

"It's fine, Mom, we'll do it," Michael said.

"I told your father we should."

"No problem. I'll handle it." The edge crept into his voice. Eventually he'd slip away from Kate and into his own silent world until they were on the turnpike heading back home, leaving Kate alone to protect herself against the little criticisms that were the familiar brick and mortar of her relationship with his parents. Edith went back to the kitchen as she and Michael pushed the beds together.

"I think she's trying to tell us something," Kate said.

"Do I need to remind you this trip was your idea," Michael said. "Let's just get the beds moved." Edith had cleared out a couple of drawers for them. Michael gave Kate the drawers and lived out of his suitcase. Kate spent the week helping out in the kitchen and shopping with Edith. She wanted to prove to Edith that she was a good wife and loved her son. But nothing she did could make up for the one fact that mattered above all others. This foreigner had taken and kept Edith's boy hundreds of miles away from her. He wasn't coming home, he didn't marry Barb Wipperman and it broke Edith's heart.

Barb was the one and only reason Kate was eager to go to the high school reunion. She had been curious about her since she first spotted that perky picture in Michael's dorm room years ago in college. It was the small part of Kate that still didn't believe she was the kind of girl who got the guy. Barb had married one of Michael's classmates and they heard through the Elna grapevine they were attending the reunion.

After Kate and Michael were engaged, she found two photo albums dedicated to Michael's courtship with Barb. Her writer's mind wanted to know the early story of Michael's life. She had a few details on the beginning of his relationship with Barb, less on the middle and just a few dry facts about how it ended. Beyond writing Kate a letter after the break up, Michael avoided the subject. Kate sensed he still felt guilty about it.

The reunion was held in the Village Hall. It was a new structure that Edith claimed cost the taxpayers too much money. The huge basement was rented out for parties. It was decorated in bright blue and gold, the colors of the Elna Tigers. The old mascot volunteered to wear the furry costume and ham it up with the DJ. The tables had alternating plastic covers in the same colors. Helium balloons anchored with small bags of pebbles served as centerpieces.

Jessie Steinerman's Smooth Tunes scored the evening. He was now the local plumber and still a part-time disc jockey. She and Michael entered as "Stairway to Heaven" had couples shuffling to their old Senior Prom theme. They walked up to the long table where the old members of the student council greeted them with nametags and gift bags. Michael shook hands, gave the guy hug to his old buddies and introduced Kate to those she hadn't already met.

They slapped on their nametags and started to mingle. Michael had been president of his class and was greeted as returning royalty. He was pardoned from any duties at the front table because of his status as a long-distance attendee. His friends gave him a hard time about missing the last reunion because he was too good for them now since making it big back east. Michael folded in easily among the people he'd grown up with, while Kate hung back and watched. She wished she had her journal with her. A few mental notes on reunions and she could pitch Esther Rosen a column on the highs and lows of looking back and going home again.

Michael looked younger than most of his old classmates. Some of the guys had thinning hair and several women were very pregnant. One couple was coming up on their tenth wedding anniversary. Kate "the observer" was on high alert. These strangers knew Michael in a way she never would. The memories of all the sleepovers, drinking parties, and moonlit drives bounced off their faces in enormous smiles and outbursts of laughter. Kate strolled to the greeting table and scanned the nametags that hadn't been claimed. She chatted with the reunion committee chairwoman, Tina Cunwhistle. Tina was an interior decorator who ran her business out of her home between caring for three small children. She glanced over at Michael.

"He hasn't changed a bit," Tina said.

"Really?" Kate had no idea where to take the conversation.

"Of course we all keep in touch with each other one way or another, and I hear he's doing great and you're a writer?"

"Just for our newspaper." Why did Kate feel the need to downplay her success?

"We were shocked when he didn't move back. But then most of us thought he and Barb..." Tina quickly pulled her foot out of her mouth. But Kate saw the opening and took it.

"Where is Barb tonight? I'd love to meet her," Kate said.

"She RSVP'd she'd be here, but Barb always runs late."

"Is she still living in town?" Kate asked.

"Oh, sure. They've got a really cute ranch house just north of town." Kate had probably passed it a dozen times with Michael. She was sure he could point it out to her if he wanted to because knowing where Barb lived was probably on Edith's top ten list of things she felt Michael had to know about life back in Elna. But Michael never once said, "Oh, by the way, honey, that's where my old girlfriend lives." Tina rearranged the remaining nametags.

"And don't you just love Michael's parents? His father is so funny."

"Funny" was the last adjective Kate would ever use to describe Carl McAllister. Kate got tangled up in an avalanche of questions, and an inner-dialogue that kept her planted by the welcoming table. She wondered what Tina saw in Michael's parents that she didn't. What drove her to force Michael to go home for this reunion when he clearly wasn't interested? Why was she so desperate to prove to Carl and Edith that she was a good person or put herself in this ridiculous situation of waiting for an old girlfriend to make an appearance? The return on investment was zero. She barely knew the people who had raised her husband. The truth hit her right there in front of Tina Cunwhistle. She would never be a part of his family the way Michael was a part of hers. She would never belong in this place or be a part of this time in his life and she had to make peace with that. Kate looked out at her husband as he laughed and told a story, undoubtedly about something he and his Elna friends had all done together. She wanted the two of them to get in the car and drive back to their own home and their own life. She wanted to tell him it wasn't his fault that his parents didn't love her the way she wanted them to, but she'd keep trying because that's what she was raised to do. Michael moved in behind her.

"Tina, mind if I steal my wife for a dance?"

"As long as you steal me next," she said.

"You got it." He led Kate to the dance floor.

"She's really nice, Michael."

"Did you meet her husband?"

"Not yet," Kate said.

"He was captain of our football team."

"With a name like Cunwhistle, he'd have to be."

"Be nice." He pulled her closer against his body. Kate felt him get an erection and leaned into it. Michael gave her a wicked smile. He loved how she made him laugh. She was his Kate. His gorgeous bride and talented wife. He was proud to show her off to his old friends, the mysterious outsider in the room with the dark hair, hazel eyes, and skin that seemed exotic among the crowd in the town hall. To his eyes, she was the most beautiful woman in the room. As he led her around the dance floor, Michael felt peaceful for the first time since they'd gotten back to town.

"I wonder where she is?" Kate said.

"Who?"

"Barb. She has an unclaimed name tag."

"One of the guys told me she was coming."

"Then you asked about her?"

"It came up in conversation."

Kate knew if the tables were turned, she would have asked about an old boyfriend, if she actually had an old, steady boyfriend in high school, which she didn't.

"Do you miss her?"

"Barb? Why the hell would I miss her?"

"Ssh, don't raise your voice. People will think we're fighting," Kate said.

Michael pulled his nametag from his jacket. Kate grabbed his arm. His face was tight. She gave him her best "Please don't do this. Don't embarrass me here" look. He led her to a quiet corner. His voice was low and measured.

"I'm here because it seemed to matter to you. I don't know why. I don't care why. It was important to you, so it was important to me. I haven't seen, spoken or thought about Barb or most of these people in years."

"I'm sorry. You married a crazy person," Kate said.

"Yes, I did. I've already seen everybody I wanted to see. Let's get out of here, okay?"

"Not back to your parents. Not yet." Kate couldn't face his mother's questions about why they were home so early.

"Okay, then let's drive to the lake and park for a while." He leaned down and kissed her. The storm was over. She slipped her hand into his and they headed out without saying goodbye to anyone. Tina had left her station as the official greeter and was swilling a beer with her husband and a group of people Kate hadn't met. The sun had just gone down in the summer sky. Michael always got over things a lot faster than Kate. He opened her car door, a gesture that had come and gone since they were married. He was about to shut it when a voice called out from across the lot.

"Michael?" A beautiful blond woman was heading toward the car.

"Hey, Barb." Michael turned, leaving Kate's door open. Kate watched them embrace. Michael kissed the woman's cheek. He didn't introduce Kate.

"Leaving already?" she asked.

"Yeah. It's a good turnout though," he said. Kate caught a glimpse of her in the side-view mirror. Barb was still prettier than Kate wanted her to be.

"It's good to see you," she said.

"You too. You're doing well?"

"I'm great, Michael. I finally get my degree at the end of the winter term."

"Terrific."

"The minute I registered for my last couple of classes, I said to myself, 'Michael McAllister would be very proud of me right now.'"

"I'm happy for you, Barb. Good luck with it." Kate was about to step out of the car.

"I guess I'll go in then," she said. "Tim's meeting me here later."

"Have fun." She watched Barb head into the Village Hall as Michael walked back to their car and finally closed her door. He got into the driver's side.

"You could have introduced me."

"You could have introduced yourself."

He started the car. "So how did it feel, seeing her again?" Kate wasn't trying to make him angry. She wanted to know.

"It felt great," he said. "And she looks – I mean, you saw her. Talking to Barb brought back a lot of great memories. Fate's a funny thing." Kate didn't see the humor in the moment. She stared straight out the windshield. "Something feels so right and then you turn one way or the other – and your life is completely different." She refused to look at him. "If I didn't suck at modern British lit, the prettiest girl in class would never have taken pity on me." Kate exhaled. "It took a while, but eventually I was smart enough to marry her."

Michael leaned over and kissed her. They left the Village Hall and the reunion. He took her hand as they drove to the shores of Lake Michigan. They parked in a remote spot and made out under the August moon.

21

Kate read Steve Yeardsley's paper over and over again and still struggled with the technical jargon. Even if she could decipher the language of injecting data and social engineering, she had two other problems. One, Michael always had his laptop with him, and two, his desktop was at McAllister Research Group. He kept an extra set of keys to the office in his nightstand, so Kate persuaded Violet to take an after-hours road trip. She had to time it carefully. Many of his people worked late to take advantage of some of the perks he offered, like free takeout if you worked after six or the washer and dryer he installed on-site so you could work and still get your laundry done. Michael had proven it increased productivity.

Kate decided she'd wait until after eight. That should give everybody a chance to wash, spin, dry, and fold their way home. Violet took some convincing.

"You want me to do what?" Violet asked.

"We're not breaking in. I have a key. See?" She held it up. "And the security guard is a sweetheart," Kate said.

"What if this 'sweetheart' reports back to Michael?"

"Then I'll come up with a great excuse why we had to be there," Kate said. "If we don't do this tonight, I lose my window of opportunity."

"The window will have good company 'cause you already lost your damn mind," Violet said.

"Please come with me, Vi."

"I'll hang out with Jake."

"Jake's covered. A friend's coming over."

"On a weeknight?"

"In or out, Vi?"

"I don't need a ski mask or that huge flashlight I keep in my car, do I?"

"Thank you! I love you!" She gave her a quick hug. Violet went home to change while Kate made Jake his favorite dinner, macaroni and cheese with fried chicken. They sat together like it was a normal Wednesday night.

"When's dad get home?"

"Friday afternoon."

"He's been gone a lot," Jake said.

"Yes, he has. Do you miss him?" Jake shrugged, not letting Kate break through his well-built teenage barriers.

"How's school?"

"Fine."

"Best Buddies Club?"

"Okay."

This was the rhythm of their conversations. Kate would try to find a small opening that would prod more than one syllable from her son. He'd grown three inches taller in just a few months. She went from hugging him goodbye in the morning to settling for a quick kiss when he bent down his head. He needed a haircut, but she'd let Michael handle it. She spent too much of her time chanting phrases like "pick up your room, take out the garbage, did you finish your homework, where are your good shoes, did you make your bed?" It's the language of all mothers and the reason they're usually voted the parent "Least Likely To Be Any Fun." Kate hated lying to her son, her sweet, innocent boy, but she had no choice.

"Aunt Violet and I thought we'd catch a movie tonight. Do you mind?"

"No."

"I asked Tom to come over." Tom was Laura's friend. He was a year younger and a senior in high school. He'd been a regular at their house as long as Kate could remember.

"I don't need a babysitter," Jake said. "I'm almost fourteen."

"He's not babysitting. He's hanging out."

"Right."

"Finish your homework and he can help you beat that video game."

"What game?"

"The new one I just bought you. It's up on your bed." Jake flew out of his chair and hugged her.

"Thanks, Mom. You're the best." It was a good thing Kate was an early holiday shopper. The bribe set Jake up to have a fun evening while she was off spying on his father.

"Can I play online too?"

"Sure, but only after you finish your homework."

"Deal." She cleared the table as Jake polished off his fourth piece of chicken. Violet picked her up at 7:45 and they made their way to Michael's office. It was ten minutes door-to- door from her house to Valley Forge Commons, the office complex where McAllister Research Group rented half of the third floor. The security guard sat at the oval desk in the center of the lobby. He had his headphones on. He never heard her use the master key.

"Hey, Phillie." Kate gave him her brightest smile. His name wasn't Philip or Phil. Kate didn't even know his name. Everyone called him Phillie because he was crazy about the Phillies. He watched or listened to every game. He had a large, stuffed green Phanatic on his desk.

He removed his headphones. "What are you doing here, Mrs. Mac?" He always called Kate that. It started at the Christmas party the first year after Michael moved his offices. Phillie had dipped into the spiked punch and by the end of the night everyone had a nickname.

"I need to use Mr. Mac's computer. Mine crashed and I can't pull up what I need from this flash drive and I'm on a deadline." Kate held up a small USB stick she brought along to prove her predicament. The lying was coming easier. She wondered if it was that way for Michael – you tell one and the others fall into place to create a new reality that seems every bit as truthful as the real one.

"No problem. You know the way." Phillie put his headphones back on as Kate and Violet walked to the elevators. They headed straight for Michael's office and booted up his computer. She and Violet stared at the password prompt box.

"Now what?" Violet said.

"Michael's not paranoid about security."

"I guess we'll find out." Kate hit a few keys.

"Here we go," Kate said. "Already logged on."

"So what's the magic word?" Violet asked.

"Mate. You know – Michael and Kate. Mate? Plus our wedding anniversary."

"Mate? Like Brangelina?"

"Yeah, but obviously much more glamorous. He uses it for everything, Vi – has for years." Kate scanned the inbox. "Michael came up with it years ago. He now takes full credit for joining hot celebrity names. It stopped being romantic when I found out he uses it for the dog's Pet Smart account."

"Search her name," Violet said. Kate entered "Marilyn Campbell" into Michael's email search box. Her stomach dropped to her toes.

"God, Vi, she's everywhere."

"Let me see." There were scores of emails from Marilyn. "Wait, look – they stopped. There hasn't been one in months and months."

"And months. That's weird," Kate said.

"Open one."

Kate scrolled back.

"Hi Michael, tried to reach you by voicemail. We need to talk. Too much info to put into an email."

"Scroll up," Violet said. Kate did. Most were copying Michael in on projects his people were working on for her agency. And then they stopped.

"There's nothing recent, Vi. Not one. These are from her corporate account, a couple from Gmail but even those are old."

"Maybe that's a good thing."

"If that perfume on her card wasn't nice and fresh," Kate said.

"Let's look at what's here," Violet said. They went through most of the messages. There was a lot of business jargon about companies and clients. They were friendly and cordial, some contained borderline inside humor for a married man with a wife and two kids, but there was no smoking gun, no absolute proof of anything. Kate powered down Michael's computer.

"Greg's friend claims people sometimes set up domains for private accounts they keep under the radar." Kate didn't respond. "I'm just saying." Violet saw the fight was out of Kate, so she dropped the subject. They left Michael's office and made their way down to the lobby. They walked past Phillie's desk. He gave them a small wave but Kate could have sworn he did it in his sleep.

Kate paid Tom when she got home and faced the barrage of Jake's questions.

"Where's Aunt Violet?"

"She went home."

"The movie's over already?"

"We didn't go to a movie," Kate said.

"How come?"

"We couldn't decide on what to see." This was technically true. She and Violet didn't have the same taste in books or movies. Violet loved science fiction and historical dramas, while Kate would just as soon be lulled into believing in a romantic fairytale with a ridiculously happy ending.

"What did you do?"

"We just went out, you know, to the mall – had a drink. Hey, I see they're coming out with a new war game for Xbox." She had no idea if this was true, but she was banking on the greed of the video game industry to tweak the latest combat game just the slightest bit so every kid would want it.

"It's on my Christmas list."

"Good. Dad and I'll talk about it."

Jake was the image of his father, with the same light brown hair, but with a twist. It had Kate's mother's texture, a head full of reckless curls that couldn't be tamed. For years she tried waxes, gels, and crew cuts that looked like his scalp was full of razor-width scars where his cowlicks divided. She and Michael finally gave up.

"School tomorrow, Buddy. Homework done?"

"Yeah." Jake's interest in Kate came in small spurts and now that he was done with her he went upstairs. Kate picked up his sweaty socks and carried them with her as she made her way to her bedroom. The light from his television was on in Jake's room.

"Five minute warning, Jake." Finding nothing definite about Marilyn and Michael made Kate cranky. If Michael was deceiving her, she was no better. She lied to her son, went behind her husband's back and put Violet in the middle of it all. She decided to take a hot shower, then call Michael and tell him how she really spent her evening.

22

Kate was wide-awake, staring at the phone. She eventually lost her nerve and any interest in talking to Michael. She didn't want to hear his voice, not even on his polite message. She decided that a simple "I love you. Goodnight" text was best. The one person she wanted to talk to had left her life too early and now the sound of that voice had permanently evaporated from Kate's memory. There was no video to remind her and no matter how hard she tried, she couldn't recall even the cadence of a simple phrase.

Kate once believed she shared everything with her mother, but it wasn't true for her any more than it has ever been true for any mother and daughter since the beginning of time. When Michael returned to school their senior year of college, they were officially a couple. Kate parsed out bits of the facts to Maryann. She described their dates with the fewest details possible. Michael rented his own place off campus and he suggested they tell her parents he had a roommate. The small studio barely fit his bed and a small card table – and the only roommate he had was Kate, even if it was only now and then. If her parents suspected they were having sex, they never asked. They believed good Catholic girls waited till their wedding night, so her parents considered Kate tiptoeing up the stairs at four in the morning still being on a date and that kept a tranquil balance in the Marino household.

Kate and Michael went back to his apartment every day after class. They peeled their clothes off of each other before the door was fully closed. She'd fall into him as he kissed her. He would lead her to the bed and throw back the covers. Michael would leave a trail of kisses from her breasts down her abdomen until his tongue stroked her and she throbbed with delight. She had to will herself not to come until he was inside of her. Kate loved sex with Michael. He joked he'd awakened a sleeping tiger. On the late afternoons he worked at the grocery store, Michael would return with flowers that the manager was ready to toss because a fresh shipment had come in. They'd cook together and spend the rest of the evening making love until they exhausted themselves. But no matter how late it was, Kate always showered and made the drive home to sleep in her own bed.

Michael often surprised her with thoughtful gifts. He celebrated the first day he saw her in class with a new paperback anthology of her favorite authors. They recreated their first non-official date at Café Monty. Cards would appear on her pillow on his bed or she'd find notes and cards in her lingerie drawer that he'd sneak into her room at home.

Michael's long silences were Kate's oasis that first year. He didn't like to argue and if that meant Kate got her way, then things always seemed to work out for both of them. And if it put Michael in a bad mood for a while, he eventually came out of it. They were together almost every day. During the winter, Kate would tell her parents she was staying with her friend Sharon because there was snow in the forecast. Sometimes she would invent a late study session – anything she could come up with to have more time with Michael.

Kate and Michael graduated with honors. They took pictures with his parents, Kate's parents, Kate's sisters, and the two families together. Maryann had sent the McAllisters an invitation to Kate's party, but they had to get back to the farm. A week before commencement, Michael mentioned to Kate that his parents planned to take him out to dinner to celebrate.

"Great. I'll see if my parents are free. I mean they'll be crazy because of the party..."

"No, I mean just the three of us, Kate." Her face fell. "But I'm sure they'll be cool with you coming."

"No, I can't. I have to help at home." She heard her mother's martyr tone creep into her voice.

"I'll call them and ask."

"No, don't. Really, Michael, it's fine."

Kate was in love and if Michael's parents wanted to celebrate with their son, alone, she wanted that too. She had been careful not to say or do anything that would bring on a dark mood or start an argument. April and the change of season marked a change in their relationship. Michael was being recruited by several companies. He had a half-dozen job interviews lined up right after graduation. They didn't like to talk about life after college, but when a large consumer products company in Cincinnati offered him a job, they agreed he had to take it.

He went back to Elna for a week after graduation, then drove back to Philadelphia to spend a few days with Kate and her family before he started as a junior marketing executive. Kate tried not to cry in front of Michael and had only broken down a couple of times in all the weeks leading up to finals. On the night before he left, he was sleeping on her family room sofa. She snuck down to see him.

"Can't sleep?"

"No." He sat up and she got on the sofa next to him. He wrapped the summer weight blanket around her.

"What time are you getting on the road?"

"Seven, eight maybe."

Kate didn't want to repeat the words that had closed him off to her the last few weeks. Words like, "I'll miss you" and "We'll talk all the time," so she sat next to him and for one of the few times in their relationship, she refused to fill the silence. She wanted to tell him to stay and find a job close to her, but she knew he was eager to succeed. Kate didn't want to move to Cincinnati and they both knew they weren't ready to get married. He put his arm around her and kissed her softly. Kate knew without hearing the words that they were saying goodbye to each other and no matter how hard she tried to stop them, the tears came.

They planned to meet up over long weekends whenever they got the chance, but Michael was working sixty-hour weeks from the start. Kate couldn't afford to fly to Cincinnati and it was a long trip in her old car. They never had a big fight or officially broke up; they just stopped being together. They called each other on the weekends, but after a few months, that turned into every other week, which became now and then. Almost six weeks went by without hearing from Michael when he got in touch with her that following December. She was thrilled to hear his voice.

"Hey, how's Cincy?"

"Snow flurries today."

"I'm jealous," she said.

"How's the writing going?"

"Slow. I'm stalking a woman at *The Journal*. She's not in love with me."

"She will be. How's the family?"

"Great. They ask about you all the time."

"Your mom sent me a birthday card."

"I know, she told me," Kate said.

"With twenty bucks..."

"For beer money, right?"

"That's what she called it."

"How's work?"

"Good. I've got a couple of interesting accounts. I might even get out to Philly early next year."

"Great. Call me, okay? We'll meet up."

"Sounds good." They talked a little longer and Michael eventually slipped in that he started seeing someone, another junior account executive. Her name was Janie or Josie. Kate said she was happy for him. She knew Michael didn't like being alone. He'd had a steady girlfriend since high school, and Kate was hit with the sad realization that eventually the next girl, at his next job, in the next city, would replace Janie or Josie. She was wrong to think they were perfect together. It just felt perfect at the time because Michael made you feel like no one could ever replace you in his life – until they did.

Business did take Michael back to Philadelphia the following March and he met Kate for drinks. He said he didn't have time to come out to the house and see her family, so they agreed to meet in Center City. Kate was dropping off another article for Esther Rosen and Michael was staying near Rittenhouse Square. They agreed to meet in the hotel bar. He was nursing a beer when she walked in. Kate stared at him for a moment, not sure she could go through with it. He looked handsome in his business suit, but she already dreaded the horrible loneliness she'd feel the day after he left so she turned to leave. But he had already spotted her.

"Kate." He moved toward her and kissed her cheek.

"You look great."

"Yeah, right."

"You do. Incredible. And your family?"

"The same. Good."

"Tell them I miss them."

There was a long silence. She didn't ask about his girlfriend and he didn't ask if she was seeing anyone. She wanted to tell him she had gone on a few dates, but she missed him. That the two of them being apart felt wrong. That she still loved him and hated thinking of him having sex with another girl. She wasn't sure she'd ever find anybody she loved as much as she still loved Michael, but his new life had taken him from her, just like their life together in college had taken him from Barb.

He wanted to know more about her writing and Kate went on about Esther Rosen's amazing ability to ignore her and how she had dug in her heels and didn't plan to stop until the editor put out a restraining order on her.

"You know we have newspapers in Cincinnati," he said. Kate wondered how Janie or Josie would have felt if she heard Michael practically invite her to come and live in Cincinnati. Kate didn't respond. Michael checked his watch. He had a flight first thing in the morning and needed to turn in early. He got her a cab to take her back to the train station.

"It was great seeing you, Kate."

"You too."

"Mind if I still call once in a while?" he asked.

"No. I'd like that, Michael." He kissed her softly on the lips, then hugged her goodbye and held on a moment longer, at least that was how Kate remembered it.

A year later she was in New York meeting a friend for drinks in a small, neighborhood bar. It had only six booths against a wall and a thick mahogany wrap-around bar. She settled into a booth. There was a mirror on the rough brick that faced her. Its original brass frame had never seen a coat of polish. It was as worn as the distressed brick. Her friend Sharon slid into the booth with a hasty apology about cross-town traffic and rain, but Kate didn't hear a word. She was fixated on the image of the man in the booth behind her that was reflected in the mirror. Without her contact lenses, she could barely make out the hazy image of Michael McAllister. His reflection stared at her as if he had no idea who she was. What were the odds they'd end up in the same New York bar? She whispered to Sharon, "Michael's here. Isn't that too weird? Think I should say 'hi'?" Sharon looked up at the man in the booth. Her eyes glazed over as if she'd seen a vision. She leaned over the table and whispered.

"Kate, it's not Michael. It's Christopher Reeve."

Kate went limp and dug out her glasses from the bottom of her purse. She didn't dare turn around and instead looked in the mirror to confirm Sharon's sighting. This is what Kate would later call in one of her columns "Dream Come True Limbo," where something so incredible happens to you, you are immobilized by shock. She took a few notes while keeping her back to Superman, stealing occasional glances in the mirror. She pretended he wasn't there and told Sharon to stop staring as if she'd never seen a man before.

"This is no ordinary man. I heard he lived around here, but I've never run into anybody famous." Sharon was halfway out of her seat, but the look on Kate's face stopped her. Kate ordered a burger and beer and made Sharon promise to keep her seat and pretend he wasn't there.

"What? Just sit here?" Sharon said.

"Yes. Pretend he's invisible." Kate had practiced the invisible drill for years; especially since Michael had left to start his career in a city she still had trouble spelling. In a family where roles were easily assigned, she wasn't the pretty sister or the lucky sister. She was the smart sister. She had spent too many years in dowdy uniforms that left her with little sense of fashion. She never mastered eyeliner or figured out whether a color looked right on her or not. Kate loved writing because her words made her beautiful and attractive to her readers. Since she started working for Esther, she spoke her mind through her column. Fighting for her words and her ideas was easy, even with her headstrong editor. But Kate the writer and Kate the woman had not yet merged. And on those rare nights when she struck up a conversation with a man at a bar, it was her career that got things rolling. Her job got her past those first few awkward moments, but she usually ended up buying her own drink and leaving quietly. She had a brief fling with a copy editor who had been hired away from the *New York Times*, but she knew it wasn't going anywhere and broke up with him after a couple of months. Unlike her sisters who had a stream of "steadies," Kate's only real dating experience began and ended with Michael.

She ate half her meal, exchanging small talk with Sharon as a familiar feeling of sadness crept over her. Kate knew that the only person she had made invisible that night, like she had done so many other nights, wasn't Christopher Reeve. It was herself.

Kate had been working at the newspaper for almost a year and her columns had gotten more reader mail than some of the veteran columnists. She had created buzz. The paper advertised her as "The voice of a new generation." Kate wrote constantly, keeping notes on future columns, and she could finally afford fun. She took in some Broadway shows and some off-Broadway hits or misses. She visited old friends up and down the northeast corridor from Boston to Washington. She was gone a lot, but when she was home, she slept in the same small bed with the window facing east. Marie was teaching elementary school and Theresa was getting serious with Frank Dedda, a good Italian boy from South Jersey. She had followed in Kate's steps at Montgomery State University and met Frank their sophomore year. Kate wondered if her baby sister and Frank would be luckier than her and Michael.

She had gotten a note from Michael saying he moved to Minneapolis. Kate was too busy at the paper to follow up, but jotted down the return address in her journal. In the security blanket world of success, when almost everything was falling Kate's way, she embraced the idea that fate was finally on her side and didn't believe it would ever turn its back on her. The small obstacles life threw her way didn't alter her belief in a limitless future. And if Kate still missed Michael, she was finally open to the possibility of finding someone new.

It was an unusually cold December that first year at *The Philadelphia Journal*. Kate was looking forward to Christmas as if she were a little girl again, except it wasn't about what was waiting for her under the tree. She was excited about the gifts she could now afford to buy and wrap up in bright bows for her sisters and parents. She spent weeks thinking about what to get for each one of them. She made the rounds of travel agencies and decided to send her parents to Italy. They had saved repeatedly for that trip over the years, until a new roof or bad plumbing emptied their savings. She arranged for them to go in late spring. It was her mother's dream trip. Now that Kate was living her dream, she wanted her mother to live one of her own.

Her mother caught another virus after Thanksgiving so Kate offered to help Maryann with her shopping. She knew what her sisters wanted, what they liked, and what would be thrown in the return pile. She had a year's worth of columns in her head so she had no trouble meeting deadlines.

Maryann was worn out and needed this trip to Italy. The brochures would be placed in order of the tour: Sorrento, Rome, Florence, and finally Venice. She imagined her mother's fingers playing over the brightly colored pages depicting the Ponte Vecchio and Doge Palace. She'd insist Kate cancel the whole thing. She could practically predict the volley of words.

"Are you crazy? I know what this costs."

"I can afford it, Mom."

"You should be saving your money."

"I am saving my money."

"Tony, did you know about this?"

"Not a clue."

"We can't take it. It's too much. Why don't you go?"

"I will one day. Let me do this for you, please. If it wasn't for your support, I wouldn't even be at the paper."

"Talk to her, Tone."

"You can both talk to me, but I'm not returning a thing. If you don't go, the whole trip will go to waste." That would stop her. Maryann hated any kind of waste and when she finally accepted the trip, she would cry picturing herself among the sites, standing in front of the Pietà, looking up till her neck ached at the Basilica at St. Peters, shooing pigeons on St. Mark's square. Kate couldn't wait to see her face on Christmas morning. Buona Natale, Mama.

Snow had fallen the first week in December and frigid temperatures settled over eastern Pennsylvania. The maple trees had shed their leaves by late November. Only the stubborn oaks refused to bow. They held onto the brown, brittle, and shriveled pieces of their former beauty. Kate came home one day from an editorial meeting and had mistaken the sound of a strong winter breeze blowing through them for wind chimes as they rattled against each other with an eerie harmony.

The house was unusually quiet. Theresa was probably with her boyfriend and Marie never came home from school until almost six. She had the enthusiasm of a young teacher. Kate shared her sister's passion for her work. She was her happiest when she was writing. Any doubt or lingering fears about her personal life melted away at the keyboard. She commanded her column like a general in the battlefield. The paragraphs marched in formation, with just enough humor to keep it from being preachy. Her first published column for the *Journal* was laminated, framed, and hung in the family room. Kate begged her parents to take it down, but they refused.

The fan letters were an unexpected bonus. People she'd never met told her she made them laugh, helped with their loneliness, or touched them in some way. Kate secretly wanted to get her own place soon, but decided to wait until after Christmas to tell her parents. They wouldn't like the idea. They'd want her to stay home, save money, and wait to meet the right guy. But the right guy was living over a thousand miles away in Minneapolis.

She looked around the kitchen for a note from her mother. It was Maryann's day off at the beauty shop. Kate assumed she was Christmas shopping. Even though Kate had handled most of it, she probably wanted to add a few of her own surprises. Nana was napping, so Kate started to make dinner. She didn't need recipes or cookbooks. Every dish prepared in that kitchen was like a home movie she could play back in her mind. Nana and Maryann mincing garlic, blending tomatoes, simmering a piece of veal to add to the gravy. The recipes came to life in Kate's mind as her hands moved through the refrigerator to find ingredients or snipped pieces of basil from the small plant growing on the windowsill.

Each family scene was unique depending on the menu. Most of the time, Maryann and Nana moved around the tiny kitchen on autopilot as the familiar aromas evolved without more than a few words spoken between them. But a more complicated dish would be peppered with a beautiful score.

"The osso buco is *shabeed*." *Shabeed* was Nana's word for it had no taste, which translated into add more salt.

"Ma, it's fine."

"It tastes like paper," Nana said. "A pinch. No more."

Nana grabbed the saltbox and filled her palm.

"Ma, what are you doing?"

"Who taught you how to make veal?"

"We're trying to watch what we eat."

"Everybody watches. My father, ninety-six, God rest his soul, never watched a day in his life." The movie always had the same ending. The two women smiling proudly as their family devoured the meal.

Kate kept it simple that night. There was leftover gravy in the fridge. It was almost five. Nana would be waking soon. She was the family night owl. Kate often heard her creeping around the kitchen or saw the light from the television in her bedroom casting a glow under the door. Her hearing was getting worse, so she often watched with no volume while saying a rosary. Most of her friends were gone. She was the last of her siblings. For years she followed the ups and downs of her television families, the Hughes clan on "As The World Turns," or that *putana*, Erica Kane on "All My Children." The young, fresh faces and sad stories became her daily companions.

After lunch, she'd announce, "Katareen, it's time for my story." She'd settle in the family room for the next three hours, talking back to the television as if they could hear her. By four o'clock Nana was exhausted by the drama and ready for a nap. So many of Nana's stories have since gone off the air. Shows she once listened to on the radio were cancelled after fifty-year runs. But it was years ago on that simple, ordinary afternoon of the quiet house, Nana's nap, and leftover spaghetti gravy that Kate learned nothing good lasts forever.

She stirred the congealed tomatoes and olive oil, and then added a cup of water and fresh basil while it thinned. She placed the frozen meatballs in the pot so they thawed in time, and washed a head of romaine lettuce. Kate set the colander on the avocado countertop. Small knife slits marked the surface in an abstract pattern. The Formica was too old to fuss over, so when they were too lazy to pull out a cutting board to slice a loaf of bread or chop an onion, another line or two was added. She barely noticed the corners and seams that had bubbled from water that seeped under it and was lifting the surface. The countertop, like most things she saw every day in that house, was taken for granted. When something was worn or tired, it happened slowly, making Kate forget what it looked had like when it was brand new.

Kate decided to wait and see if her sisters were coming home for dinner before she set the table. Nana was finally moving around upstairs when the front door opened.

"Hey, Marie, get your lazy ass in here and help!"

Tony entered the kitchen alone.

"Where's Mom?"

"The hospital. She had a checkup. The doctor wants to run tests."

"Why? What's wrong?"

Tony sat down at the table. She poured him a glass of wine.

"It's that flu," Tony said. "She can't shake it, so he wants to check her blood, things like that."

"Can I go see her?"

"Sure. I'm going back after dinner. We'll bring her some real food." Nana shuffled in and Tony told her the news. She nodded and whispered to him in Italian. Marie called and planned to meet them at the hospital. Theresa wasn't coming home for dinner. She and Frank were going to a movie. Tony decided he'd tell her when she got home. It was a quiet meal. They did the dishes quickly and afterward Kate, Tony and Nana piled into the car and headed to the hospital with a Tupperware container of food for Maryann. She was sitting up when they got there, freshening her lipstick.

Kate laughed. "It can't be that serious if you're worried about lipstick."

Tony unpacked the two peignoir negligees she hadn't worn in years. Marie hung them up in the closet and put her mother's favorite slippers by the bed.

"Good, you brought the pink one."

"And the blue..."

"If I'm here that long. Dr. Hunt says one, two days max."

"What do they think it is?" Kate asked. Nana pulled out her rosary beads and sat at Maryann's side.

"Ma, enough with the rosary. I'm fine."

"You need anything else from home?" Tony kissed her forehead.

"My make-up bag. I just have that tube."

"I'm not bringing you anything else so you can look pretty for the doctors."

"Have you seen that young one coming in and out of here? Kate, he's on rounds later."

"Ma, stop," Kate said.

"You had this same 'bug' when you were seven. Sick off and on. How long, Tone?"

"Long."

"I don't remember Kate sick," Marie said.

"You were too little."

They stayed until visiting hours were over. Maryann promised to eat after they left. She was scheduled for more tests first thing in the morning. They sent her home three days later in time to put up the Christmas tree. Tony picked a gold theme that year. The balls, lights and tinsel garland – all gold. He placed the tree in the center of the picture window.

"This one's the best ever," he said.

"You say that every year," Maryann said from the couch.

"But the gold, Mare, it's like the sun right here in our living room."

"Would it hurt to put some lights on the outside?"

"How many times do I have to tell you? It takes away from my tree." It was the same argument every year. Tony hated to do any Christmas decorating outside the house. Except for his obsession with the perfect tree with the perfect theme, centered perfectly in the picture window, the rest of the decorating was left to Maryann. It was a crazy December. Kate handed in her last column of the year on the nineteenth. Marie was busy at school, directing the holiday pageant and Theresa was spending every free moment with Frank.

Kate received dozens of cards from readers. They came in large, inter-office envelopes. The paper collected them every few days and forwarded them to the house. Maryann was spending more time in her room, and Kate would sort through the stack and read them to her. Whatever her columns inspired came back in an odd collection of notes, pictures and the occasional marriage proposal.

"See, I told you. Esther Rosen wasted all that time because she was jealous."

"She wasn't jealous."

"She knew you were better than the writers she had," Maryann said.

"If she was so jealous, why did she hire me?"

"I said jealous, not stupid."

Maryann took her daughter's hand. Something felt unusual. Kate looked at her mom's fingers entwined in her own. Her quarter-carat engagement ring was twisted toward her palm. Her fingers were thin and her skin had a yellowish cast.

"What's going on, Mom?"

"Read the next one."

"Please, tell me."

Kate looked at her mother in a way she hadn't in a very long time. As Kate was enjoying her new job, new money and new friends, the house became a place to change her clothes before she flew out the door again. Marie and Theresa were in and out as often as Kate. While they had become young women, the house where they grew up seldom changed. Its sculptured carpeting and wild onion wallpaper in the kitchen, along with the water stain in the front hallway ceiling, chipped porcelain in the tub, and theme-colored Christmas trees would be reminders of the life they had as children and the things they'd talk about years later as adults.

"Is it cancer?" Her daughter, who saw the truth in life and the truth in people and wrote about it, knew. Maryann nodded and Kate began to cry.

"Ssh, no tears. They don't know everything yet."

"What kind?" Kate asked.

"Does it matter?"

"It matters, Mom. They have different treatments for different kinds and..."

Maryann cut her off. "Don't tell your sisters. I don't want to ruin their Christmas."

"Mom, they have to know."

"They will. I go back to the hospital on the twenty-sixth. We'll know more then." She lifted her hand to brush away Kate's tears.

"Can you keep this our secret, Kate? Honey, please."

"Does Dad know?"

"He knows, and Nana. She's worn out three sets of rosary beads over nothing. Don't you worry. These doctors are smart. I'm not going anywhere."

Kate got into bed with her mother for the first time since she was a child. Maryann winced when she held Kate closer. Kate saw her mother's pain as she gently settled her head against her mother's shoulder. Maryann kissed the top of her head and her flesh-worn collarbone pressed against Kate's cheek.

"Don't sit here with me all day. Go out and find something to write about."

Kate barely spoke above a whisper. "I love you, Mom." Maryann stroked her hair.

They were all together opening presents on Christmas morning. Maryann didn't go to midnight Mass the night before. Kate went with her father and grandmother. Her sisters were in and out visiting friends. The presents Kate picked out were a huge hit. Theresa loved her sweaters and tape player. Marie was thrilled with her tickets to see *Cats*. Kate had put the Italy brochures back in her nightstand. She'd gone out and bought other gifts for her parents instead – a new clock radio, a bracelet for her mother and a jacket for her dad, more practical things.

Kate, Nana, and her sisters pulled off the enormous dinner later that day. Maryann insisted everyone come, all the aunts, uncles, and cousins. Aunt Millie fought tears and told Kate to "be strong" and that's when Kate realized they all knew. The entire extended family had kept this secret from her and her sisters. The air in the house turned stale. Not even the delicious holiday meal masked the putrid smell of sickness. How had she not seen what was right in front of her?

Maryann stayed in her room. Tony went missing during dinner. Kate slipped upstairs; their door was open.

"Just a little bite, baby."

"I can't. Maybe later."

He had a plate of food and kept coaxing her mother to eat something. Tony believed if she kept something down, she'd get better and life would be good again.

After the extended family left, later on Christmas night, they told Marie and Theresa about Maryann going back to the hospital in the morning. And in that moment, they saw what Kate had seen, and the three of them sat on the bed and cried. Tony was downstairs with Nana. He couldn't bear the shared sadness of his girls.

Maryann went back to St. Peter's Hospital the next day. An extensive biopsy was scheduled. The surgeon finished more quickly than predicted. Kate assumed that was a good sign. His white coat was wrinkled and there were a few speckles of dried blood by the slit for his pocket. Kate wondered if it was her mother's blood.

"How'd it go, Doc?" The red-embroidered name above his breast read Dr. Bernstein, surgical oncology.

"I'm sorry, Mr. Marino. I sewed her right back up." His head was down. He didn't look Tony in the eye. Dr. Bernstein's lips continued to move. He spoke in cancer's foreign language of "... nomas" and "metastases" and a suspected subtype that spread like wildfire. That was the only word Kate remembered – wildfire. Nothing would stop it. They could try chemotherapy but it would yield no results. Maryann fell into a coma two weeks later.

On a dark January morning, Kate couldn't sleep. She left the house quietly and was at the hospital by four o'clock. She sat by her mother's bed as the nurses moved in and out, touching Kate's shoulder as they glided around the IV pole and monitors. Maryann's breathing made a garbling sound that Kate blocked out with silent prayers. It took a few moments before she realized the sound had stopped. Her mother had died. She didn't call for a nurse. Kate held her hand and felt Maryann's spirit leave her as if it was a physical thing she could reach out and hold onto one last time. Kate felt like she witnessed what must be the exact opposite of a child being born into the world.

Cancer ate her mother alive. An alien living inside of her body waited until it was ready, waited until it was starving and when it woke up, it devoured her. Nana had nieces and nephews who'd suffered similar deaths. She blamed herself. The family curse. Tony signed papers for an autopsy since they didn't know where the cancer began. He needed to know for his daughters.

Tony's boss lent him his Mercedes Benz to drive those next few days as if having a hundred thousand dollar car would make up for one dead wife. Kate drove with him to pick out the casket. She traded in the Italian vacation for the most expensive solid cherry coffin they had and a small plot behind their church. They met with the priest, ordered flowers, chose hymns, and arranged for the luncheon afterward. Kate was grateful there was so much to do. They would lay her mother out in the beautiful turquoise silk dress she'd bought for Gina Palmieri's wedding next month. Gina, a cranky "old maid" at twenty-eight was Maryann's best friend's daughter. Gina was marrying a third cousin. Nana said if the wedding ever came off, it would be Maryann's first miracle.

Kate and her father drove back from the undertaker in silence. Tony's eyes never left the road. He'd aged twenty years in the last four weeks. She heard him walking around his room at night. The television went off and on. He hadn't slept in days.

"Nice car, Dad."

"Nice of Bob to let me use it." Hollow words were better than no words.

"Mind if I try the radio?" He shook his head.

She flipped the switch on the eight-speaker, perfectly balanced sound system midway through a song. "Hey, did you happen to see the most beautiful girl in the world..." Kate tried to shut it off, but Tony stopped her. The singer continued. "And if you did, was she crying, crying." Kate looked at her father.

"Dad come on, please." The awful song wouldn't end. "Hey, if you happen to see the most beautiful girl/that walked out on me/

tell her I'm sorry./Tell her I need my baby./Won't you tell her that I love her." Tony put his head against his hands on the steering wheel and burst into tears.

"Pull over!" He couldn't hear her. Kate grabbed the wheel. "Dad!" He looked up and quickly pulled to the side of the road.

"I'm sorry, Kate. I'm so sorry."

"It's okay."

"She never went to the doctors. She never listened. I should have made her listen."

"Daddy, it's not your fault. It's nobody's fault." She reached over to hug him. His fingernails dug into her shoulders.

"I'll drive home." Kate touched his arm when they met in front of the car.

Nana insisted on a wake the night before the funeral. Tony wanted an open casket. They expected a big crowd, so Father McGrory let them hold the viewing in the church. They stood guard next to her body: Tony, Nana, Grandpa Joe, Kate, Marie, and finally Theresa. Frank Dedda sat in the first row, getting up every few minutes to check if Theresa needed anything.

Maryann's face was bloated from the autopsy. The cutting and the disease made her look like somebody else, someone Kate didn't recognize. The family shook hands, kissed hundreds of people and comforted them. Her aunts and uncles brought them water and stood in line now and then to greet the mourners. They were at the church for three hours and people were still arriving. By the end of the night, Maryann's entire family, her brother, sister-in-law, Tony's brothers, their wives, and the nieces and nephews had all joined the receiving line. Kate was sure her mother would have loved the sight of all the boys and girls she helped raise, standing over her body like she was Princess Grace. People stayed to talk and catch up with each other and mostly share stories about her mother. All of Kate's childhood friends from our Lady of Perpetual Help Elementary School came. They loved her mother. Maryann listened to their problems with boys or their parents. They slept at her house, stayed for days and went to the Jersey Shore with them for summer vacation. They called her Mama Mare.

It was after ten by the time the crowd thinned. Tony wanted only the six of them there when the undertaker closed the casket. The Mass of Christian Burial with its strong incense and formal readings was the following morning. The closed casket, covered in a white burial cloth, had to be traditionally placed in the center aisle. What was left of her family would sit in the first pew with no space left for where her mother should be.

The last two mourners knelt in front of her mother's body, making the sign of the cross. The stained glass windows were black. The images of the Virgin Mary, baby Jesus, saints and martyrs were obscured by the darkness. Kate looked into the void that broke the dimly lit granite and marble walls. Mr. and Mrs. DiAntonio, Nana's closest friends, were hugging Nana, speaking Italian. Kate made out a word here and there. Words like "tragedy" and "too young." Frank was alone at the back of the church waiting to walk Theresa to the car. The pews were empty.

The undertaker was growing impatient. Kate caught him checking his watch. She hated him for that. The DiAntonios had moved on to Tony. No one else was in line. There were no more stories being told, no one was laughing.

"Your mother was like a daughter to me," Mrs. DiAntonio said.

"I know, Zia Carmen. Thank you for coming." Kate's words were rote, lifeless. They'd say the same words to her sisters, and her sisters would say the same words to them. Then it would be time to close the casket on her mother's face, that wasn't her mother's face. The DiAntonios headed toward the side exit. Everyone was gone.

The undertaker nodded toward Tony and the casket as the heavy doors at the back of the church creaked open. He stepped back once more, annoyed. Kate moved to the first pew to get something from her purse when she heard footsteps coming up the long marble aisle. She was thinking about driving home in that stupid Mercedes. She hated that car. It didn't have her mother's smell or the lists she crammed into the glove compartment or food wrappers that spilled out from under the seats. Tony complained constantly about Maryann's car being a garbage dump. Now he couldn't bear to be in it. The footsteps stopped by her pew.

"Kate?" She looked up at Michael, standing there in a brown suit, not sure what to do or say next. They hadn't talked in almost a year. He glanced at Tony, Nana, Grandpa, and her sisters. They smiled when they saw him. She stepped out of the pew and he opened his arms. Kate went into them and wept harder than she had in days. She cried because her life would never be the same. She cried because she already missed her mother's voice and knew that one day she'd forget the sound of it. She cried because Michael was holding her again. She tried to pull back but Michael held her tighter. He smelled of citrus musk, the kind she bought him years ago. He leaned down and gently kissed her cheek.

"Who told you?"

"Your dad called. I tried to get an earlier flight but it was crazy, storms in the Midwest..."

"How did he know how to find you?"

"Your mother must have told him. She called me on my birthday."

"She didn't tell me," Kate said. Maryann was protecting her. She knew how much Kate still missed Michael.

"But she didn't say anything about being sick."

"She didn't know," Kate said. "Do you want to see her?" He nodded. She took Michael's hand and led him to the kneeler in front of the casket.

"What are those," he whispered. He indicated the travel brochures she'd taken from her purse.

"A gift." They knelt in front of Maryann's body. Michael closed his eyes and said a prayer. Kate carefully placed the Italy brochures next to her mother's lifeless hand.

"Merry Christmas, Mom." She kissed her mother for the last time. The cold, frozen, opposite-of-life skin offered no warmth, no memories. Michael rose and moved to the rest of the family. They hugged him like he'd never left. Tony thanked him for coming and kept calling him "son."

"It means a lot to us, Mike. To Mrs. 'M' too."

"Are you coming to the Mass?" Marie asked.

"Yeah. I took a couple of days."

He turned to hug Nana. She took his cheeks in her hands, moved at seeing him. He didn't want to break down in front of her. Michael felt it wasn't fair to have Kate or her family comfort him. He wanted to tell them how much he missed them and Maryann, and that being with their family had been the best part of his life so far. Instead he channeled his parents' stoicism. Edith often said to him, "When has getting upset ever helped anybody?"

He explained he was staying at a hotel near the church and he'd see them all in the morning, and then moved back to Kate.

"They're about to close the casket," Kate said.

"I'll let you and your family say goodbye." Another awkward moment passed and he walked out of the church. The undertaker was already folding the blankets around her mother. He removed the spray of flowers with the silver cardboard "Mother" label on it. He took the single red rose from Maryann's hand. Tony wanted it placed on the coffin during the Mass. He carefully removed the dried flower rosary bead arrangement from the foot of the casket. They went one by one up to the body for a final goodbye, and then stepped back, holding each other up as the bald man in his generic black suit and lily-white hands slowly closed the lid. It sealed softly as if the sides were lined with velvet.

23

Michael was floored when Tony Marino called him at his office in Minneapolis. He liked Kate's father, but always felt a little intimidated by him. Maryann was the one who called Michael and sent cards on his birthday. Michael assumed that's how Tony had gotten his number. Tony got right to the point. He said Kate's mother had cancer. It spread quickly and she had died the day before last. Michael couldn't believe it. He always liked to think of the Marinos sitting around their table laughing and arguing, frozen in time the way he remembered them.

Michael was working his way up in the market research department of a national soft drink company. He had been dating Claire O'Brien for a while. He met her through one of his friends at work. She was a nurse at Abbot Northwestern Hospital. She was taller than Kate, much taller, and had bright red hair with freckles. She was sweet and fun, but Michael wasn't in love with her. The guilt he felt about his lack of feelings for Claire competed with his nagging loneliness of being in a new city and not knowing many people.

He and Kate had lost touch, but he wondered why she didn't call him when her mother got sick. Maybe she had found someone else too. Michael wasn't sure what to do. The wake was the following night. He'd have to get a quick flight to Philly, but he wasn't sure he belonged there. It wasn't as if he and Kate broke up, they simply drifted away from each other. He couldn't start his career in one city and date a girl that far away. Kate was focused on her writing, and Michael had a ten-year plan of where he wanted to be in his career and it didn't allow him to be stuck in one geographic area. His parents warned him long-distance relationships never panned out.

"Just look at you and Barb," Edith said. "Everybody thought you two were perfect for each other."

"We weren't perfect, Mom," he replied.

"We thought you were. And Michael, maybe your next girlfriend could be just a little taller. That Kate was just too short for you."

His mother judged Michael's happiness by the height of the girl and where she lived in relation to the farm, but Michael felt something had gone out of his life after he left Kate. And no matter how hard he tried or how many girls he dated, he hadn't found it again.

His cubicle was filled with pictures from different trips he'd taken. There was skiing in Colorado, a scuba vacation to Belize. He hadn't dated anyone seriously enough yet to bring her along, but he and Claire planned to go to Jamaica next month to escape the cold Minnesota winter.

He sat in his office debating what to do. He could send flowers to the funeral parlor; write cards to Tony and the family, maybe even a personal note to Kate. But Tony had called him. This woman who continued to love him like a son, even after he stopped dating her daughter, was gone. He remembered her hugs when he came and went. She said he always had a place at her table and he believed her. He had helped Tony with small projects around their house. Kate's father taught him about sanding floors and plumbing and fixing cars. They loved him because their daughter did. And that love had no boundaries and no strings attached.

When he and Kate grew apart, Maryann never asked him what happened. All she wanted to know when she called was if he was happy. He last spoke to her on his birthday back in September.

"How did you remember?" Michael asked.

"How could I forget," she answered.

"I know I'll never forget the lady who put ten pounds on me."

"Best ten pounds you ever gained."

"I'd kill to have dinner at your place. I haven't found a good Italian restaurant around here yet."

"It's a long way to go for pasta, Mikey."

"Not just any pasta."

"The door's always open. You know that. Are you having a happy birthday?"

"So far. I'm going out with friends tonight."

"Good for you," she said.

"So, you're doing okay? You happy, Michael?"

"Yeah, I'm fine. The job's good."

"I started drinking that stuff because of you," she said.

"Diet or regular?"

"Regular. I hate the diet stuff. Are you coming to Philly soon?"

"I don't think so. Most of our big markets are on the west coast and the south. But if I do get East, I'll stop by."

"You better. We miss you. Happy birthday, Michael."

"Thanks. I miss you too."

"Love you, honey. Take care of yourself."

"I will. You too, Mrs. Marino." That was their final conversation. And even if he had known that at the time, Michael wasn't sure he could ever tell her how much she still meant to him. Since he left Kate and her family, he fell back into old patterns he'd learned in childhood. He was more careful about letting people into his life. But Michael was touched at how easily Maryann said she loved him. He regretted not calling her or sending a card at Christmas.

He picked up the phone and made an airline reservation, then called Claire at the hospital and told her something came up with work and he had to leave town. He wasn't sure she'd understand why it was so important to go to his ex-girlfriend's mother's funeral. He decided a small lie was more convenient than the truth. He'd send Claire flowers from the road to make up for the dinner date he'd miss. The cost of the flight was outrageous and it looked like the weather wasn't going to cooperate, but his decision had been made.

He was at the airport first thing the following morning. His flight was delayed almost five hours as a winter storm messed with air traffic. Once he landed, he picked up a rental car and drove out to the suburbs. He wasn't sure he'd make the viewing. It was almost ten o'clock when he got to the church. If the family were gone, he'd go right to his hotel and attend the funeral Mass the next day. The parking lot was empty except for the hearse and a couple of cars. He rushed up to the wooden doors. The smell of incense and wood polish reminded him of the time Kate had taken him to Our Lady of Perpetual Help for a midnight Mass their first Christmas together. He had followed her lead and learned to kneel and stand in the right order. He read along with the prayers in the Mass book. Kate put her hand over his. She smiled in a way he hadn't seen before and had not forgotten since.

Kate didn't notice him enter the back of the church. She was digging for something in her purse. Michael thought she looked even more beautiful, even in her sadness. He walked toward her and she looked up at him. She didn't speak, but went into his arms and he held her while she cried. She still fit perfectly against his body, and he knew in that moment that he would go back to Minneapolis and resign. He'd break up with Claire, pack his things, and find an apartment and job closer to Kate. Michael wasn't a mystical or religious person, but he felt that somehow Maryann Marino had her hand in all of it.

It was in that cold, sad church as he hugged each one of them – Kate, Tony, Nana, Grandpa Joe, Theresa, and Marie – that Michael McAllister felt like he had finally come home.

24

Marilyn Campbell hated chasing men, but Michael was proving to be such a challenge that she had no choice. Her plane landed in a little more than an hour in Dallas. The next item on her list was deciding where she was going for Thanksgiving. She still hadn't confirmed plans. Her mother wanted her to fly to Florida and have dinner with her and her new husband, Cal. Marilyn liked Cal. Of all her mother's husbands, number three had staying power. He indulged Phyllis' frequent visits to the plastic surgeon for an injection here and a minor-lift there. He had more money than the first two combined and this improved Marilyn's relationship with Phyllis. Before Cal, Marilyn was her mother's personal ATM. She hadn't seen her father since she was eleven, and the last she heard from him, he was running a motel in South Dakota. She still had a box of old photos of the two of them together that she took out when she had one too many martinis. She lets herself cry for five minutes, and then puts them back in the storage unit in her high-rise. The only clear memory left of her father is the smell of his aftershave that was unfortunately still on the market. Her condo, with its clear view of the art museum on one side and the city skyline on the other, took years to find. She had rented in several trendy neighborhoods in the city until she discovered the perfect location. One of the partner's wives recommended a decorator. Marilyn filled out a personality profile and gave the design team free reign to create her living space. The contemporary, sleek result suited her sharp angles. The neutral colors, or absence of color, was cool and inviting. Pale tones against white with a sharp black accent piece here and there gave an impression of controlled serenity.

She asked the flight attendant for a scotch and decided not to let the cheap plastic cup bother her. She sipped it slowly, thinking of her and Michael meeting in her room later that night.

She had made a detour through the suburbs earlier, hoping to catch a glimpse of his wife. She searched for Kate McAllister's image on the Internet and found the magazine stock shot that she'd seen already and a few images from speaking engagements, but Marilyn preferred getting a first-hand impression. Kate really didn't factor into the future. She was simply a minor detail Marilyn wanted to keep on her radar screen. She certainly wasn't envious of Kate. She hadn't been jealous of anyone except the little girl who took her spot in the television ice cream commercial years ago. Marilyn didn't feel a bit of remorse when she read that same girl had been arrested in a crystal meth lab sting several months earlier.

Marilyn wondered if a decorator had a hand in designing Michael's home. If they did, it was embarrassingly personal for Marilyn's taste. She hadn't walked past the center hall, but she saw a glimpse of the dining room and an even smaller one of the kitchen at the end of the narrow corridor that branched off from the center hall. Michael's wife was obviously in love with color. The dining room was a deep burgundy, and robin's egg blue reflected off what looked like honey-colored cherry cabinets from the kitchen. Marilyn noticed the fabric on the small settee was expensive. It looked like a professional find but the chipped porcelain umbrella stand was either an old family hand-me-down or a flea market special.

Marilyn was sure that Michael, in his perfectly tailored suits, must feel like a stranger in that house. She saw that type of disconnection all the time with the men in her circle. They were aggressive and dynamic at work then went home to overstuffed rooms with sentimental pictures scattered along the tables and walls. She could never understand which part of their lives were truth and which were fiction. How do you choke the competition and beat them out on a solid deal by day, and then go home and play board games with the kids on a plaid sectional by night? It seemed hypocritical. Marilyn was the rare breed that didn't divide or compartmentalize her life to society's expectations. There wasn't a *work* Marilyn and a *domestic* Marilyn.

She never apologized for anything and didn't understand what people meant when they said they were lonely. Her life was too busy for loneliness. Her days could use more hours, her weeks more days, her months more weeks. She was in the gym at four-thirty in the morning so she could be the first one in the office. Her nickname was "Lights Out" because she was always the last to leave. Fortunately she didn't require much sleep. After she left the office, she usually dropped by Bistro Provence for a quick bite or to meet a client for drinks. Her first boss once told her that nobody succeeded at anything by working forty hours a week. If that was her measure, then Marilyn was a huge success. Her laptop, two phones, and briefcase allowed her to move geographically from place to place without ever leaving work and work never leaving her.

She touched down in Dallas and wheeled her carry-on through the terminal when her cell phone rang. It was Michael. She waited till the last possible moment, and then picked up.

"Hey, stranger."

"Marilyn, sorry, I have a few minutes between interviews."

"I'm on my way to the hotel. See you there. Oh, and by the way, nice house, Michael." She would have given her shoe allowance to see the look on his face.

"What the hell were you doing at my house?"

"Leaving you a present."

"Did you..."

"Meet Kate? No. Her assistant didn't let me past the front door. See you at the hotel."

She hung up before he could respond. She knew at moments like these he hated her, but later when she sat across the table from him and took his hand to assure him everything would be all right, he would calm down. Michael couldn't afford to stay mad at her. Marilyn felt that everything in her life thus far had been a dress rehearsal and this was her grab for the whole package. Her phone rang again. It was her mother, probably about Thanksgiving. She let it go to voicemail. She had a lot to be thankful for this year, but the last person she wanted to share it with was her mother.

25

Michael was livid that Marilyn went to his house, but he hadn't heard from Kate all day. Hopefully she didn't make much of the visit, but he highly doubted it. Marilyn wanted answers and promises, but more than anything else, she wanted things to go her way. Michael told her he was in no position to make promises yet, but Marilyn was an impatient woman.

Impatient women surrounded Michael. Kate's act-on-impulse, just-say-how-you-feel, get-things-done style often clashed with his slow, methodical way of approaching life. He had ignored Kate's one and only question about Marilyn's business card and now things were getting messy and slipping from his control. But Michael knew there were too many people to consider to simply blurt out the truth and clean up the mess later.

Luckily Kate was busy with the upcoming holidays. That bought him more time. As soon as he returned to his hotel, his cell phone rang.

"Hi, I was just about to call you," he said.

"Liar. I'm in 1214. Come up." Marilyn said.

"Marilyn, I'm beat. I started at seven this morning."

"We'll make it an early night, or morning. I promise." Michael was too tired to argue so he showered quickly then rode the six floors up to Marilyn's room. She looked incredible when she opened the door. Her V-neck sweater and tight slacks accented every line and curve of her perfect body. From the moment she shut the door, he forgot all about her dropping in on Kate. Time got away from them the way it always did. When he left her suite and stepped back out into the corridor, it was after three in the morning. He glanced down at their room service tray full of dirty dishes and stained wine glasses and made his way back to his own room.

Michael hadn't felt this guilty since the long drive home after his junior year of college. He and Kate had made love for the first time earlier that afternoon; they dressed quietly and took separate cars back to her house. He put his things in a corner of the basement, and then took the boom box up to her small bedroom while she took a quick shower. It was the first time he'd been alone in her room. He lingered in the space and fantasized about taking her in his arms again and making love to her under the faded daisy comforter. He wanted to stay in Pennsylvania and find a job, but he had promised his parents he'd go home.

"What are you doing?" Kate came from the bathroom wrapped in a towel. He held up the boom box.

"I thought I'd set it up for you." He found an outlet for the box. "Maybe I should wait downstairs." He couldn't stop looking at her bare shoulders and wet hair falling down around them. Beads of water had collected above her breasts.

"Good idea."

He ran down the steps as Kate's mom entered the hall from the kitchen, wiping her hands on a *mopeen*. Michael had picked up some Italian-American slang over the Marino kitchen table. Kate explained that a *mopeen* is a dish cloth, like a small mop.

She told him Nana was always making up words that were part English, part Italian. Michael imagined trying to explain a *mop-een* to his own mother.

"Now why would they call it that?" Edith would say.

"Because it's fun, Mom. Not real, just fun." But his mother was suspicious of "Eye-talians." To her they were all gangsters or worse, Catholics. He was sure she'd be skeptical of Kate and her "foreign" family, but Michael loved being with them. He loved when Kate's mom put her hand on the back of his neck and hugged him when he came in and when he left. He liked that her dad asked about school and his plans after graduation. But most of all he liked how they kissed each other for no reason – going out to the store, leaving for a walk, or coming back in from work.

He wanted to talk to Kate about what happened back in his room, but not with her mother around and he had to get on the road before it got much later. Maryann was holding a large brown bag.

"This is for you. Some sandwiches and those coconut cookies you like."

"Thanks, Mrs. Marino, but I'm fine."

"Take it. You need something to keep you awake."

"Thank you."

"And make sure you tell your parents how much we love having you around here."

"I will." No he wouldn't.

"And there's a thermos of coffee, black."

"Mom, he'll be fine," Kate said as she came down the stairs dressed, her hair was still wet.

"And you're the one driving halfway across the country?"

"I'll bring the thermos back in August."

"It's old. Don't worry about it. You be safe. We'll miss you, Michael." Maryann pulled Michael into a hug and kissed his cheek softly. "You're a good boy."

"I'll miss you too, Mrs. Marino. I better go."

"I'll walk you out," Kate said.

"Thanks."

Michael and Kate walked to the car.

"I'll write, Kate. Call too, if I can. It's just my folks are crazy about the phone bill."

"It's okay," she said.

"No, I will. I promise."

"Did you mean it, Michael? When you said you loved me?"

"Yes. I do. I love you, Kate. I love you so much."

"I love you too." It was the first time she had said it to anyone who wasn't related to her.

"I wish I didn't have to go."

"If we hang around this car, my mother will know something's up," Kate said. "You better go."

"Are you okay? I mean I didn't plan on this afternoon."

"I wanted it too, Michael, for a long time. Just go, please?" She didn't want to cry. Michael put the food bag on the passenger seat. His back was to her.

"I'll talk to Barb as soon as I get back."

He kissed her softly, got into his Ford Torino and left. On that long drive, Michael realized since he'd met Kate his old life felt like a movie he was watching from the last row of the balcony. Barb began fading from his heart a few weeks after he spied the pretty, petite brunette in his English class. He had twisted and turned his feelings and thoughts into some kind of logical order until he convinced himself that Kate would never be more than a friend no matter how much space she took up in his life. Her exotic eyes and easy laugh were just a distraction. He was promised to another girl and he kept that promise. His life in Indiana was separate from his life at college and up until that afternoon he had never once cheated on Barb.

Michael got groggy and stopped to pour coffee from the thermos before he reached Pittsburgh. He was exhausted. He took an exit and drove to a secluded area and shut his eyes. He didn't wake up till morning, and then got back on the road. He had a lot to juggle. His boss expected him to join the painting crew on a new housing development as soon as he returned to Elna. He was also needed on the farm. Michael could handle all of that. He was used to managing his time and meeting deadlines. He wasn't used to disappointing people. Michael knew the first thing he had to do when he got home was to sort out what had just happened with Kate and then decide what to do about Barb.

Michael had been vague about his plans. He didn't tell Barb exactly when he'd be getting back to Elna. He had called her over the weekend before he left Pennsylvania, but she was out with her girlfriends. He left a message with her father saying his exams were pushed back a couple of days. It was a small lie, but he was in no rush to leave Kate. He wanted to stay with her until the very last moment and the cleaning crew was ready to come in and close his dorm for the summer.

He finally pulled onto the farm's gravel driveway and the dust kicked up under his tires. Trixie was barking from the porch and ran to greet him. The barn had a fresh coat of red paint. He could see his father on the tractor out in the fields. The cows were idly walking around in the pasture. There was a cool breeze and it wasn't unusual for the wind to blow right through you, even in May.

Michael stepped onto the porch and looked out at his father. He seemed small in the distance. He didn't notice Michael was home. He stepped into the living room and everything looked exactly the same as when he left after winter break.

"Mom?" Michael moved into the kitchen. "Mom?"

"In the basement. Be right up."

The basement was an organized maze of laundry, canned goods, and old furniture that was still "too good to part with." The basement door was off the kitchen. He heard his mother's footsteps land lightly on the treads. She broke into a smile when she saw him.

"It's good to have you home, son."

"It feels good to be home." He tried to sound excited.

"I think you put on a few pounds back in Pennsylvania."

"Maybe a couple."

"They say that cafeteria food is all starch."

"I've eaten a lot at a friend's house lately."

The images of Mrs. Marino's homemade pastas and veal scallopini made his mouth water.

"Well whatever it is. It agrees with you. You needed the weight."

"I saw dad out in the field."

"He should be in soon. Go get your things. I just started a load of wash. I'll add to it."

"I can do it later," Michael said.

"No use wasting the water. Go get it and I'll stop the washer." There was no point in arguing with her so he headed toward the door. "Barb called an hour ago, wondering when you were getting home. I told her I wasn't sure – 'he doesn't clear his plans with me anymore,' I said. I promised to give her a buzz. I told her to come for dinner."

"Tonight?"

"I know you're probably dog-tired from the drive. What time did you leave Pennsylvania?"

"Early this morning."

"Must have been more like the middle of the night," Edith said. "That poor girl is so excited to see you. Now go get those clothes."

Michael walked out to the car as Barb pulled up in her father's truck. She waved and honked the horn several times. She looked beautiful, already tan and her blond hair was longer than he remembered. She flew out of the truck and into his arms. She kissed him, forcing her tongue into his mouth.

"I was on my way into town when I passed your car on Highway J. Didn't you hear me honk?"

"No, sorry. I could barely keep my eyes open. I literally just got here."

"I was going to turn around and follow you but I stopped to get us something." She went back to the cab of the truck and handed him a brown bag.

"Look inside. It's a present." He opened the small bag. Barb had bought a box of condoms.

"I thought we could put those to good use," she said. "I've missed you so much, Michael."

A half-hearted "Me too" escaped Michael's lips.

After leaving Marilyn's room that night he felt the same kind of weariness he felt that day in Indiana with Barb. The weariness that comes from knowing that the cost of any new beginning is usually a drawn out and complicated ending. It brings the unlikely combination of elation and fear that fills the heart with anticipation while weighing heavily on the mind.

26

Since coming up with nothing at Michael's office, Kate took another stab at understanding Steve Yeardsley's "Penetration and Intrusion." Michael would be home tomorrow afternoon. It was time to get serious, so Kate called Greg for Yeardsley's number.

"Hey, Greg, it's me," she said.

"Did you get that paper?" Greg said.

"I got it, Greg. I just don't know what the hell he's talking about and what's up with that title?"

"I know. It's totally Steve."

"I want to meet with him." There was a long silence. "Is that a problem?"

"I'm not sure. I'll have Steve call you."

"I don't have a lot of time on this."

"Let me see what I can do."

"Thanks. We can't wait to see you, Meredith, and the kids next week," she said.

"We're looking forward to coming home. Kate, I've got to run to a meeting. Either me or Steve will be in touch, okay?"

"Make sure he knows I'm up against a deadline."

"Will do. Oh and tell Jake I'll meet him online tonight."

"Is there something I should know?" Kate asked.

"We play *Call To Honor* online. The kid's a great sniper."

"It's a relief to know he has a career path."

"If you don't hear from Steve by noon, call me and maybe I can step you through his paper."

"Thanks." She waited a moment. "But Greg, he's got to call me. Okay?"

It was an hour earlier in Chicago. Hopefully Greg would call his friend right away. She had planned to tell Michael everything last night but came to her senses after a long shower. She couldn't bring herself to admit she was so insecure she snuck into his office and raided his inbox. But she didn't feel so terrible that she was ready to call off her pursuit of Marilyn Campbell. She killed time waiting for the call by cleaning out her briefcase. The soft leather messenger bag had been a Christmas gift from Michael two years ago. It probably set him back a fortune, but in Kate's eyes it came up a little short as a present from her lover. She got bored picking through the folds of the bag and collecting discarded gum wrappers. She moved to the sunroom to survey her traditional Thanksgiving dining room. The same architect that oversaw the house renovation had designed it when Michael's business showed its first big profit. The room lit the entire back of the house. It was where she and Michael shared coffee on weekend mornings and read the paper before the kids came down. The view, even in the dead of winter, was peaceful and serene. There wasn't a lot of furniture to be removed. She decided she and Violet could handle it. She went out to the garage and cleared a space for the wicker chairs and sofa. The phone rang as she crossed back through the kitchen. Kate jumped on it before checking caller ID.

"Steve?"

"Who the hell is Steve?" Michael said.

"Hey, how are you?"

"Tired. Sorry I didn't call back last night." Kate hadn't realized he'd called at all. "It was a long day. How did Jake get off?"

"Fine. I took him early so he can check in with his math teacher."

"Jake said you and Violet were at the movies. That's why I didn't try your cell. How was it?"

"We didn't go. The night was kind of a bust."

"Sorry."

"It's not your fault, Michael." But it was his fault. This whole mess was his fault.

"So who's this Steve character?"

"A friend of Greg's from Penn. I'm researching a column." If Kate knew anything about lying, it was to keep it simple. Her research proved liars typically give long, intricate explanations, but telling the truth is usually done in a couple of words. "This guy is a computer whiz. I'm thinking of a piece on how they've taken over our lives."

"Sounds good. And try not to obsess about the holiday. Everything will get done," he said.

"I'm not obsessing – much."

"Did you make a list?"

"Not yet."

Even with a list, Michael would call her a half dozen times from the store. They'd go back and forth about quantities, costs and brands. Kate hated grocery shopping, but Michael didn't seem to mind the packing and unpacking of carts and bags. He once did a lot of market research for food companies. Going grocery shopping was like a mini-business trip. It could take hours by the time he finished stopping at end cases, and examining brand packaging, the photography, and the lettering of dessert pies and frozen vegetables. He'd question if a design were good enough to entice a consumer to try something new. Kate just wanted to buy milk and eggs. She didn't give a damn what they came in, so to avoid arguing, he did most of the food shopping.

"I better run. I'll call later so I can check in with Jake," he said.

"Great. He'll like that. Bye."

"Love you," he said.

Saying "love you" had become the equivalent of a simple "goodbye," more habit than emotion. But Michael was a good father. He would call Jake as promised. She made peace years ago with Jake being more Michael's child than her own. He would tell his father things he'd never disclose to Kate especially since his teenage hormones kicked in. Michael would then fill her in, and warn her not to panic. Why did he always think she'd panic? Michael was still on the line. He hadn't hung up.

"Kate, are you okay?"

"Fine, why?"

"You sound funny." Kate wanted to shoot back, "And you sound paranoid," but she didn't want to alert him about her mission with Greg's friend.

"I need to get a jump on this column. You know how I am." Call waiting beeped through. The ID announced "private caller." Kate assumed it was a charity disguising its number and ignored it.

"Want to get that?" Michael said.

"I'll let it go to voicemail." But then she thought of the computer guy at Penn.

"They're not giving up. Give me a sec. I'll get rid of them." She hit the flash button.

"Hello. Hello…"

The voice was barely above a whisper.

"Hi, Mrs. McAllister? This is Steve Yeardsley. I'm a friend of…."

"Steve, hi – I'm so glad it's you. Thanks for calling me so quickly."

"Greg said it was important."

"Can you hold just one sec, please?" Steve didn't respond so she hoped that was a yes. She hit the button again to return to Michael.

"I've got to run." She didn't even bother with a goodbye as she hit the button once more to return to Steve.

"Steve, hi, sorry..."

"Still me, Hon. Your boyfriend's on the other line."

"I told you. It's research. This guy's impossible to reach. I really need to talk to him."

"Should I be worried?"

"No, Michael, should I?" Kate said.

Michael laughed. A laugh is not an answer.

27

Steve Yeardsley called Kate to tell her he couldn't talk to her. He was at a conference all day and wouldn't have another break till after eight that night.

"Can you call me then?" Kate asked.

"No." He offered no other explanation but agreed to meet with her on Friday morning at his place near the university as a favor to Greg. He told her he wasn't familiar with her column. He rarely read print media and got all of his news on the web like a civilized human being. He would see if he could help her with her research, but his time was very valuable. Kate quickly agreed to meet Steve first thing Friday morning. When Violet got in a few minutes later, she offered to pressure Greg to see if he could nudge Steve to take a break from his conference and figure things out today, but Kate told her something in Steve's voice didn't invite spontaneity and she didn't want to risk him cancelling on her.

They spent an hour on the computer but were punching the same keys and getting the same results. They were no closer to discovering if Michael had a secret email account.

"You know what this is," Kate said.

"Frustrating?"

"A sign of age."

"You're still a kid," Violet said.

"No, Vi – a kid would know how to do this. They're wired in all the time. My computer is a glorified typewriter. I email because it's pretty basic and I have a Facebook page because the magazine makes me. Bet I could call Laura and she'd figure this out in five minutes. It used to be a bad knee or aching back meant you were on the downward slide. Now it's not knowing how to Tweet. Or thinking it's something birds do."

"Let's take a break. My eyes are going crossed," Violet said.

"I'm sick of it too. Want to clean out the sun room?"

"I thought you were waiting for Michael," Violet said.

"I'm tired of waiting for Michael."

"Then let's do it." Violet was also ready to be done with Michael's shenanigans. The sooner Kate knew one way or the other, Violet could help her pick up the pieces and choose a direction. The in-between time is the worst. Violet remembered it being that way with Eddie. She knew she should have put her foot down about his drinking months before she locked him out, but it's the yearning for what was that keeps you from seeing the way it is and has to be.

In the fifteen years she'd been working for Kate, Violet had only a handful of conversations with just Michael. They both loved Kate and the children deeply, but whenever their conversations ended, Violet walked away feeling she knew little more about him than when they had started.

The women put their downtime to good use and focused on the holiday. Kate and Violet moved the wicker furniture into the garage. They swept the travertine tile floor but had to wait for the rental company to deliver the tables and chairs before they could set it up as a banquet room.

"Why does an empty room always look so big?" Violet wondered.

"Imagine how an empty house looks," Kate said.

"Don't go there. I don't care who's leaving smelly cards for Michael, I can't see this house ever being empty with your people coming and going like they own the place. Now go pull out the silver. Don't think I didn't see the tarnish on those tines the last time you used it."

Kate got a step stool and pulled the silver chest out from the butler's pantry cupboard. Together they buffed, polished, and rinsed each piece until they shone brightly. They chatted about Greg's kids and seeing Laura in a few days. It reminded Kate of all the holidays she and her mother spent getting ready, ticking off all the big and little jobs one at a time. Once they were done, they carefully placed the tableware back in the chest.

"Feeling better?" Violet said.

"A little."

"By tomorrow, you'll know what you know," Violet said.

"Why does doubt always get in the way of a good thing, Vi?"

"Cause that's doubt's job. Let's wait and see what Greg's friend can do."

"Do you want to come to his place with me?" Kate said.

"No. It's best I work here. You've got a ton of fan email to answer. But the second Michael's home, I'm out of here."

"Sounds fair. So what's next?" Kate said.

"Next we wipe off the serving platters, dust off that hutch and control what we can control. Tomorrow will take care of itself."

"Maybe I'll do something with Jake later."

"That's a great idea for both of you." Kate wasn't sure Jake would think it was so great, but she made a plan and would let him decide. After they finished up in the kitchen, Kate checked online to see if the slasher movie Jake mentioned he wanted to see was still in the theater. She figured there are worse things in life than adultery. A guy with a machete and Oedipus complex could be chasing you through remote woods where they'd be lucky to find you before you turned into liquid fertilizer.

Violet opted out of going to the movie, but stayed for dinner. She made her famous chocolate chip pancakes and Jake was thrilled to have another face around the table. He and Violet shared a love for anything sweet – doughnuts, chocolate, cookies, and especially a river of maple syrup on their pancakes. Violet always pretended to be mad when Jake raided her private stash of goodies she kept in one of the kitchen drawers. Every time Kate tried to get Violet to join her at the gym, they'd chase the same conversation in circles.

"And do what?"

"Exercise, Vi. It's good for you."

"I read. I exercise my brain. More people should worry about what they put in their head than what they put in their body."

"It wouldn't hurt you to move around more."

"I move just fine. I've seen you after one of those workouts, moaning and groaning like my great aunt Jenny. No thank you. I've got my own knees, my own hips, even my own teeth – nothing's been replaced. Why mess with a good thing?"

"What about your cholesterol?"

"What about it?" Violet asked.

"Do you even know what it is?"

"Sure I know. The doctor mentioned taking some of those pills. I told him, if you fix one thing, you mess with another." Kate would give up because Violet was one of the most stubborn people she'd ever met. And despite her devotion to rich desserts and anything swimming in butter, she was in remarkable shape. Her body never changed, there were no wild swings in her weight. It drove Kate crazy. Violet never once looked at a food label or worried about what she ordered at the diner. To Violet, an egg white omelet was an insult to the chicken.

Jake begged Violet to come with them to the movies, but she wasn't a fan of violence in any form. After they cleaned up, Violet left and Kate and Jake took off in time for the 7:45 show. Since it was a Thursday night and none of his friends were likely to be at the theater, he figured it was okay to go with his mom. The movie lived up to Kate's low expectations but after two buckets of popcorn, Jake thanked her for taking him. Violet had been right. Spending the evening together was a perfect idea. She and Jake laughed on the way home about the obvious plot and predictable characters. He went right up to bed and took a shower without her reminding him. There were no messages on the answering machine. Kate assumed Michael must have been tied up with his clients or maybe tied up by Marilyn Campbell. She knew she'd never close her eyes so she took half a sleeping pill to help her fall asleep.

She was groggy in fifteen minutes. Her stress and fear melted away into a warm place of peace. She wasn't angry or resentful. She existed in the space created by the wonders of pharmaceutical intoxication. It created a world without a beautiful other woman, secret email accounts, and insecure wives. Kate's eyes grew heavier and she soon drifted off. It was the best night's sleep she had since Laura had left for school.

28

Kate looked over at her son as she dropped him off at school on Friday morning. Jake had a soft growth of dark hair over his lip and Kate decided to buy him his first electric razor for Christmas. The drop off line was longer than usual because of the rainfall. It wasn't really rain, more like a cross between a mist and drizzle as if Mother Nature couldn't make up her mind.

Jake was growing up, not just because of his height or the deeper tone of his voice, or even because of the stubble on his chin. He was starving for independence. It silently radiated off him, announcing he would soon find his own larger social crowd to confide in and need more than his family. And when that time came, it would cement his final steps away from her. It was one more thing Kate dreaded in her changing family dynamic.

She looked at the other kids getting out of the cars in front of her. Some of the boys were already six feet tall and a few of the girls had the bodies of supermodels. Still others were a foot shorter than Jake, looking like they'd taken a wrong turn on the way to the elementary school. Jake was still in-between those two worlds. He didn't have the manly look of a Kurt Miller, who Michael told her, that Jake told him, was the guy all the hot girls wanted to date. She didn't know Kurt Miller, but she knew her son would grow into a good man. That he'd be kind and attentive to his girlfriends and that his softness and sensitivity wouldn't always be the curse they are now.

They inched their way toward the overhang. Jake pulled his hoodie over his head as the car stopped.

"Have a good day, Honey."

"You too." He reached for the door handle.

"Hey," Kate said. He leaned closer and tilted his head toward her. She kissed the top of it, getting a mouthful of navy blue cotton. She let go and he exited the car, meeting up with a friend on the sidewalk.

Before she left the house, Steve Yeardsley had called to remind her he was expecting her. She tried to convince him to come out to the house, but the computer genius didn't drive. He is also adverse to trains and buses and has never been on the expressway. He prefers the two-lane River Drives and when he does leave campus, it's by bike.

Kate faced at least an hour's commute on the Schuylkill Expressway during rush hour. There were the two guaranteed fender-benders in the rain that brought everything to a halt from the Conshohocken Curve to City Line Avenue. Things were worse than she expected. She had been on the road a half hour and hadn't gone three miles. She dialed Steve to tell him she was running late.

"How late?"

"I don't know. The radio says it's bumper-to-bumper the entire length."

"I teach a class."

"What time?" Kate said.

"Three."

Three? She could be in New York and back by three and have time for lunch.

"That shouldn't be a problem," Kate said.

"But I have a class at three."

"I got that," Kate said.

"Okay. So I'll see you soon?"

"As soon as I can. Steve, I really appreciate this."

"Class at three," he repeated.

"Three – right." She hung up. Kate eventually made it to the six-lane spread into Center City that condensed into three lanes when she veered right toward South Street. She finally got to University City. She was way behind schedule and hoped she would catch on to Steve's methods quickly. Much of the area around the campus had been revitalized into an amazing urban community with cafes, restaurants, and bookshops. Students with backpacks and professors with overstuffed briefcases rushed from the storefronts on their way to class. Kate could see herself in exactly this kind of neighborhood when she retired, surrounded by young people in a bustling neighborhood. She and Michael had once talked about buying a place in the city when the kids were gone. A place where you didn't have to get in the car every time you wanted a cup of coffee or a quart of milk.

Steve's building was about seven blocks from campus. It was one of Philadelphia's grand houses before being chopped up into apartments. Paint chipped off the dark green shutters that framed the windows. Any urban renewal of the area looked like it literally stopped short at Steve's doorstep.

The heavy oak front door led into a small lobby with filthy black and white granite tiles. She found his name along the row of white labels, stuffed through tarnished brass holders, "Yeardsley, S." She pushed the intercom button.

"Yeardsley." His voice crackled through the small speaker.

"Steve? It's Kate McAllister, the writer. Greg Evans' friend."

"Come up. I've got a class at three." The door buzzed loudly and she rushed to pass through before Steve changed his mind and took off for that class. The building was a walk-up and he was on the fourth floor. Her briefcase was heavy and the strap cut into her shoulder. It held her notes, her laptop, the large file Steve had sent, and a small gift she brought to thank him for his time.

His door looked like it hadn't seen a coat of paint since John Adams crashed there after a long day at the Continental Congress. She knocked softly. He opened the door as far as the chain link lock would allow. He looked Kate over from head to toe.

"Steve?" His pale face was scarred from years of acne. He had something that resembled a moustache above his lip but it was hard to tell.

"May I see some identification please?" Kate dug into her briefcase and pulled out her driver's license. Steve took it quickly, and after a few seconds, unlocked his door. He handed it back to her and went to his desk. Kate closed the door and looked around. She didn't remember ever being in the presence of genius before and pledged to avoid it in the future. The walls were covered with decrepit bookcases. There wasn't a square inch of space on the shelves. Kate scanned them quickly. They held the usual great works of literature, along with history, biology, astronomy, economics, and philosophy. Apparently there wasn't an area of academia that didn't interest Steve Yeardsley. One whole wall, however, was devoted to technology. He was clicking away at a desktop computer. He hadn't looked at her since she'd entered. She took out the scented candle she'd brought him and placed it on the bookshelves.

"This is for you."

"Right, thanks." Two cats milled around his legs. The Oriental rug on the floor was worn thin. It could have been an antique, worth a small fortune, or something he salvaged from curbside garbage. Kate couldn't tell. A small bathroom was on one side of the room. It had white subway tiles with a mosaic floor that had yellowed with age. There was a hot plate in one corner. There was no kitchen or bedroom. A futon was tucked by one of the two floor-to-ceiling windows. They filled the room with filtered light that penetrated the grime on the inside and outside panes, casting a sepia tone on everything in the room. Kate didn't know if she should sit or wait for further instruction. Without warning, Steve shut down his computer, closed all the manila files on his desk and stacked the books neatly.

"Sorry about that. I do one thing at a time. Never more, never less." She had no idea what he had been doing, but he seemed to have finished that one thing and all of his attention was now on her. His plaid shirt and jeans were standard university issue, but he was wearing sandals in November. The apartment was chilly but Kate chalked it up to the old leaky windows. His thinning hair was long and tucked behind his ears.

"You got the information? I sent Greg the information."

"And he sent it to me, but as I said on the phone, I'm not very computer savvy. I had a hard time following it," Kate said.

"Good man, Greg. The university was sorry to lose him." Greg had left Penn over fifteen years earlier but Steve made it sound like it happened last week. She couldn't imagine the two of them hanging out and having a couple of beers together.

"He speaks very highly of you." Kate glanced at her watch. It was already past ten. Jake got home around three. He usually took the bus in the afternoons. She told him she had a doctor's appointment and may not be there when he got in. Another lie.

"You brought a laptop?"

"Yes." Kate took it from her briefcase and booted up quickly.

"Good. I don't like to co-mingle data on my own network. You never know."

"No you don't," Kate said. "May I?"

"Yes, yes, of course." She placed it on his desk.

"Greg says you're writing a column on hacking?" Steve asked.

"More or less."

"Then I have to warn you from the outset. I never hack. Hacking is illegal. I gather perfectly legitimate information that is otherwise not attainable to the average person. There's a line, Mrs. McAllister."

"Please call me Kate."

"And I never cross that line."

"Understood. I'm sorry. I didn't mean to insult you."

"I am never insulted." Her computer hummed to life. Steve stared at her intently.

"Do you want to have sex?" Steve looked from the musty futon to Kate. She wasn't sure she'd heard him correctly so she ignored him.

"Sorry, my computer's pretty slow. All that anti-virus stuff."

"Slow is good," Steve said. "So, do you want to have sex? The computer work won't take long." This time there was no missing the question. Kate didn't want to get on his bad side, but she didn't want to have sex with him either.

"I can't. I'm married." That's all she had.

"I know. I saw your ring."

"And your paper seems like a lot of information to get through."

"It isn't as hard as most people think."

"But you've got that class at three," Kate said.

"Right. Damn it. You're right. Class at three." He glanced at her laptop. Kate had found the magic words to change the subject. It wasn't her marriage or their work together; it was that class at three.

"This laptop needs a good cleaning, maybe you could come back when I don't have class and I can strip it for you," he said.

"I don't want to put you out more than I already have." He fondled the lid's hard shell and ran his hand over the sides and the front where her wrists rested when she typed.

"Still – nice machine."

"It's showing its age, but then who isn't?" He looked at her and practically said "you."

"Steve, I want to pay you for your time. It must be very valuable."

"Greg mentioned something about turkey."

"Pardon?"

"He told me he's going to your house next week."

"For Thanksgiving," Kate said.

"I like legs, thighs. Breasts can be dry." A headline flashed through Kate's mind. "Syndicated Columnist Found Raped and Murdered in University City Apartment. Suspect Claims He Had a Class at Three."

"True," she said. "The trick is in the basting." Finally her screen came to life. She prayed the blue light and musical tones would distract him. She decided to call Greg later and ask him what the hell he was thinking introducing her to a sex-starved "leg man."

"Greg says you're cooking?"

"What?"

"Thanksgiving."

"Yeah. It's a tradition with family, friends." He took a couple of technical books off the shelf that he'd written.

"Most of my family's in Portland," Steve said.

"Great city. So, Steve, if somebody was trying to hide an email account..."

"Oregon, not Maine," Steve said. She took her copy of his research paper from her briefcase and put it on the desk.

"I don't fly," he said.

"Shocking," Kate said.

"Besides, we don't get a lot of time for Thanksgiving. I'm back in the computer lab on Friday. I'd cook, but a bird on a hot plate..."

"Would you like to join us?" The words flew from her mouth before she could stop them. She had channeled her mother. The idea of anyone being alone on a holiday, even a horny computer whiz, was wrong. And Michael already knew Steve's name and her cover about researching a column so it could work.

"I'll have to check my calendar," Steve said.

"I understand."

"But I think I'm free. I'll need a ride."

"Of course you will," Kate said. "I'll have Greg pick you up." Serves him right, Kate thought. Now that he'd angled an invitation to Thanksgiving dinner and his holiday plans were firmed up, Steve's interest in her project spiked. He tapped on her keyboard like a concert pianist while flipping through the pages of one of his textbooks. She recognized the pages from the material he sent her. She stood over his shoulder. Small scabs on his scalp were visible through his hair. He scratched at them. In the "life doesn't play fair" scheme of things, a man with an oozing scalp just hit on her while Michael was being chased by a blond knockout wearing three-inch heels.

Steve worked fast, mumbling about pathways and domains.

"Is this the best you got?" Steve smiled, then went back to muttering about cross-references and data fields while his fingers ran across the letters – adding and deleting, adding more.

"And you're using your husband as a template for the article," Steve said.

"Yes. He set up a secret email account so I could explore the topic."

"Interesting," Steve said. He had no idea. Steve began talking to the machine as if it was a child. When he did speak to her, his eyes never left the screen.

"Turn to page fifty-three in that handout." Kate did. "This is where it gets fun. If I inject the right data into the proper field." He looked like he was in a trance. "Let's search domains, common subsets. We'll try McAllister, Michael right? And you're Kate."

"Short for Katharine with two "a"s.

"Kids?"

"Yes. Laura and Jake." Steve waited for the computer to catch up to him.

"Nothing. Let's keep going. Pet?"

"Just Dexter, or Dex. He's a very friendly mutt. Oh, and Trixie was his dog years ago."

"Still nothing," Steve said. "Anything else, other names, interesting facts, extended family, friends?"

"There's Evans of course. Greg, his mother Violet, wife Meredith, oh and the Campbells. Marilyn's a dear friend, more like a sister really."

"Like the soup?" he said.

"Exactly."

"Like the soup," he muttered. A small grin hinted at success. "And we're in. Something or someone called McAllisterCampbell parked a domain." Kate felt like she was going to be sick. "There's no website. It appears to be used for email exchange only. It could be a completely different company or a strange person not related to your project. It may be a partnership of any number of people. McAllister is a common name. There is a very strong chance it's not the mystery account your husband established for you. We don't know. Here, see for yourself." He spun her laptop around and there was her husband's name, linked to Marilyn's somewhere in cyberspace where neither thought it would ever be discovered. Kate couldn't speak.

"You still don't have access," Steve said. "No password, no access. Whoever it may belong to, won't want you cracking into their account."

"But I know who it belongs to."

"You only think you do. A password is the only way to find out for certain."

"I made my husband promise not to give me the password so I could find out how hard it is to get in."

"Fascinating," Steve said, but he couldn't have sounded less fascinated.

"Let's say I wanted to crack it, out of curiosity."

"That's where this train stops, Katharine with two 'a's. I told you I'd help you find a domain based on my expertise. I won't hack into it."

"That's not what I meant." It's exactly what she meant.

"But I can tell you that 85% of the population uses the same password for just about everything. Sometimes they use combinations of familiar old ones. Many times it's as simple as one-two-three-four." Kate placed her fingers on her keyboard. "No. Not here, Kate. Never here," he said.

She was past her allotted time with Steve. He picked up one of his textbooks and flipped through nonchalantly. She was boring him. His voice was flat. "Once you get it in, if you get in, you'll be able to read everything they have sent, received, deleted, or permanently deleted. Just to warn you, some people are security nuts. They change passwords every month, week, day, sometimes a couple of times a day. I make it a practice to change mine hourly." Kate didn't doubt it.

"Can you write the steps down for me, exactly as you went through them to get to this domain and email it to me? I'm not sure I could recreate it. Oh, and don't forget how to erase the search from my hard drive."

"What time is dinner next week?"

"Cocktails at four, dinner after. I'll have Greg pick you up around three-thirty."

"Three would be better."

"You're right, of course. Three is better." She wrote down her email address.

"When does the column come out? Will I be in it?"

"I'm just doing the leg work now," Kate said. "But absolutely, you'll be in it. It takes a few weeks to go through the publishing channels. Probably after the first of the year." She shut down her laptop and put everything back in her briefcase.

"Steve, I like to keep my research confidential, so I'd appreciate it if our visit didn't come up around, say the Thanksgiving table."

"No problem." He went back to work at his desktop. Kate thanked him and said goodbye. She let herself out, found a seventy-five dollar parking ticket on her windshield, and drove home on autopilot. If this was the slow death of her marriage, it seemed appropriate that "McAllisterCampbell" sounded like the name of an Internet funeral parlor. The expressway was wide open and she made it back to Valley Forge in half an hour. She tried breathing slow and steady the way Justin had taught her to do in the gym when her heart raced out of control. If she got hysterical, she'd never be able to figure out the password and Kate's goal was to hack into it and download the entire email account before Michael's wheels touched the ground.

29

Michael's plane took off on time from Dallas/Fort Worth International Airport late Friday morning. Marilyn jumped on a different flight. The perks of logging so many miles meant he was bumped up to first class and had room to stretch out on the flight home. The conspicuous absence of support staff and other moderators on this trip created a buzz around his office. He diverted their workload to different projects, but noticed conversations were halted when he passed by his employees in the corridor.

Michael planned to tell Kate his plans after the New Year, but since things had heated up so quickly with Marilyn he had to rethink his timetable. The only thing he knew for sure was that Kate deserved to hear the truth from him. Thirty thousand feet in the air and over twenty-five years later, Michael felt a disturbing and familiar wave of guilt. It was the same feeling he had on his first night back home from college after having made love to Kate the day before in his empty dorm room.

"One more year to go, babe. I can't believe it. You'll be a senior," Barb said. The four of them were sitting at the dinner table, but all Michael could think about was getting back to Kate. His parents contributed little to the conversation. Michael's father served himself first and was practically finished by the time his mother eventually joined them at the table. They exhausted the subject of his senior schedule and job at the grocery store off campus. His mother finally broke her silence.

"Michael, you remember that Stoltzfus boy?" Edith asked.

"Who?" His mother would store up all the gossip and hard-luck stories while he was gone and try to connect them back to Michael. It was her way of keeping him connected to her and life in Elna.

"You went to school with him. He left in the tenth grade."

"I read about him in the papers, Mrs. McAllister," Barb said.

"Michael, he was short for his age. The kids used to tease him. You remember," his mother said.

"What about him?"

"Dead," she said. "A motorcycle accident, Highway 56. No helmet. He was always reckless."

Michael was too preoccupied to push back on her implication that it was the Stoltzfus kid's fault for dying. To Edith, everything and everybody was at fault for whatever horrible thing happened to them. She never considered that he could have been driving carefully, moving along at the speed limit when a random animal crossed his path or a drunk driver swayed over the yellow line and never saw him and just kept going. Maybe the Stoltzfus kid deserved just a little sympathy for dying at twenty years old.

"Barb, did you write him about Jason Reeman?"

"I meant to."

"Drugs." Edith could deliver any piece of bad news in one syllable.

"He's in jail," Barb said. "But he should be out in a year."

"I heard at the beauty shop he was selling it," Edith said.

"I knew that kid was a bum. Never liked him or his old man." Michael's father was the exclamation point on these conversations. The final dose of judgment on whomever hit rock bottom.

"What are you so quiet about?" His father turned to Michael.

"Tired, I guess. It's a shame about Bill Stoltzfus."

"Bill, that was his name," Edith said.

"Was he drinking?" his father asked.

"I wouldn't be surprised," Edith said. "Barb, pass the mashed potatoes." Edith served his father a second helping as Michael wondered if it was possible to deliver his bad news to Barb in just one word.

Barb stayed after dinner to watch "Dynasty" with his mother while Michael unpacked. It was cool when they finally stepped off the front porch, and an amber haze covered the moon. He walked Barb to the pickup truck and she slipped her hand into his. He thought about not telling her about Kate. He could kiss her lightly when he opened her door and put if off at least another day or two.

"How about a movie tomorrow night? The whole gang wants to see you."

"I can't. I have work the day after," he said.

"We'll go to an early show." Michael knew most of his college friends would have no trouble sleeping with Barb all summer and then go back to Kate and pick up where they left off.

"Barb, I can't go to the movies."

"Why not?" He didn't answer. "You've been weird all night, Michael. What's going on?"

"Nothing."

"You barely wrote all semester and when you called, it was like you couldn't wait to get off the phone."

"That's not true." But it was true.

"Who is she, Michael?"

"What?"

"The girl," Barb said. "Is she why you didn't come home for spring break?"

"Spring break was one week. It didn't make sense to spend two days in the car. Besides, I had to work."

"I don't need this shit, Michael." Barb opened her door. Michael grabbed it tightly. He paused and lowered his voice.

"I'm sorry. I am seeing someone. A girl at school."

"You son of a bitch." She jerked the door from his hand and slammed it shut. She crossed her arms and leaned against the truck.

"I didn't want to tell you over the phone," he said.

"Cause you're such a great guy?"

"I'm not a great..."

"Shut up. You don't get to talk. I've waited three years, Michael. Three years of my life. Plenty of guys have come on to me."

"I know." They were the only two words he could think of to say.

"No you don't know, you fucker. I've turned down so many chances with other guys I lost count. I waited for you!"

He had no defense. He was wrong. There was nothing he could say, but Barb had one last thing left to say.

"Do you love her?" Michael waited to answer her for as long as he could. "Do you? Yes or no, Michael?"

"Yes. Barb, I'm sorry," She began to cry. "I am really sorry."

"You're not sorry. You're a complete shit and a liar, Michael McAllister. A fucking liar." She got into the pickup and spewed gravel at him as she peeled out of the driveway. He looked up at the house. His mother was watching from the front door. He went for a walk into the fields. He pushed his hands deep into his pockets and got lost in the smell of the crops and the damp earth. When he got back, his parents were watching television. They never asked him about the scene in the driveway.

"I'm going to bed," he said.

"Goodnight," Edith said.

"'Night son, good to have you home." Michael went into his bedroom and wrote Kate a letter. By July, Barb was engaged to Tim Tickner, the former high school basketball star. The guy she once complained about being all over her. The guy who was her "man" in the cheer. "Tim, Tim, he's our man…" became her "man" after all.

Michael's flight emerged from a huge cloud. There was no turbulence as the captain cleared them for use of electronic devices. "Can I offer you another beverage, sir?" Michael hadn't noticed the flight attendant beside him. He was lost in the irony of returning home all these years later with another secret that would change his life.

30

Kate flew through the front door and headed for her office. Violet was waiting for her.

"What did the Boy Wonder have to say for himself?" Violet asked.

"He promised to email me a hacking for dummies list. Excuse me, not hacking, that's illegal – penetrating for dummies." Violet checked Kate's email on her desktop. "It's here already."

"He's got a class at three," Kate said. Violet looked confused.

"Don't ask," Kate said.

"Should I print it?"

"No. I don't want it around. Put it in the junk mail folder and I'll decide what to do with it later. Read from my desktop, but we'll do all the digging on my laptop. I don't want to co-mingle data."

"Co-mingle what?"

"Nothing." Violet studied the steps before reading them off to Kate. "Still doesn't seem that easy. And why couldn't he have emailed this in the first place?"

"Steve is a hands-on kind of guy." Kate sat down on the loveseat wearily as her laptop came to life.

"Are you okay, honey?" Violet asked.

"Michael's got a secret email account, Vi."

"Are you sure?"

"Positive. Steve found it at his place. It's called McAllister-Campbell dot com. That's why the emails between them at his office stopped cold last February."

"That's still not proof of anything."

"Right. Worst case, he's having an affair; best case, he's having a cyber affair that will turn into an actual affair sooner or later. Either way, I have to figure out the password to get to his inbox," Kate said.

"Mr. Computer Genius couldn't help?"

"It's crossing the line," Kate said. "Oh and he wants to have sex with me."

"Excuse me?"

"In exchange for his help, but he settled for a drumstick on Thanksgiving instead." Violet helped her unpack her briefcase.

"You should have had the sex," Violet said. "We don't have room for one more at your table."

"We'll squeeze him in."

"I'd like to know where."

"One crisis at a time, Vi. We still have some time before Michael lands. I want out of these clothes before we get into this." Kate went upstairs and pulled on her sweats. The bedroom was as uncluttered as it ever gets. Her books were stacked neatly on her nightstand, Michael's trade journals on his. The sport watch she gave him on his last birthday was on the dresser and a pile of clean clothes he promised to put away was still on the chair.

She sat on the bed, drew her knees up, and then sprawled out on Michael's side of the bed. The bed they'd made love in, conceived their children in, and watched endless baseball and hockey games in – this bed told the stories they didn't share with family or friends. Her trust in Michael was eroding quickly, but there was just enough left to try and battle the invisible cracks that once again spread across the ceiling. The ones she saw in her parents' bedroom when she learned her mother had cancer and overran the examining room on the day her baby's heartbeat was silent. They were stopped miraculously when she got the phone call that Jake was growing strong and healthy inside of her. The cracks always left just enough life in their wake, so Kate could put one foot in front of the other, taking shallow breaths because there wasn't strength for more. No one has discovered the word for the excruciating pain that pierces the tissue under your sternum and camps there, radiating and burning along that direct line to the heart. If her fears about Michael and Marilyn were true, this would be the first time her children would feel that pain. Michael was everything Jake and Laura knew about what a good man is and even if she tried to protect them from the truth, they would know. Laura's heart would break right beside Kate's, while Jake would find a way to blame her. With or without facts, he'd align with his father. It would blow up the tenuous relationship with her precious teenage son. Jake and Michael had their inside jokes, team statistics, and hoops in the driveway. She had little in the bank with Jake. Her jokes stopped being funny to him, and getting sentimental about his outgrown tee-ball shirts was not cool. It was only one o'clock in the afternoon and she was already worn out. She forced herself to go back to her office.

Violet had the account up when she got back downstairs.

"I followed his directions and found the domain."

"Impressive," Kate said.

"I also tried every password I could think of. I used that 'mate' thing and all kinds of combinations."

"Maybe you're thinking of the wrong 'mate'," Kate said. She moved to her laptop. Violet watched Kate closely and struggled to find something to say that would help Kate feel better. She swallowed any negative thought she ever had about Michael and said what Kate needed to hear.

"I've seen all kinds of men in my life and the ones that cheat, cheat. If Michael was that kind of man, he wouldn't wait over twenty years to start."

"Or maybe he didn't wait, Violet. Maybe in the tornado of raising kids and building two careers and spending weeks on the road, it was easy. Michael had his mini-vacations with God-knows-who, and I was too naïve or up to my eyeballs in carpools to see it. I always told him, 'Things happen.' If you want someone else, fine. Just don't let me be the last to know.' So why am I the last to know? Do you know who I am, Vi? I'm poor Barbara Jean Fucking Wipperman."

"Who?"

"His girlfriend when we met. She was the last to know too. Michael never told her he was falling for me just like he didn't have the guts to say in the restaurant the other day, 'Kate, we've got a problem. That card you found? I've been seeing that woman'."

"Don't start writing this story till we know how it ends," Violet said. They got back to work. Kate tried dozens of combinations using Marilyn and Michael's names: Marchael, Marimike, Michaelyn. She added the date when the emails stopped in his office account. She tried inserting his birthday, the kids' birthdays, switched over to his favorite sports teams, and favorite vacation spots without success.

"It's no use, Vi. Think of something else. Something cute between the two of them. How about Mikey's whore? Or stupid Kate. That's a good password."

"Stop that. We need more than a perfumed business card and a sketchy email account that we can't crack before you know what you don't know."

But Kate's crashing self-esteem and thick ankles convinced her Michael didn't love her anymore. While he was out in the world of people who make deals and grow profits, he'd found someone else who shared that world with him. Kate's job required a total of ninety-two steps from her bedroom to the kitchen to her office. That was her world. There weren't people filling a room or meeting around a conference table waiting on her input. There weren't weekly trips to every city in the country. The pin-map of her job had one pin – home. Her columns traveled the country and sometimes the world, but Kate rarely did.

"We can't do it, Vi. He'll be home soon. Why don't you head out? You don't need to be in the middle of this." Kate had a headache and wanted to close her eyes before Michael and Jake got home.

"We'll figure this out. Don't worry." Violet hugged her.

"Can we figure out my column too?"

"It'll get done. It always does." Violet was right. Kate never missed a deadline. Not during her mother's illness, not after giving birth or an emergency appendectomy. She certainly wouldn't miss one over this.

"And if Jake needs a place to hang out later, I can cancel my ballroom dance class."

"Thanks, but he's got a school dance tonight. We'll be fine." Violet gave her another hug before she left. Kate took some ibuprofen, went up to her bedroom and closed her eyes for an hour. She was startled by the feeling she was not alone. She turned over and saw Michael unpacking.

"When did you get here?" Her voice was groggy.

"A few minutes ago. You okay?"

"What time is it?"

"A little before three. Where's Jake?"

"He's taking the bus. How was your flight?"

"Long. Roll over, I'll rub your back." That had always been Michael's prelude, his code for "let's have sex."

"Michael, Jake will be home soon."

"And what? He'll see me giving you a back rub?" Physically he was sitting by her side but she couldn't discern his mental position. His voice was kind but lacked intimacy, polite but not loving.

"Remember our first time, Kate?" Michael asked. She had no idea where he was going with this or why he'd be thinking about it now.

"We were kids, Michael."

"Just a little older than Laura," he said.

"Okay, now I feel old, and a little disturbed."

"No, no – don't – we were packing up my room – remember? It was what, the fourteenth, no fifteenth of May." Kate remembered feeling embarrassed and awkward that afternoon. She remembered Michael being gentle, but if someone put a gun to her head and asked her to recall the date she first made love with him, she'd be screwed and not in the way Michael remembered. Something in his voice seemed sad, as if he was talking about an ending rather than their beginning. He abruptly changed the subject.

"Why don't I surprise Jake and pick him up at school," he said.

"He'd like that," Kate said. "But text him to make sure he didn't get on the bus."

"Will do." Michael's phone hummed. He stopped in the doorway and glanced at it quickly.

"A message?"

"Yeah, a text. Nothing major – work stuff. Something came up from the Dallas trip."

"How was Dallas?"

Michael suddenly became agitated. "Hot for this time of year. It's hot in Dallas. See you in a bit." He left like bloodhounds were chasing him. He just got off the plane. Kate wondered what could have come up that was so damn important? Her mind was suddenly like an old fashioned steel safe, one with a big dial that spins around and clicks when you hit the right number, then spins and clicks again and again. The clicks kept coming, faster and faster. Her tumbler stopped and clicked, then clicked again. What did Steve Yeardsley say? Passwords are names, dates, and places – combinations. People change them, sometimes daily. Dallas is a place. Kate flew to her office and booted up her laptop. Jake's school was only four miles away. She had to work quickly. She typed in every possibility she could think of: Dallas, Michael, Marilyn, the day, their last names plus Dallas, first and last names together, Michael/Marilyn/Dallas, the date, a combination of initials. Five minutes turned into ten that turned into fifteen. She couldn't find the right order. She added underscores, no spaces, spaces with slashes, without slashes. The choices were infinite.

Her concentration was invaded by other thoughts – the look on Michael's face when he got that text, the odd way he talked about the two of them back in college, and the way he rushed out of the house like a child caught doing something wrong. She took out her anger on the keyboard. Her fingers flew across the letters. "Fuck you, Michael." Enter. The machine gave her the technical version of the finger: "The password you entered is invalid. Please check the spelling or contact your system administrator." Kate talked back to the screen. "What did he say? Yeah, right, it's... 'Hot in Dallas!'" She ran the letters together as one word and added the date. The machine suddenly hummed and the screen changed, lighting a new page. She was in. Her face flushed with anticipation and dread as scores of emails between Michael@McAllisterCampbell. com and Marilyn@McAllisterCampbell.com scrolled down the page quickly. They began on the same day his correspondence with Marilyn had ended on his computer at his office. Michael had obviously changed his password not only since the trip to Dallas, but at some point earlier in the day since the date was part of the access code. Somewhere buried in his subconscious, a small piece of the truth had escaped his lips. It came out like a casual weather report because something or someone had him so rattled he never even realized the information had just fallen into the wrong hands.

31

It seemed as though ten months ago, Michael and Marilyn Campbell agreed that what they had to say to each other was so important it had to be hidden from Michael's coworkers and most importantly, his wife. Kate decided to read a few emails now, then print all of them when she had more time and file them away as evidence. A quick scan would give her something concrete and real immediately. The first one was titled "Us." She clicked it open. "Hi Michael, reply as soon as you get this. I want to make sure we're set up properly so no one gets suspicious."

"We're home!" Kate flipped her laptop closed as the front door slammed. Michael and Jake entered her office. "Jake feels like tacos tonight."

"Hey, Mom." Jake dropped his backpack in her office.

"How was your day, honey?"

"Fine." He headed toward the kitchen for a snack.

"Bet he was glad to see you."

"He aced his social studies test," Michael said.

"He had a social studies test?"

"And a presentation in science. Oh, and Carol Tucker wants to know if he's going to the dance tonight. He asked if he could borrow my razor."

"You got all that on the way home?"

"And it's not cool to get to the dance before eight, so we have plenty of time to hit Chica's for tacos. Sound good to you?"

"I'm not very hungry." She needed alone time with her laptop. "You guys go. He really missed you this trip."

"Hey, your laptop is still on," he said.

"What?"

"It's closed but the blue light is on. See." Kate was amazed at how he managed to notice nothing about her for months, but the tiny light on her laptop didn't get past him.

"Violet was using it earlier. She always forgets to shut down. No matter. I have so much work to do. I'll grab something here."

"Okay, Kate, slow down and tell me what I did."

"You didn't do anything." That I know of yet, she thought. "Not everything is about you, Michael."

"I get the feeling this is."

"Your feeling is wrong. I'm on a deadline. I've made five starts to five shitty columns. I'm exhausted and worked through most of the night. I've got tons of people coming next week. And lest we forget, your folks arrive on Tuesday to pick apart my inadequacies with that subtle charm I've come to know and love. And we don't have any damn groceries in the damn house."

Michael treated her like he used to treat Laura when she had one of her three-year-old tantrums. He waited with his arms folded.

It was a standoff. Kate was lying to Michael about the computer and going to dinner with him and Jake; while he held the ace of lies about him and Marilyn and their techno-copulation and showed not a sign of it. At this point, Kate believed Michael was that rare person who could pass a lie detector test without breaking a sweat.

She wrestled with telling him what she knew. But if by the rare and highly unlikely chance there was a logical explanation as to why he was corresponding with another woman in a way that Kate was never supposed to find out, she'd have attacked him in the two places he guarded most closely – his integrity and his shame. That feeling of never being quite good enough was passed down from his parents, and he'd resent Kate for spying on him, which she had, and not trusting him, which she didn't, and questioning his character, which she had been doing for days. If Kate had been given the choice at that very moment, she'd take that fight over the one where he admits to having an affair. Kate wanted to be armed with three things before she pried open her marriage with a rusty screwdriver: information, the element of surprise, and the upper hand. She wouldn't settle for parsed out bits Michael would give her of the what and the whys of him and Marilyn.

But the one thing Katharine Marino McAllister wanted more than anything else was the blind faith she had in her husband and their marriage just a few days ago – their flawed, imperfect marriage that began with a passionate love affair and evolved into what she believed was comfort, caring, and an intimacy that takes decades to achieve. Holding Michael's hand in bed at night filled her with sublime contentment. But she wondered if what she called happiness, Michael called boredom. Her comfort, his misery. There were times she was glad he was on the road, but Kate knew she was happier when he was home. She slept better when he was beside her and she had never wanted the entire house to herself for the rest of her life.

"Okay." He touched her shoulder. "Why don't I shoot a few hoops with Jake while you go to the gym. That always makes you feel better. Maybe you'll have an appetite when you get back."

Sure, Kate thought, send the fat wife off to the gym so you can call your girlfriend and tell her you're home safe and sound with the old cow. Michael went looking for Jake. She lifted the lid on her laptop and got out of the email account and shut her computer down, then grabbed her sneakers and bag. She was about to put her laptop into her gym bag so she could finish what she started over at Violet's place.

"Why are you taking your computer to the gym?" Michael was watching from the doorway.

"Why aren't you in the kitchen?"

"Jake's still eating. I thought I'd go through the mail first."

"It's on the desk. I've been so stuck this week, I thought if an idea hit me, I could get a start on the column."

"At the gym?"

"You never know." She was bad at this. She had to concede or face looking ridiculous. Michael took the computer out of her hand.

"Maybe if you stopped thinking about it, inspiration would hit between shoulder presses and lat rows."

"You're right. It never helps to push it." She put the laptop back on her desk, gave him a quick kiss and left for the gym. She could think of worse things than spending an hour with a twenty-something guy built like granite. But the only thing Justin had ever written to her on his business card was the time of her next appointment.

32

Halfway to the gym, Kate took a hard left up West Valley Road, crossed Old Eagle School Road and took the long, winding hill straight to the top till it crested at the Strafford train station. She'd never get back into the city by car at this time of day, but she could hop on the R-5 line and be there in twenty-five minutes. With luck, she'd be back home in time for tacos.

She flew into the ladies room at the tiny station to freshen her make up and run a brush through her hair. She was in sweats, but good ones, stylish and ridiculously expensive.

She knew the address of Marilyn's firm – Lewis, Kramer, DiMayo & Campbell, by heart. One Liberty Place, Philadelphia, PA. If Marilyn could knock on her door unannounced, Kate could do the same. She had written her cover story in her head on the way to the station. "I was in the area and heard so much about you from Michael, I just had to drop in and say hello. I am so sorry I missed you the other day, Marilyn, but deadlines are unforgiving beasts." Kate would rehearse and refine her planned performance on the train.

Hoards of commuters getting an early start on the weekend came off the inbound train. Five minutes later her train pulled into the station. The silver car lumbered down the tracks, lurching right and left, making stops in Wayne, St. David's, Radnor. The small towns were streaks of brick, stone, and stucco dotted with local shop signs. This was the same train line she had taken to the city to pester Esther Rosen with her latest columns so many years ago. She knew the names of the towns like a poem she was forced to recite as a child. Villanova, Rosemont, Bryn Mawr, Haverford, Ardmore, Wynnewood, they sounded like beautiful English villages sleeping under majestic oaks, elms and tulip poplars.

She was on the "local," stopping at every station until she reached Center City. She felt comforted surrounded by strangers who didn't care about her floundering marriage. Their lives and their problems were as much a mystery to Kate as hers was to them. She ran through her story again. She would not lose her nerve. This was no time to think of consequences. She got off the train at 30th Street Station and took a cab to Marilyn's building. She rode up the elevator, smiling confidently at the executives who hopped on and off.

Kate paused at the double glass doors of the advertising agency. The partners' names were etched into the glass, but at closer inspection it was a cheaper technique made to look expensive. In case Lewis, Kramer, DiMayo & Campbell had a reversal of fortune, their names could magically disappear as if they had never stepped foot in the highest priced piece of commercial real estate on the block. The industrial carpet cleaner left a pleasant aroma in the corridor. A young woman, not much older than Laura, was behind the large desk in the reception area. Small wooden business card holders were placed in a pleasant symmetry across the long run of exotic teak.

"Can I help you?" she asked. The tasteful nameplate read, Heather Nichols.

"Hi, Heather. I'm here to see Marilyn Campbell." The girl looked confused.

"Do you have an appointment?"

"No, I'm a friend actually, a new friend." Kate was surprised by her sudden confidence and candor.

"Then she's not expecting you?" she said.

"She's definitely not expecting me." Kate spotted Marilyn's business card. Fourth in the pecking order of seniority, not far from Heather's reach. It was a clone of the card found by the dry cleaner in Michael's suit pocket. Kate reached for one. It smelled more like the carpet cleaner than seventy dollar-an-ounce perfume.

"Your name?" Kate was stumped. Of course they'd ask her name. She paused a moment too long.

"I'd much rather surprise her."

"I'm sorry. I'll need your name."

"Kate McAllister. I gambled dropping in on her, especially on a Friday, but I was hoping to catch up. I mean I'm not even dressed..."

"No, I love that suit. My mom has one just like it." Heather was getting on Kate's nerves. "I'll try to track her down. Hopefully she's not still in flight," Heather said.

"Where was she off to this time?"

"Dallas." Kate's expression didn't betray her shock.

"A great city – Dallas – but hot. My husband was just there," Kate said.

"McAllister? Michael, right? He's your husband?" Heather asked. Kate forced a smile. "He's in and out of here all the time. God, he's a nice guy. You're lucky."

Lucky was hardly the way Kate was feeling.

"Marilyn usually comes straight to the agency from the airport. I'll try her cell. Why don't you wait in her office?"

"Thank you. That's very nice," Kate said.

"No problem."

Heather led her down a long corridor and stopped at Marilyn's door. "Make yourself comfortable. Can I get you anything? Coffee, tea, water?"

"No thanks, I'm fine." Heather went back to her post. Marilyn was in Dallas. Michael was in Dallas. The tipping point of coincidence versus fear, and suspicion versus truth, had just swung toward reality and fact. The office was large, befitting Marilyn's position. Her huge desk and overstuffed leather chair on coaster wheels was flanked by a wall of bookcases, in the same rich teak that decorated the lobby. Most of her books were about getting what you want, swimming with sharks, making your way in a man's world, breaking glass ceilings, the power of yes, the power of no, the power of maybe. Dozens and dozens of self-help business bibles, guaranteed to lift you up the corporate stairway to paradise.

A large window let in natural light and overlooked the street. There was a small conference table with six chairs, and a fully stocked bar, short on alcohol and long on vitamin water, power drinks, organic fruit juices, and diet iced teas. Kate scanned the wall art. An AB from Bryn Mawr, a Wharton MBA, and too many professional awards and certificates to count. Kate felt surprisingly calm in Marilyn's world. The more she knew, the more prepared she felt to deal with her. She was tempted to go through the desk drawers, but Heather seemed very light on her feet.

Kate was debating how to open the conversation with Marilyn. She considered a warm smile, pretending that Michael had told her everything, that she was far from shocked it had come to this, and of course Marilyn would have no problem with Kate. This approach could do one of two things: Force Marilyn into silence or allow her to unburden her soul to the heroically stoic, but soon to be ex-wife.

The phone rang. Marilyn's messages were obviously going to voicemail. She didn't recognize the name on caller ID, and the volume was muted. She sat behind the desk, gave in to temptation and tried to open a file drawer. It was locked. The top of Marilyn's desk was pristine. A leather insert held a Montblanc pen placed strategically on a pad of linen notepaper with her name embossed across the top. Kate held the pen, probably an exact duplicate of the one Marilyn kept in her purse, the same one that she used to write Michael's message. A beautiful Waterford Lizmore double old-fashioned glass was off to the side next to an unopened bottle of sparkling water. Another call came through. The name scrolled across the LED screen, Michael McAllister. This time Kate didn't hesitate. She scanned the options on the phone quickly before it was too late. She gambled and stabbed at the flashing button and hit the volume control. She heard Michael's voice, already leaving a message. "I just got your text. Sorry we didn't have more time this morning..." Kate picked up the handset and cut through quickly.

"Marilyn Campbell's office. Kate McAllister speaking."

"Kate, what the hell are you doing there?" His voice was soft and even.

"I'm sorry, Michael, Marilyn isn't in the office. But the receptionist is checking if she's back from Dallas. Oh, that's right. You were in Dallas. Sounds like you two may have run into each other."

"Kate, come home," he said.

"You might want to try her home or cell. I assume you have those numbers."

"Come home."

"Jesus Christ, Michael, nothing good has come out of Dallas since Kennedy was shot!"

"Please," he said. Kate hung up. Her hand found it's way to the crystal glass and her fingers clenched it tightly, suffocating the hand-blown crosscuts in the pattern She hurled it like a major league pitcher and it bounced off Marilyn's award as "Advertising Executive of the Year – New Products Category." Heather showed up at the door moments later with a very tall security guard who looked like he could play right tackle for the Philadelphia Eagles.

"I spoke to Marilyn. We need to ask you to leave," Heather said. The smile was gone from her face as she surveyed the damage.

"Get to your feet, ma'm," the guard said.

"Either you leave with Milt, or we'll be forced to call the police." Perky little Heather had muscle. Kate rose from the chair and moved toward the doorway.

"Be gentle, Milt. This is my first time."

"Pardon?"

"I've never been tossed out of anywhere." Kate was secretly impressed with how quickly she racked up another "first" in her life.

"Let's go." He put his hand on her elbow.

"Marilyn missed a couple of calls. You might want to tell her to dial into her voicemail," Kate said.

"What do you want from Marilyn?" Heather said.

"You should ask Marilyn what she wants from me." Kate went willingly with Milt. They had a pleasant conversation on the elevator about his two kids living with their mother in Buffalo. He apologized for escorting her out, but they had to be careful. Not long ago they found a homeless guy living in the men's room. They had no idea how he was getting in.

Kate walked the entire way back down Market Street to 30th Street Station and got on a westbound train toward home. It was already past six. The young man sitting across from her was inhaling an oversized chicken and beef taco.

33

Michael waited as long as he could for Kate to get home. It was getting late, so he ran out to get some take out Mexican while Jake called to see if any of his friends were going to the dance. He tried Kate's cell phone from the car, but she didn't pick up. They ate in silence. Jake had three burritos and a chicken taco. Michael barely touched his.

"You okay, Dad?"

"Yeah, fine why?" Michael wasn't even close to being ready to sit them all down and explain himself, but he was suffocating. Kate had gone to Marilyn's office. How much did she know? Michael watched Jake devour his food. His lean body and soft blue eyes were Michael's. But he had his mother's heart; so much of Jake's compassion and sweetness was Kate. From the time he was in kindergarten, he'd share his lunch with a kid who forgot his. He'd change the channel if his sister wanted to watch something else. He was as kind and selfless as any adolescent boy could be expected to be.

Jake went upstairs to get ready. His bedroom was three varying shades of blue, painted in wide horizontal stripes. Sky blue blended into midnight blue that bled into navy blue along the stark white baseboard. Metallica posters and an Italian flag, a gift from Kate's dad when Italy won the World Cup in '06, draped his walls. He swilled mouthwash over his teeth and gums and took his cell phone off the charger. He checked the directory to make sure he had Carol Tucker's number saved, then flew down the steps.

"Is Mom home yet?" he asked.

"Not yet. I'll bet she stopped at Aunt Violet's."

"Did she call?"

"No. I tried her, but her phone's probably dead. She never remembers to charge it," Michael said.

"And she's always on me about mine."

"You ready?" Jake nodded.

"Can we pick up Ben?"

"Sure," Michael said as they headed for the garage.

The car sounded its usual beeps and alarms as he started the engine. Jake looked straight ahead, putting his ear buds in place.

"Meeting anybody special at the dance?" Michael asked.

"What?" He pulled one ear bud out.

"Friends, Jake. Who's going besides you and Ben?" Jake shrugged. "Carol?" Jake's face turned scarlet.

"Maybe, I think so."

They drove quietly for a few minutes. Jake didn't bother putting his music back on, but shot a quick text to his sister.

"Weird shit going on, Lars. Mom's AWOL." He hit "send" when Michael's voice cut through the silence.

"Buddy, you know how I've been gone a lot. Even more than usual. I'm working with a lot of new clients, new people."

"You missed the turn," Jake said.

"Ben lives off Crescent," Michael said.

"That's Mark, Dad. Ben's on Oliver." Michael looked up at the street signs and turned around.

"I'm just saying things are always changing."

"What things?" Jake said.

"With me. With all of us. Life would be pretty boring if it didn't, right?"

"I guess." Michael picked the wrong time to have this conversation. He wanted Jake to have fun and enjoy the dance, maybe even talk to that girl he liked.

"Sorry, pal. Pretty boring stuff, huh?"

"Ben's road's the next one on the left," Jake had no clue what his father was getting at and it wasn't like his mom not to be home for dinner, but he was too busy trying to work up the nerve to ask Carol Tucker out to the movies on Saturday night. Michael reached over and squeezed Jake's shoulder. He smiled at his dad, who tried too hard to smile back. They finally picked up Ben and got to the dance.

Michael dropped Jake and Ben off at the middle school. A couple of hundred kids had packed the entranceway. The boys were in the standard uniform: worn jeans and t-shirts with unbuttoned long-sleeved shirts over them. The girls were in short skirts that barely reached the top of their thighs. Their pencil-thin legs were cut at the knee or ankle by sheepskin boots with large round toes. Eskimo street walkers, Michael thought. Their spaghetti-strapped shirts exposed bare shoulders. They cut in front of his car as he waited patiently. Some of the girls looked older than Laura, with raccoon eyes shaped by jet-black eyeliner.

Michael inched his way toward the school exit lane. Once he was back on the road, he pulled over and dialed Marilyn. He knew she'd be waiting for his call.

34

There was a small scattering of cars left in the Strafford station parking lot when Kate stepped off the platform. It was well lit and quiet. Kate sat in her car. She hoped Jake had gotten dinner and a ride to the dance. She thought about Michael's voice on the phone, when Kate had picked up instead of Marilyn. It was a combination of quiet fear and controlled defiance. Maybe that's what shock is. She gripped her hands around the leather wheel. She was cold, but didn't want to start the car. She checked her phone. She had four missed calls from Michael.

Kate wondered if he was still waiting for her to come home. She closed her eyes and remembered seeing a woman on the news that ran down her husband in their driveway, and then put it in reverse just to make sure the job was done. It was tempting, but the thought of spending the rest of her life in prison was not. Divorce was expensive, but at least she would keep half their assets, including the house. She'd go after his business too, that ought to be worth something. She helped him get it off the ground.

She stayed at home so he could fly around the country and sleep with women like Marilyn Campbell. Kate imagined a small army of Marilyn-look-a-likes. What if the McAllisterCampbell account was duplicated a dozen times with a dozen different women who didn't leave their business cards behind? Her head hurt.

Kate started the engine and had visions of Michael standing in the driveway, waiting for her to pull up and her pushing the accelerator pedal all the way to the floor. It would be cleaner than carving him up like a turkey. She could hose down the driveway without worrying about stains on the carpet. That fantasy was soon replaced by the image of a stainless steel toilet, tucked openly in the corner of a six-by-nine cell and the face of a sadistic matron getting off on watching Kate pee.

It was getting late and Kate felt like she had nowhere to go. Theresa would be at the school gym watching Little Tony play basketball and Marie and her family were in New York for a long weekend. She could go to a hotel, but Jake would be home after the dance. She didn't trust Michael to answer his questions. Violet was at her ballroom dancing class. She pulled out of the parking lot and drove west along Lancaster Avenue past Strafford into Devon then into Berwyn. The car was on autopilot. She pulled into the visitor's parking spot in front of the nursing home and signed in at the register. It was quiet. Most everyone was already asleep. She glanced into the TV room. Her father was alone, watching a hockey game. He was slumped slightly forward in his wheelchair. His last stroke had been minor but his speech was slow to return.

"Hi, Dad." She kissed his forehead. He tried to curl his lips into a smile. "The Flyers winning tonight?" He was still handsome with a head full of thick, gray hair. His skin was smooth for his seventy-nine years.

"Did you eat?" He nodded. "I'll bring you some pasta tomorrow. Sound good? Laura will be home in a few days. We'll pick you up Thursday for Thanksgiving."

It had become harder to take him out of the nursing home, but Kate was not about to let her father spend a holiday eating processed turkey and food service potatoes, not if she could help it. "One of the boys will be over to get you. I'll be busy with the bird." She stroked his hair. "Know what I was thinking about on the way over? When I was in college and I brought Michael home and how you just liked the guy right away, even though we weren't dating and he already had a girlfriend. You said he was a good boy. Then when he came back after Mom died, you never asked why we broke up or what he'd been doing. You said it took a big man to show up and do the right thing." She saw curiosity in Tony's eyes. "Guess I'm a little sentimental tonight. The holidays do that – you know, the way they did with Mom." She saw a hint of sadness in his eyes when she mentioned her mother. "Want me to help you get ready for bed?" He squeezed her hand. He was embarrassed when she or one of her sisters helped care for him. "Why don't I get that pretty nurse you like?" He nodded. Kate hesitated for a moment. "Was it ever easy, Pop? With Mom, I mean, I know you fought like hell sometimes. We heard you all the way down in the rec room. But did you ever think it wasn't worth it? That you just wanted to walk away?"

Tony gave her a blank stare. He got confused at times. Kate felt selfish coming to him when he needed his rest.

"Sorry. I'm being a nudge. I better get home." He looked tired. "I'll tell the nurse to come get you after the second period." He nodded.

"I love you, Dad. I'll come by tomorrow with fusilli." His grip on her hand tightened. He looked up at her, struggling to find what – a word, a gesture, and then, it was barely audible, but clear as could be when he replied, "No."

35

Laura reread Jake's text. She'd felt a weird vibe floating up from Pennsylvania for the last couple of days. Her roommate was off at a party with her boyfriend. Laura was bored with parties. She had gone to a few, but there was a sameness to them. She ran into the same people, they played the same music, served the same beer, and had the same regurgitated smell about them. Her pre-party ritual seldom varied. She would pull a half-dozen outfits from the closet, discard the ones that didn't work on the floor, do her nails and make-up and by the time she finally walked to the party, she'd have to push her way through the door after shelling out more money than she could ever possibly drink. Most of the guys were already high or loaded and the girls were worse. Laura usually left early and ended the night in a coffee shop or alone in her room. She needed a new routine, a new group of friends. There were a few girls she had met in the library and physics lab that seemed nice. She'd see what they did on weekends when she got back from Thanksgiving break.

She slipped into her plaid, flannel pajama pants with "Lacrosse" written down the right leg in bright gold letters. A light snow was falling. She put on the Vassar sweatshirt she had bought on her first campus tour and put a mug of water in the microwave. She decided on green tea with jasmine and placed her iPod into the sound dock. Her mom was a Van Morrison nut and now, she was too. She started with "Moondance." Her room was chilly. The heater never kept up with the draft coming through the window. She thought of catching up on a few shows on Hulu. Her body melted into the memory foam topper on her dorm bed as she waited for the mug to stop spinning on the carousel. The microwave was small, with little power, so everything took three times longer than it did at home. She closed her eyes as Van sang, "Well, it's a marvelous night for a Moondance, with the stars up above in your eyes. A fantabulous night to make romance..." The microwave chimed and she danced her way over to it. "And all the leaves on the trees are falling to the sound of the breezes that blow." She dipped her tea bag into the LAX mug, a gift from Jake. "Can I just have one more Moondance with you, my love." Of course, Van, Laura laughed to herself.

"Laura, you there?" Will Tiernan's blunt knock interrupted her moondance. Her back stiffened. What was he doing knocking on her dorm room on a Friday night?

"Just a sec." She heard her mother's voice telling her to be nice. Don't get impatient. She needed that ride on Wednesday, and she was an expert in dismissing Will without being too rude. Laura turned down the volume and opened her door. He was holding two large take-out cups of overpriced coffee.

"Can I come in?" He held out the other cup. "I brought you a macchiato. Oh, you're uh, already having something."

"It's just tea. Thanks." His outstretched hand hung in the air. "I'll drink the coffee later." Laura put the cup aside as Will looked around the room. His eyes were a lighthouse, looking for a spot to illuminate his way with Laura. He stopped at her bedspread, bundled up and tangled with her sheets and an old afghan throw Nana had crocheted years ago. Will noticed her looking at him and his face flushed.

"Do you want to sit down?"

"Uh, yeah, sure, " he said. "I really like Van Morrison too." Did he think that was a sign that they were meant for each other? He was annoying. He sat on her bed, not her roommate's perfectly made bed that hadn't been slept in for over a week – no, her bed. She turned her desk chair around and put her feet up on the other side of the bed.

"So how's it going?" he asked.

"Fine."

"For me too." He sipped his coffee, making a loud, sucking sound. She held her mug to her face and carefully took a long sip of her tea.

"I wasn't sure you'd be in," he said.

"I'm not in the mood for a party."

"An upper classman in my comp class told me about one at Sigma later, if you change your mind," he said.

"Thanks, but I won't. I need to start a research paper." She caught him looking at her bra on the hook behind her door. He turned scarlet. The list of things wrong with Will grew exponentially in her mind. He hadn't grown into his huge feet. He was still only a few inches taller than Laura but tried to make up for it by always sitting up straight. He had the kind of posture her mother had nagged her about her whole life. He took another long sip, mercifully a silent one.

"Laura, about our trip home," he said. Here it comes. He wants to see her over break. Could they go out for a bite, maybe a movie? Excuses flooded her mind, like paper firing rapidly into a collator; they came to her quickly and brilliantly. Family was in town, she promised her brother they'd hang out, she and her girlfriends were thinking of going to the shore for a mini-reunion, she promised her mom she'd start their Christmas shopping together, they had tickets for a Broadway show. It was so easy and he would have no way of knowing if she was telling the truth. Will seemed lost for words, as if he couldn't find the right connectors in his brain to make them come out of his mouth. Laura ended his misery.

"Don't worry, Will. I'll be ready when your folks get here. And thanks for the coffee. I'll really enjoy it later."

"Actually, I was wondering if you could be ready a couple of hours earlier." He couldn't let it end on a good note. He had to add a wrinkle and mess with her timing. "My economics professor cancelled my twelve o'clock and Carrie doesn't have class on Wednesday. Laura was confused. Who was Carrie? "My girlfriend's spending Thanksgiving with us. It'll be a little tight, but I think we'll still all fit."

Will Tiernan has a girlfriend? Laura tried to picture what kind of girl would consider him attractive and fun. She never saw him with other girls, except for her and maybe some of the members of Key Club last year.

"Sure, no problem. I'll be packed and at the curb. Text me when you're close."

"Cool." He gulped the rest of his coffee and left. Laura turned up her iPod and picked up the cup of coffee he brought her. It was still warm. She held it over the plastic covered wastebasket to throw it out. She changed her mind and decided to save it for later. She glanced out her window as Will moved across campus through the snow and crossed the quad outside her dorm.

36

Kate's car found its way home. Twice deer darted across the road, but she was used to driving well below the speed limit this time of year. It was their mating season. Michael told her that when a buck was chasing a doe in heat, nothing would stop him. No shit. Kate was only a few miles from home. She and Michael had found their house right after Jake turned one. They agreed they wanted something old and with character. They doubled the equity in their starter home and had a considerable budget with enough money left over for renovations. They looked for over a year. They went to open houses and searched the listings. Kate was waiting for that feeling you get when you walk through a strange door and know you're home. The house didn't have to be perfect. She preferred the opposite of perfect with just enough of what they wanted, so her imagination could do the rest.

They were about to give up and add onto their bungalow when she saw a small "For Sale by Owner" sign. Its driveway was practically a street of its own that set the house back two

acres. It was gray stone with white clapboard siding, a traditional late nineteenth century colonial with a porch off the
living room and another small porch off the kitchen entryway.
She rang the doorbell and met the woman who explained her
husband had been transferred to Atlanta. They had lived there
only a couple of years and hated to leave. They had plans to
remodel but never got to them. Kate said a silent "thank God."
They hadn't gotten much traffic since it was out of the way, so
they planned to put it on the market the following week. Kate
called Michael at his office and he met her there within the hour.
It was out of their price range but with a long-term mortgage
and a huge hit to their savings, they made an offer. They had
a verbal agreement with the couple by that night and moved
in eight weeks later.

They refinished floors and woodwork. They rebuilt the kitchen
porch and landscaped around the entire house. They picked out
the spot where they'd build the pool one day. They had the stone
pointed and repainted the chunky wooden shutters a high-gloss
black. Over time, they remodeled the kitchen but kept the details
within the period of the house. She and Michael collected dozens
of magazines and built strong relationships with the architect and
construction crews who constantly came and went.

The doorway over her office and the living room was arched
with five-inch molding. The only real change they made to the
footprint was adding the sunroom off the kitchen. The house was
the perfect blend of old and new. She and Michael debated and
decided on each change, no matter how small. It was a perfect
time in their marriage, if there ever was such a thing. The house
became an extension of their love for each other and their children.
It was grand and it was simple. There wasn't a chair or sofa that
you couldn't curl up in, even the ones in the living room that was
rarely used except on Christmas morning.

Kate pulled into the driveway and continued toward the back
of the house. Michael's car was gone. He'd forgotten to put the

door down. She couldn't remember if Ben's parents were picking up from the dance. She texted Jake to be sure.

The house was empty. She hung up her coat, and noticed Michael's black cashmere jacket wasn't in its usual spot. Her phone rang. It was Laura. She picked up on her way to their bedroom and put on her "mom" voice.

"Hi, honey."

"Hey"

"What's going on? You okay?" Kate asked.

"Yeah, fine. How are Dad and Jake?"

"Fine." Kate didn't know what to make of her small talk.

"What am I missing at home?"

"Not much. Just the usual. I'm nuts because of the holiday. I'm behind on my deadline. Your brother's at a dance and your father is somewhere. I just got in from visiting your grandfather."

"How is he?"

"A little better I think," Kate said.

"I can't wait to see him." Laura sipped at the reheated coffee Will had brought her.

"Maybe you should get out of the dorm," Kate said.

"I didn't call for advice, Mom." Kate was in no mood to fight with her daughter. "You'll never guess who stopped by earlier. Will Tiernan." Laura thought her mother would go into a list of Will's saintly qualities so it could be used one day at his future canonization, but Kate didn't reply. "He brought me coffee."

Kate wanted to tell her daughter to run because even nice guys like Will are as hard as hell to live with and they'll break your heart in the end.

"And it looks like I'll be home a little earlier on Wednesday. He wants to leave before noon."

"Great. I can't wait to see you."

"I miss you, Mom."

Kate closed her eyes, missing her daughter every bit as much.

"I love you, sweetie. I'll see you in a few days."

"Okay. Oh, I almost forgot. Guess what? Will's got a girlfriend. She's having Thanksgiving with his family."

The Friday night phone call finally made sense to Kate. Always available and adoring Will had tired of waiting for Laura and moved on without her. Laura was sad because she didn't want Will to want someone instead of her. They exchanged a few more words and then Laura said she had to get back to work. Kate was relieved. She could only handle one heartbreak at a time.

She went up to their bedroom and decided to take a bath. She ran the water as hot as she could stand it. The countertop was littered with Michael's hair gel and vitamins. His comb lined up next to Kate's straight iron and deodorant. She wondered what was on Marilyn's bathroom counter. Did Michael have a duplicate comb and toothbrush that matched her décor or did he keep her bathroom as pristine and uncluttered as her Liberty Plaza office? For all Kate knew, he had a whole other set of clothes and books and music he enjoyed with her.

Kate undressed slowly. She brushed her teeth and casually put her brush back in the stand next to Michael's. His had a trace of encrusted dried toothpaste. It needed a good cleaning. She took the brush and swished it against the pink mold inside the toilet bowl feeling very clever to have cleaned two things at once. She swirled the brush around the water vigorously. "There, that ought to do it." She replaced his toothbrush in the stand, removing her own.

Kate finished undressing and put her cell phone on the narrow tile border around the soaking tub. Michael hadn't left a note or tried to reach her again. She immersed herself in the scalding water with a mixture of discomfort and pleasure. She had blown the Marilyn Campbell affair wide open and made herself even more unattractive and insecure to her husband. Whatever happened in the next twenty-four hours would have a potential cast of characters far beyond her and Michael. There were the kids, the inevitable school counselors, therapists and attorneys – his and hers. Financial advisors and mediators would play supporting roles, along with a chorus of shock and venom from their extended families who would line up on one side or the other with support or condemnation depending on whom they believed was at fault. Jake and Laura would live the rest of their lives in pairs. Everything would come in twos – two holidays, two vacations, and two places to call home. She had left the bathroom and bedroom doors open. She heard the front door slam.

"Kate!" She counted his footsteps on the stairs – one, two ... eleven, twelve. She was naked and vulnerable.

"Kate?" She didn't answer. She was lost in the dim lights and fog, calmed by the scented candle that promised serenity. Michael appeared through the mist like an apparition. He sat on the edge of the tub.

"We need to talk." Kate recognized the scent of perfume coming from his shirt. She slid underneath the water and submerged her entire body to clear her nostrils of that putrid smell.

37

When Michael showed up at Marilyn's door earlier that evening, he was not the same man she was with the night before. He was shaken so she poured him a drink the minute he got there. It had already been a hell of a day. She had a long flight back from Dallas, and her receptionist called to report Kate McAllister had a temper tantrum in her office. Marilyn wasn't interested in the theatrics but would have loved to have been there when she was escorted out.

Michael sat on the edge of her white leather sofa, hands clenched. Marilyn softened and put her hand on his arm. "I'm sorry this is so difficult for you."

"I've been lying to her for months."

"Michael, this will work out." Her words sounded as hollow as the ones he had said to Jake earlier. He put down his scotch and surveyed the room. He saw how detached Marilyn was from her life. The room was sterile. Anyone could move in without changing a thing because there wasn't a hint of a personal touch that made the space her own. Marilyn was beautiful and charming when she wanted to be. When she had first contacted him about work, he explained that his firm was completely booked, but she wasn't a woman who accepted the word "no." He didn't remember how she managed it, but eventually Michael agreed to personally oversee her projects. She joined him on the road and sat in the back room with him as his best people interviewed consumers. Later over drinks, she shared some of her plans with Michael. Lewis, Kramer & DiMayo would soon have a new business model – hers. She was short on details at first because she wasn't sure she could trust Michael. Her objective was to gain that trust and make him her confidant. And once he was convinced he needed her as much as she needed him, the rest would be easy.

Although they had worked on and off together for several years, they'd been inseparable since last February. They shared several clients, so meeting was easy. Marilyn had made the first advance when Michael desperately needed something new and exciting in his life. Too many of his days were swallowed up like a dull poison that made him numb to any highs or lows. Marilyn was his antidote.

She went into the kitchen as Michael realized he'd have to ride out this storm with Kate until he and Marilyn were ready to go public with their relationship. She came back with a small platter of cheese, pâté, and crackers.

"My version of cooking. Eat. You look like shit." He sipped his scotch. "She's got balls, Michael. Showing up at my office like that? By the way, you owe me a very expensive glass."

Michael retreated into silence. Nothing she said helped. He was foolish to try and find comfort here.

"Kate will accept this," Marilyn said. "She doesn't get a choice and it doesn't matter when or how she finds out. We just need a little more time."

He got up and swallowed the rest of his drink.

"You okay to drive home?"

"Fine." Marilyn kissed him tenderly and gave him a brief hug. "If she throws you out, you know your way back."

He rode the elevator down to the lobby. The doorman nodded discreetly. He was used to Michael coming and going. He stepped out onto the street as snow flurries swirled around him. It was too early for any serious snowfall, but the temperature had dropped ten degrees since he'd driven into the city. By the time he had gotten behind the wheel, it was already nine-thirty. The car had been a present from Kate. She surprised him on their twentieth anniversary. It was the most generous gift he'd ever received. They took a long trip to upstate New York, soon after he got it. Kate said she wanted to take their pulse as a couple. Michael had no idea what she meant. She wanted something from him, but he couldn't figure out what it was. The ride through New Paltz, New York was like driving through a watercolor. Kate said she wanted more conversation, so he gave her words. She wanted his feelings, so he told her he loved her. But the rest of it – the anger, the frustration, the daily bouts with inadequacy and frustration – weren't given away to anyone. They were his problems, not hers. He talked to people for a living, but he could no longer figure out how to talk to his wife. It was much easier and straightforward with Marilyn. She didn't give a damn how he felt about anything. All he had to do was show up.

Michael was relieved to see Kate's car parked by the kitchen door. Maybe there was still time to talk to her before Jake got back from the dance. He spotted her purse thrown on the table beside the large envelope Marilyn had dropped off the other day. He ignored it and called out for Kate. He took the stairs one by one.

He saw the light from their bedroom. He dropped his coat on the bed. Her suitcase wasn't out, drawers weren't open, clothes weren't scattered on the bed. Maybe things weren't as bad as he feared. Small billows of steam filtered through the bathroom light. If she heard him, she made no sound. He walked into the bathroom. Kate was lounging in the oversized tub. Her body was sprawled out and her eyes were closed, but she knew he was there. He stood for a moment and took in her body. He loved to watch her undress. He didn't tell her this. There was no reason to keep a simple pleasure to himself, but she struggled with her weight and innocent comments he made in the past had hurt her, so he decided saying nothing was better than saying the wrong thing.

His caution had eaten away at their marriage, leaving a festering remoteness that had grown slowly and politely over time. Michael had forgotten the freedom he'd felt in the early days with Kate's family, where feelings flew like clay pigeons waiting to be blown apart and scattered through the crowd. He was the quiet observer then, and they had accepted him into their family without hesitation. Now, as his eyes took in Kate's body, he understood that there had only been one constant in his life, and that was Kate. Michael was still deeply in love with his wife. With all the mistakes and hurts they brought to each other over the years, Michael was still desperately in love with the girl he met in modern British literature. He cherished the life they had built together. But Michael had forgotten how she needed to be loved. He had to find his way back to her. He sat on the edge of the tub. She opened her eyes.

"We need to talk."

She slid her body entire body under the water. Michael rose and walked back downstairs, unsure if he could ever repair the damage his silence and caution had caused.

Jake texted Michael. He wanted to spend the night at Ben's house. Michael was relieved. After leaving Kate in the bathroom, he spent four hours staring at the Discovery Channel. He dragged himself upstairs to bed. Kate had locked their door. He decided not to knock, hoping she was able to sleep.

He didn't want to stay in the guestroom with his parents coming into town. It would make more work to erase the signs that their son wasn't sleeping with his wife. He went back to the family room instead and stretched out on the sofa. This time he kept the television off. The table behind him was soldiered by pictures of the kids at all different ages. Jake's first Little League pose, Laura digging at the beach, Jake mugging with Laura at her high school graduation. His eyes fixed on the only photo that wasn't of their children. It was a picture of Kate and her mother taken at the Marino kitchen table with Michael barely noticeable in the background. He tried to remember when it was taken. It could have been any Sunday he dropped in for dinner or midweek when he'd leave long after midnight. The photo was old and fading. He looked at the woman who didn't live to become his mother-in-law and suddenly recalled her soft smile and how she had called out for him to be in the next picture. He remembered every kindness she'd shown him. He smiled at the memory of finding cash hidden in his textbooks to tide him over till his next paycheck and the mountain of food she would pack for him to take back to his apartment so she wouldn't have to worry about what he'd eat. More than anything Michael remembered how she loved him because her daughter did. And then he knew exactly what he had to do.

38

Michael woke early the next morning. He fixed the coffee pot and went to the grocery store. He returned over an hour later with almost everything they'd need for Thanksgiving dinner. No matter what came next, he was sure Kate wouldn't cancel the holiday. He put away most of the staples but kept out what she'd need to start cooking ahead of time. Twenty pounds of potatoes for a casserole, fresh green beans, bags of cubed bread. He arranged them in a corner. He'd control what he could control.

Kate smelled the coffee from her bedroom. What the hell was Michael doing? This wasn't a normal Saturday morning. He didn't get to make coffee and lounge around in his robe. She threw on her sweats and opened the door with a force that threatened to rip it from its hinges. She heard him moving around in the kitchen. She stopped in the doorway. His back was to her. He was kneeling in front of the spice cabinet.

"Is this for real?" Kate said. Her eyes were swollen from crying.

"Are you ready to talk?" he asked.

"Get out, Michael."

"No."

"Then I'll go," she said.

"Go where, Kate? Jake will be home in a few hours. Coffee?"

"You shopped?"

"I promised I'd get it done."

"Just get out and go to your whore."

"She's not a whore." Hearing him defend that woman blanketed Kate in irrational rage. She grabbed a carton of eggs off the counter.

"Put those down." She opened the styrofoam container and hurled an egg at him. It shattered against his jaw.

"What the hell are you doing?"

"Get out."

They came rapid fire – to the chest, the midsection, at his feet. Egg whites and yoke seeped through and ran down his shirt and pants.

"Kate, stop!" He grabbed her wrists. "You threw enough shit yesterday in her office."

"She told you?"

"Last night."

"I smelled her on you."

"We talked, that's all."

"This time?"

"Your stunt could have ruined everything."

"Let go of me." Kate struggled to free her hands.

"Not until you promise to listen," he said.

"To how I don't put out like she does? Because I'm stinking tired at the end of the day or because I don't give a crap about your needs? Who the hell has time to worry about your needs?"

"I'm not sleeping with Marilyn."

"Bullshit," Kate said.

"It's true."

"Fuck it, Michael. I found the secret emails." Michael was stunned. "Or did you think I was too stupid to figure it out?"

"What emails, Kate?"

"The McAllisterCampbell account. Cute title. Your idea?"

"Sit down, please." He released his grip, took a towel, and wiped the shells and dripping egg off his face and clothes.

"I had no idea you were in Marilyn's office when I called yesterday."

"You think? That's a pretty shitty defense. Christ, it's a good thing you're not a lawyer. I handed you her card days ago. I read it, Michael. You know I read it."

"We went out to celebrate a deal that night."

"That's what they call it now? 'A deal.' I'm really out of circulation."

"I've done positioning work for her..."

"No shit."

"And for other clients."

"Other clients too? Any visual aids of this positioning work?"

"Dammit, let me finish."

"That's what she said. Sorry, Jake and I watch too many of *The Office* reruns – oh, that's right – you're not here – because we're alone all the time. Maybe Marilyn can teach me some of your favorite positions for when you drop in around here between "business" trips." Michael remained calm.

"My firm takes a product and prepares a marketing strategy. We step the client and the advertising team through it. It's a huge leap between concept and getting to market. It's been a great angle for the business and a huge success."

"What the fuck does this have to do with you screwing that bitch?" The phone rang.

"Let it go," he said.

"It could be one of the kids," Kate said.

"Please, don't answer." Kate checked caller ID.

"Perfect. It's your mother. Should we tell her to bring her pickled eggs this year since I just went through ours."

"I'll call her back." Edith's voice on the answering machine cut through the tension.

"I guess it's still too early for you east-coasters. It's your mother. I'd appreciate a call back. Dad and I are getting in bright and early Tuesday morning."

"Make her shut up," Kate said. Michael muted the volume on the answering machine.

"Do you love her, Michael?"

"No." He took a step toward Kate.

"I guess nothing fucks up a good affair like the wife finding out."

"Kate, would you please shut the hell up!"

Kate looked out at the brown leaves settling on the patio furniture that never made it back into the shed. The sun was trying to break through gray November clouds. Michael sat at the table.

"I'm sorry I haven't been honest with you, but I want to try now, if you'll let me."

"You've got two balls and a mouth, sure, go for it." Her anger and sarcasm made Michael want to storm out, but he knew if he did, Kate would see it as proof that he was having an affair.

"At first I told myself what I was doing with Marilyn was okay. I wasn't hurting anyone. In the end everyone would be happier."

Kate grabbed a kitchen counter stool and threw it against the wall.

"You want to destroy the place. Go ahead, but it won't change the truth!" She grabbed another. This time Michael yanked it from her hands and took her by the shoulders.

"Stop it!"

"You're a lying piece of shit!"

"Who the hell are you to accuse me of cheating? I never even look at women on the road, and let me tell you, there are plenty of chances."

"You called her name, Michael."

"When?"

"In your sleep – the night before you left."

"I did?"

"Whispered it in my ear."

"Probably because she was hounding me about the final draft of a deal."

"You didn't sound hounded."

"Christ, you're hanging me for saying the woman's name? I was living this thing full time, all the time. Marilyn is pretty damn difficult to manage and half the people at the office are already pretty pissed at me for off-loading projects because she chewed up so much of my time."

"Poor thing. How could you stand being 'hounded' by a tall, beautiful blond?"

"I'm pretty goddamn angry at being accused of something I didn't do. Have I shut down? Yes. Have I been lying? Yes. But not the way you think. I screwed this whole thing up, but that's a long way from banging a woman I barely like."

"Don't be crude."

"Did that just come out of your mouth? And don't talk to me like I'm one of the kids."

Michael held onto her. His knuckles were white. He closed his eyes for a second. Kate saw his rage rise up, then retreat. He released his fingers.

"You said you lied."

"Kate, I put my life in separate boxes. I always have. Home, work, travel. It helps me sort things out before I make any big decisions."

"Wait, we played this game in college," she said. "I'll sleep with Kate, and then break up with my girlfriend. I'll sleep with Marilyn and then break up with Kate." She threw a bag of cubed stuffing bread. It split open and the bread flew across the room like down feathers. "Violet never liked you anyway." That had nothing to do with a damn thing, but Kate was lining up her support team. She wanted to hurt him. She didn't want to use the kids yet, but if it got ugly, everybody was fair game.

"You told Violet?" Michael said. "Who else? Your sisters?"

"No. I don't want them to know I was stupid enough to marry a cheating bastard."

"Kate, I swear this is the truth. I am not having an affair with Marilyn Campbell or any other woman. I haven't been with anyone else since that night I came back to you – that horrible night of your mom's wake. I love you. Only you. I am so sorry I shut you out. It was stupid and it was wrong."

"Wait – let's get back to putting your life in all those little boxes. What box did sex with Marilyn get put into? Hers?"

"Did you not just hear what I said? Okay. Forget it. Come with me. If you want proof, I'll give you proof."

"I'm not going anywhere with you."

"To your office – now." Kate stared at him defiantly. "Don't make me pick you up and carry you like a child." She waited a few moments, then followed him out of the kitchen.

"Show me," he said. She looked at him blankly. "After you know everything, if you still want me to leave, fine, I'll go. I promise. But not until you hear this from me and not read it in some damn email account or on a meaningless business card. Boot up your computer." She didn't move. Michael swung behind her desk and turned on her desktop.

"I'll get you some coffee."

"I don't want the fucking coffee," Kate said. He physically put her in her desk chair. "Log onto the account. I assume you know the password."

"I don't want to read them, Michael."

"You wanted to read them yesterday. That's what you were doing when I came in, wasn't it? Log on." Kate followed Steve Yeardsley's instructions and logged onto his email account.

"But I need your word that what you're about to see stays between us, nobody else can know. I mean it. Look at me. Nobody, Kate. I don't care how much you hate me right now. I don't care that you tell your sisters and Violet everything about our life; this is my business, our business. If you can't promise, I'll change the damn password right now, and this time you won't have a prayer of figuring it out."

"Don't threaten me, asshole." Her tears bounced off the keyboard.

"I'm sorry. It wasn't a threat. But you have to promise, Kate." She stared at him silently.

"Go ahead. Enter the password." She did.

"Start with the first one. It's short."

"I got that far yesterday." Michael stood behind her and pointed to the screen.

"Then try that one," he said. Kate read silently, and looked up at him confused.

"Keep going. Every one." Kate took her time going over each and every word. She went in order while Michael moved to the kitchen and came back with her coffee. She had read a dozen of them.

"How far are you?"

"Not far enough," Kate said.

"Fine. Scroll up to that date." He pointed to it on the screen. "Now open it."

Her finger clicked on the mouse and opened the most important cover message between her husband and Marilyn Campbell. Buried in the secret email from the McAllisterCampbell.com domain. The subject line read, "Let's Do It." Kate read the first few lines, then kept reading. It was long, but built a persuasive argument for Michael to walk away from the life they had built together. Kate eventually got to the bottom line. Then she fainted.

39

Kate woke up in bed and soon drifted back to sleep. When she woke again, she was outstretched in a cushioned lounge chair under a tented canopy protected from the blistering sun. It was oppressively hot, but a soft breeze came off the water. A tray of all her favorite foods was beside her. She was sipping a piña colada and gazing at the island fare of fresh fruit and shrimp salad sandwiches. To her left was another tray of food, odd for the locals. Mounds of linguini in red clam sauce and steaming Italian bread competed for her attention.

A young man was there to twirl the pasta on a fork and feed it to her. Another approached her with a plate of pignoli cookies. She took one or two, then clapped her hands to dismiss him. When did she die and become Cleopatra? The manservants were rock-solid young men whose life work was obviously to look inviting to women. Kate was in a bikini. She was a forty-six-year-old woman with a swimsuit model body. Obviously eating five thousand calories a day didn't hurt her a bit. A tropical breeze washed over her and with one more clap a scantily clad young man knelt by her side and reapplied the tanning oil that smelled like fresh bananas and mango. His hands worked the muscles in her back and neck the way Nana would gently knead her pasta dough. He unhooked the back of her bikini and removed her top, all the while his fingers played softly across her muscles. He moved his hands lower to release the tension in the small of her back. She got aroused as his fingers slid under her bikini bottom and then things got really interesting.

She heard a familiar laugh in the distance and turned her head to see Michael and Marilyn walking down the beach. Marilyn whispered something in his ear and they pointed toward Kate. She waved at Marilyn like they were old friends. Michael was in the board shorts she bought him for their canceled trip to Bermuda. More voices washed onshore. The deserted beach was filling up with tourists who laid out towels and unloaded picnic coolers. Kate recognized one, then another. She shot up and wrapped a towel around herself.

"Katharine Elena Marino, you put that top on right now, young lady!" Her mother glared at her and looked at Michael.

"You let her go out like this?" He and Marilyn exchanged another laugh.

"Let her go Mare, she's having fun," Tony said. Kate looked at her father kissing her mother. Others cropped up around Maryann. Laura and Jake were throwing a Frisbee. Her sisters were spreading out a picnic with their families. Nana was all in black, sitting in a plastic strap chair. Grandpa Joe, in a gray suit and black oxford shoes, was walking along the shoreline with his head down. Violet and Greg were coming in the other direction with Meredith and the little ones. The sun was high and it was warm. The Caribbean blue water was inviting. Kate got up to join them. Her mother was as beautiful and healthy as Kate remembered. Her father was holding her while Nana scolded them for being so affectionate in front of the children. Kate took a few steps closer as her mother looked up and Nana said "Vieni qui." So many people were talking at the same time. Conversations ran into conversations, faces blended with other faces. Laura dove in the sand to grab the Frisbee. Greg spun his son in a circle. Jake raced at the water's edge with his cousins. Michael and Marilyn were at the perimeter watching them all. Kate moved closer and her mother opened her arms. Kate ran to them. She had missed her mother's embrace. She missed the way she said her name and the smell of her skin. Maryann held her daughter tightly. "Love you, baby." "Love you too, Ma. I miss you so much." Kate opened her eyes and Maryann was gone. They were all gone.

She didn't know how long she'd been asleep. She was exhausted and probably still in shock. She heard Michael downstairs, talking to Jake. She glanced at the clock. It was two in the afternoon. The sky was a pale gray compared to her blue and white tropical dream. She picked up the bedside phone and called Violet. She got the answering machine and hung up. Michael made her promise not to tell anyone, but he of all people should have known how bad Kate was at keeping secrets.

40

A few hours earlier, Michael moved her to the desk chair in her office. Kate had never fainted before, not even when she was pregnant. Technically, it wasn't actually a faint, but she felt like she was spinning inside a top. She couldn't catch her breath and the room was fading out in the distance.

"Honey, are you okay?" Kate was dazed and foggy. "Kate, did you read it?" he asked.

"This has been going on with her for how long, nine, ten months?"

"Give or take a few weeks."

"And you thought it was okay not to tell me? You've traveled around the country with her?"

"I wasn't *with* her," Michael said.

"Her perfume costs more than our car, Michael."

"Don't exaggerate," he said. "You're mad because Marilyn's ad agency wants to buy my firm?"

"No, Michael. I'm mad because I'm the last one to know."

"You're not the last, far from it. Kate, look, right there. See? We clear almost twenty million dollars on this deal. Did you miss that part?" The five-ton stone had been lifted from Michael's chest. He felt free – finally.

"She's buying you?"

"No. Her firm is buying my firm. At least that's the plan. I couldn't risk it getting out. Clients would get antsy and bail on us. And I had to make sure my people were protected. No layoffs. It's in the deal."

"What about you?" Kate asked.

"I stay on as a consultant for a year, two tops, and I get paid for it, a lot. Kate, if she can talk her partners into the buyout, Marilyn will control a huge part of her agency's business and how they run things. Since they promoted her to partner, she has been on the hunt for an angle, a way to set herself apart and be on top. Literally."

"And you're the angle."

"My firm is."

"But why did she come here, Michael, with her hooker bras and stripper panties?"

"Her what?"

"In the envelope downstairs," Kate said.

"That's what's in there?"

"With a note about you getting a closer look at them on the road."

"Jesus, I don't believe it. Kate, look, they're prototypes from one of her clients. They make lingerie. We're testing those products next month. They went out to consumers weeks ago. I'll show you my schedule. Monday the twelfth in New York, Tuesday and Wednesday in Chicago. The following week I think it's Tampa and Los Angeles. I'm not sure. I'll be listening in while women who mean absolutely nothing to me talk about how they like wearing those panties. I'm bringing Pete, Lori, and Deborah with me on the job. Call them. Be my guest."

"But why come here? What was her point?"

"Marilyn is anal. Hell, she invented anal. Those pieces are top secret, if you can believe it. They aren't on the market yet. She probably didn't want to risk any of my people who are not involved with that project opening it up at the office, so she left them here for me. On top of it, she got the added bonus of checking out how we live. The woman worships at the altar of complete control."

"She obviously controls you."

"That's not true."

"Does she know I helped start that company? That it was our money? That we remortgaged when things were slow those first few years? That I'm alone almost every damn week of the year, and now you keep me in the dark on this?"

"Honey, I know. I'm sorry. This is no excuse, but Marilyn hasn't even presented the idea to her partners yet."

"Now I feel much better. Me and her business pals are on the same playing field."

"That's not what I meant."

"And what if they shoot it down, Michael?"

"They won't. It's good business. When she lays it out to them, she wants it to look like it's a new idea, or better yet, their idea. She'll offer to handle the negotiations, but it's practically ready for our signatures. We've already come to terms and she looks like a genius, taking the problems out of what could be a long, drawn-out process. Honey, this is one of the best things that's ever happened to us."

"Stop calling me 'Honey.' 'Honey's' husband doesn't make a decision that will change the rest of their lives and keep it between himself and his girlfriend."

"She's not – dammit Kate! Marilyn wants McAllister Research Group. Our numbers are strong. It's a huge coup to put us under her agency's umbrella, but we can't afford a leak when we're this close."

"All those late-night negotiations with Marilyn must have been exhausting." He refused to be baited.

"Yes, they were, but I was never unfaithful to you, not once, and I fucking resent you thinking I was." He sat beside her on the loveseat. Kate's anger ebbed.

"Why didn't you tell me, Michael? And please don't give me the bullshit about top-secret deals."

"I almost did that first week, but you went off on a speaking tour and then it got easier to keep it to myself, not because I don't trust you."

"You don't..."

"I do in almost everything, but face it, Kate – I know you. The Marino sisters have no secrets.

"Okay, I get your point, but give them some credit," she said. "Hell, give me some credit."

"All right, look – that's not it, at least not all of it." Kate waited for him to finish. "If you knew, if anyone did and the deal fell through, I didn't want to feel like a failure. I didn't want to let you and the kids down."

"That's the most fucked up thing you have ever said to me."

"Thanks for your understanding."

"Michael, even if it fell through, you've still built a great business. You'd still be you. It wouldn't change anything."

"Yes, it would – for me – it would. But you never got that. I don't want to fail. I need this deal, Kate, and I want it for so many reasons, I lost count. I want it for me, you, the kids. But more than anything I wanted to be the one who came to you with the best news of our lives, not fuck it up this way." Michael looked genuinely sad, but Kate wasn't ready to help him feel better.

"Tell me about her," Kate said. "She must think I'm a goddamn loser."

"Actually, Marilyn's flattered you're jealous."

"She said that?"

"She didn't have to. I read her pretty well."

"So what's she like? Besides being a beautiful, overly ambitious control freak who keeps a very neat office. At least till yesterday."

"That's pretty much it. Marilyn is all business all the time. Quirky, and yes, neat, no – more like sterile. You could perform surgery in that condo."

"You've been to her condo?"

"Yes," Michael said.

"How many times?"

"I don't know. We've held meetings there." Kate couldn't take it all in. She felt like a contestant in one of those hot dog eating contests. She kept swallowing more and more information until she couldn't ram one more piece down her throat, but the details kept coming.

"She's not a bad person, Kate. I know you don't want to hear that, but it's true. I am so tired of my life running me. I want more time with you and Jake while he's still here. We'll finally have that. I handled this all wrong, but I don't regret selling the company. I do regret hurting you."

"I need to know something, Michael. You said there's no affair. I want to believe you."

"I swear it's true."

"But if I dropped dead tomorrow, would you be interested in Marilyn Campbell?"

"Before or after your funeral?"

"Shut up and answer the question," Kate said.

"If anything ever happened to you – no. I would never look at another woman until the day I died. Jesus, Kate, can't we enjoy being rich for at least five minutes?"

"Answer the question."

"Okay, here's the God's honest truth. If you were gone, I would never go out with Marilyn, not even on one date. Besides, I don't think her girlfriend would like it very much." For one of the few times in her life, Kate McAllister was speechless.

41

Michael was worn out like a last-place marathon runner. The toll of deception and secret negotiations showed on his face. Kate hadn't seen it until now because she had stopped looking at her husband. When she finally came back downstairs and into the family room, Michael was going over the terms of the deal. The secret papers were spread out openly for the first time.

"Still hate me?" he asked.

"A little. I need more than a few hours," she said.

"I'm not the bad guy, Kate."

"Yes, you are, but now you're a rich, bad guy." She sat next to him and he handed her a paper.

"It's not final yet, but here's the standing offer." Kate looked it over. All the zeroes made her dizzy again.

"Where's Jake?" she asked.

"In his room playing video games. He wants to go the movies. I think he's meeting that girl there. He dropped a few hints."

"Pretty soon he'll be gone too," Kate said.

"And then you're stuck with me." Michael couldn't tell if his wife thought that was a good thing or a bad thing. Kate hated to think of her children dropping in and out of their lives. She hoped Jake would marry a girl that she'd fall in love with too, and that Laura's husband would have all of Michael's good qualities, and few of the ones that still drove her crazy.

"He says he needs a haircut," Michael said.

"You're kidding."

"I'll run him to the mall."

"See what you can get out of him," Kate said.

"He'll tell us about her when he's ready to tell us."

"It's that kind of thinking that got us into this mess." Michael ignored her comment and kissed her softly.

"Noted," he said. Kate pulled back.

"And the days of you answering me in one syllable are over."

"I've been warned," Michael said.

"And don't use words that tell me zero."

"Okay, Mrs. Writer, what should I have said?"

"How about something like, 'you know, Kate, from now on, I want you to know what's going on with me and how I feel about everything especially something as huge as walking away from a company we built together.'"

"Agreed. And that's a one-syllable joke. I love you, Kate. I'll try. I will. I'll get so good at it, you'll be begging me to stop talking."

"Yeah, right."

"Why don't you get your shower and I'll open a bottle of wine."

"It's a little early," Kate said.

"I want to celebrate."

"Me too. So why don't you take Jake for that haircut first and get him something to eat and we'll celebrate when you get back."

"Sounds good," Michael said. He kissed her again and left to find Jake. Kate waited until she saw them pull onto Conestoga Road, then grabbed her keys and left the house.

Violet had been in on this from the beginning and had held Kate up when she was feeling her worst. Kate wasn't about to keep the news from her now. If she was keeping score, and Kate was, she had just lied to Michael. But he had been lying to her for a very long time, so they weren't even close to being even. She felt a little guilty about breaking her promise so soon, but that didn't stop her from heading straight to Violet's townhouse.

It was a ten-minute ride and the narrow two-lane road was covered with leaves from a brisk fall shower. Kate remembered the uproar when a developer wanted to put multiple-property housing on one of the grand old estates that dotted the Main Line. Neighbors were irate. It would ruin the historic integrity of their town. It would be an eyesore and what kind of people would it attract? For all their noise and superior blathering, a beautiful community was built, hidden by mature trees on the far side of the estate. Only thirty townhomes were built in the style of the historic homes in Society Hill. Authentic brick with wooden shutters and arched doorways stood side-by-side. The window wells were deep, and dormers capped the attics that ran the span of the houses. The community had a town center with a fully equipped gym, a small organic market, a restaurant, coffee bar, two clothing boutiques, and an independent bookstore. The same people who fought against the development frequented the shops and outdoor café. They praised the restaurant so much it made it hard to get a reservation. It was a self-contained town within the town. The homes had high-end price tags. Violet was very careful with her money through the years and had a strong portfolio. Esther started her off early with her broker, who had gone on to advise Violet over the years. She had moved most of the furniture from her old place and treated herself to a new dining room set when she bought the townhouse. It was spacious and compact, the kind of place that was bigger than you realized once you walked past the front door. It had plenty of room for Greg and his family when they came to visit. Kate hated showing up unannounced but she knew if she called, she'd spill the news over the phone and miss out on the look on Violet's face.

Kate drove into Jefferson Square and found an empty spot in front of Violet's. Her car was there. She must have been shopping. She never answers her cell phone when she's browsing in a store. She says it takes all the fun out of spending money you shouldn't. Kate rang the bell. No answer. She rang again and waited a few minutes. She peered into the front hallway. Violet probably had her noise-canceling headphones on; whenever she was doing anything around the house she piped her favorite music through them. She was worse than the kids. Kate dug into her purse and sifted through the old receipts and spare change looking for her ring of house keys. Kate still hadn't completely processed the last twenty-four hours. She didn't know what it meant to all of them. They weren't hurting financially, but there were always downturns in Michael's business and print media was changing quickly. Kate was raised to worry about money. The company buyout defied her imagination, and things weren't even close to being better with her and Michael. Kate had a lot of her own issues to overcome and the Marilyn Campbell mystery had exposed real problems in the marriage. They obviously had a communication problem. They went through long periods where they were pleasant roommates in a relationship that used to be passionate and dynamic. She still couldn't understand how Michael could keep something this huge from her. He'd engineered his exit from his company without discussing it or considering their future beyond the time the check cleared. He had crawled into bed at night with this on his mind. It never came up when bills were due and they had to sell stock to pay Laura's tuition and the cost of her father's nursing care. It never came up over dinner when there were gaps in the conversation, and there had been plenty of gaps. Even when she asked about work, he would say it was fine – the same. She got workout clothes for her birthday, very nice workout clothes, but wouldn't a multimillion dollar buyout garner her more than spandex? Just last month she mentioned their friends the Schmidt's bought a shore house. Kate didn't want a house at the beach. What she wanted was the two-hour drive alone with her husband where they entertained the joy of having one. Kate wanted to be in the Michael-Marilyn club. After the high of having a fortune blew over, they would still be left with the gulf between them. She planned to suggest couples therapy. Michael would resist. It wasn't like him to open up to a stranger, let alone to a stranger who may tell him things about himself he didn't want to hear. His low tolerance for criticism and drive for perfection didn't invite introspection, but Kate knew it was already a condition of her forgiveness and willingness to put their marriage back together.

The key turned smoothly in the lock. The house was quiet. She didn't want to sneak up on Violet and give her a heart attack. She called out softly.

"Vi?" She walked through the living room. Everything was in its place. Kate drove Violet crazy with her constant clutter. No matter how much Violet buzzed through Kate's house, she couldn't get everything as organized as she'd like.

"Violet, it's me." Kate passed through the kitchen and den. She peeked out the back door. A raven was emptying out the birdfeeder, scaring away whatever sparrows remained. She tried Violet's cell phone one more time and heard the ringtone in the distance playing "You Can't Hurry Love" by the Supremes. It stopped. She dialed again and followed the sound up the stairs, tracking Diana Ross all the way to Violet's bedroom. She listened for running water from the shower. She slowed down at the landing as if the soles of her shoes were weighted and gravity wouldn't release them from the carpet runner. She kept one hand on the banister; the other clutched her cell phone. The bedroom door was ajar. She looked over the landing down into the living room. She stared at the front door, willing Violet to walk through it, arms loaded with bags from the overpriced community boutique. "Vi…" Kate peeked into the bedroom. Violet was asleep, her cell phone on the nightstand. She was perfectly still. Kate moved closer.

She sat beside her dearest friend and touched Violet's cool cheek. "No, no, no," she said softly. Kate rested her face against Violet's forehead. She murmured softly and the words sounded like those old prayers she had learned back at Our Lady of Perpetual Help. "Wake up, wake up. Please, Vi, wake up." But Violet didn't wake up. She must have passed peacefully. Violet got the death everyone prays for and very few get. Kate cried silent tears as she covered her beloved friend. Kate hated that she was cold. For one of few times in her life, Kate wasn't frantic. Her thoughts and movements were slow and methodical. Something she didn't quite comprehend had happened. A nuclear explosion had been set off and destroyed her without a sound, and yet she was alive and breathing and smoothing the covers over Violet's still body. This would be her last time alone with Violet, her dear Violet, and she wasn't ready to say goodbye. She knew what she should do. Her mind was telling her to dial 911, but that was the last thing she wanted to do.

Kate went down to the kitchen and made a pot of tea. She'd clean up the mess before anyone saw it. She spied Violet's iPod and scrolled to her favorite playlist. She placed it in the sound dock and the music filled the townhouse. She then fixed two mugs of Earl Grey, one for her and one for Violet. She went back upstairs and put Violet's on the bedside table. She slowly sipped hers and then told her the whole story of Michael and Marilyn and the twenty million dollars. She told her about Jake having his first date with a girl and Laura looking forward to coming home. She promised to set up college funds for Greg's kids and stay close to him and his family. She promised that he'd always have a place at their Thanksgiving table. She thanked Violet for being her best friend and for loving her and believing in her as a writer when no one else at the newspaper did. She wanted Violet to know that without her, Kate's life would have been less – less in everything that she held close – things like love, friendship, honesty, and compassion – and that she was the one person who filled up the lonely times with her laughter and common sense. When she finished her tea, Kate kissed Violet softly on the forehead, then straightened up what little things were out of place around the room. She closed the People magazine that had fallen to the floor and placed it on the bedside table. She put Violet's medicine bottles away neatly in the bathroom cabinet. She hung up the robe that was lying at the foot of the bed.

Kate's tears continued but she moved quickly now. She went downstairs and washed out the teapot and the mugs. She put everything where it belonged, shut off the music, and then called Michael on his cell. She calmly told him what had happened. He dropped Jake off at home, made a credible excuse, and rushed over to Violet's. Kate ran to him when he walked through the door. Michael held her just as he had that awful night of her mother's wake. His tears fell onto her. She took his hand and led him up to Violet's bedroom. Michael didn't ask any questions. He didn't tell her what to do or insist they call 911. He followed Kate in silence. He stopped in the doorway, then looked at Kate and saw how much she needed him to do the absolute right thing for her even if he wasn't sure what that was. She let go of his hand and went back to Violet. She sat beside her and took Violet's hand again.

Michael entered the room uneasily, but followed Kate's lead and walked around to the other side of the bed. He was uncomfortable not calling the authorities, but he would wait. He would know when to do it because something, a look or a gesture from Kate, would tell him it was the right time, and she was ready, but not now. He pulled up a chair and took Violet's left hand in his. And in that moment, Kate knew that Michael McAllister was still a good man. When her life was shipwrecked, he knew what she needed and never questioned those needs. Sitting there with Violet, she watched as he held her dear friend's cold hand. He would let her have this time with Violet. They would stay there together until Kate was ready to let go.

42

Kate and Michael refused to cancel Thanksgiving. Marie and Theresa offered to have it at their houses, but it was out of Kate's control because Michael took over as soon as they followed the ambulance to the hospital. Violet was pronounced dead at the scene. He called Greg. They hated giving him such tragic news over the phone. He was on the next plane to Philadelphia. Meredith and the kids would meet him on Tuesday.

Michael broke the news to Jake when they got home. He sobbed like a little boy and spent the rest of the day in his room. That night, he got into bed with Kate and Michael for the first time in years. They talked about Violet and laughed more than they cried. Michael and Kate decided to drive up and get Laura themselves on Tuesday and tell her then.

Michael's parents came out immediately after they found out what happened. Edith and Carl were at their best when they were needed. What they couldn't say in words, they put into action. Michael's brother practically ran the farm now, so they packed up the car and drove to Pennsylvania the moment Michael hung up the phone.

Greg was executor of Violet's will and he and Kate each knew about the safety deposit box she kept at Valley Forge National Bank. There they found her will and instructions on exactly what kind of service she wanted. Organized, detail-oriented Violet had left no doubt about her final wishes. She wanted to be cremated. This was unheard of in Kate's family. They clung to the concept of the open casket, but she wouldn't argue with Greg. Violet rejected the single portrait of herself next to the urn. In a letter they found she wrote, "It's not my damn graduation, it's my funeral, and if I have to be up there smiling like I'm happy to be gone, then I want all of you with me, surrounding that picture like our photos are having a party." And she listed every single photo that had to be there. Greg and his family, of course, but she also wanted Kate, Michael, and the kids along with nieces and nephews and some friends from the old neighborhood. She instructed them on where to find the less-obvious pictures squirreled away in her attic. They found a deed to a mausoleum crypt for her urn. "Don't you dare put me on a mantle or bookshelf. I'm not a work of art. This goes for you, Greg. I'm a Philly girl so don't get any ideas about hauling my ashes out to Chicago." Greg laughed at his mother's no-nonsense approach. She organized her funeral like she'd been organizing Kate's life every day over the last fifteen years. Violet had known Kate wouldn't agree with all of her decisions, but she'd also known Kate would honor and respect them. The service would be at the Methodist church Violet attended since moving from the city, and the pastor agreed to have the funeral the morning after Thanksgiving. He was well versed in Violet's wishes; apparently she'd met with him several years earlier to discuss the matter.

Kate insisted Greg and his family stay with her. Greg agreed, knowing it would be difficult for his kids to stay at their grandmother's or a hotel after such a loss. Since Meredith's parents had moved into a retirement community, Kate's house was the perfect choice. There he would be among people who loved his mother as much as he did. Young Greg was almost eight and Missy was four. They had strong memories of Violet, who'd visited Chicago as often as she possibly could. Kate would help keep those memories alive.

Michael's parents arrived, as promised, by late morning after driving through the night. Kate had the coffee ready as usual when they got there.

"So sorry for your loss, Kate." Edith held her for a brief moment. She had been not so secretly jealous of Violet for years, but never said so out loud. Violet laughed it off. She liked Edith and got a kick out of her. She ignored her digs about the kids having two grandmothers. She was flattered Edith saw her that way. No matter how often Kate and Michael carted the kids out to Indiana, Edith knew Violet was in the trenches every day. Violet got Jake past his night terrors. She went to all his ball games and took Laura to get her braces checked. She spent countless nights sleeping over when Michael and Kate were out of town. Jake and Laura loved her and Violet loved them.

Michael handed over the day-to-day business of McAllister Research Group to his number two-person. He took off the entire week and with Kate's sisters' and his mother's help, he commandeered the holiday. Michael immediately put Edith to work. She was a remarkable cook, and for all his chauvinism, Carl was great in the kitchen as long as he followed his wife's instructions.

Kate was grateful that Edith was happy to get her hands dirty and help Michael pull off dinner with his in-laws. Her disapproval of Kate's entire family coming to dinner along with Greg and his family would be stifled. Kate couldn't wait for her to meet Steve Yeardsley, the computer expert, who helped crack the Marilyn Campbell affair. Edith's eyes would scrutinize him and later comment on him being an "odd little fellow."

Kate and Michael left early Tuesday morning to get Laura. They had called her on Sunday and asked if she could talk to her professors about missing class on Wednesday. They added a positive spin about wanting to be the ones to bring her home for her first holiday and how it was easier for them to come up a day earlier. They kept Jake home from school. He begged to go to the airport with Greg to get Meredith and the kids. Michael had some business things to tie up. He was on his cell phone with Marilyn almost the entire trip to get Laura. He was open and relaxed. Kate heard bits and pieces of their conversation. Marilyn didn't know Kate was in the car. She was keeping Marilyn's secret a secret from Marilyn. The balance of power had shifted. Michael looked over and smiled at Kate. He knew how much she was enjoying her clandestine role in whatever happened from this point forward.

When her parents got up to her room, Laura was braced to hear the worst. She was sure they were going to announce a separation or divorce. Her mother looked as if she'd been crying for days and her father was obviously exhausted. He held her mother's hand and put his arm around her when they broke the news about Violet's death. Her father, who measured words like a chemist, spoke clearly and calmly. Laura sobbed as they carried her bags down to the car. Violet had sent her a box of goodies the week before and she called to thank her. It was the last time they'd spoken. Laura held onto her mother as Michael put the suitcase in the car. Kate opened the back passenger door. She got in beside her daughter. Laura put her head on Kate's shoulder and wept most of the way home.

The house was full when they got back from Poughkeepsie. There were more tears as Laura hugged Greg, Meredith, Jake, and her grandparents. Lots of food had been sent from friends and family. Kate's sisters, their husbands, and their children had come over to see Laura and be there for her, the way Kate's family had always stood together in good times and in bad. They stayed up late into the night and told Violet stories. Everyone agreed to come back on Wednesday to get ready for the holiday.

Kate sleepwalked through the next day. She helped Michael and his parents dust and set up the rented folding chairs and tables. She worked in the kitchen and practiced the Bible passage she'd read at the service. Violet left no instructions for a eulogy, but she and Greg needed to say a few words. Violet would protest, but this was one argument she wouldn't win. Kate was going to say goodbye to her whether she liked it or not.

Michael had a long conference call with Marilyn on Wednesday. He took it in their bedroom. Kate walked in halfway through their conversation. He held his fingers to her lips to warn her not to talk. Downstairs was a circus. Her sisters and Edith were arguing over how much to season the soup. The kids were making place cards and her brothers-in-law were practicing staying out of the way. Meredith had taken Laura to the mall to get a dress for the service. Kate was glad to be out of the confusion. She looked around at her old, sturdy furniture. It would be with her till they carted her out of that house. She'd never part with it, not for the latest transitional style, not for twenty million dollars. It was reliable and sturdy, like her mother and Violet and Kate. It held secrets. It stayed strong.

Michael's tone of voice changed. "You're kidding. No, Marilyn, I'm not uncomfortable with the idea. I just wasn't expecting it." Kate sat up.

"Yes, okay, of course, come. No, no problem. I'll handle Kate. I have so far, haven't I?" Kate stuck out her tongue. "No, she's calmed down. I told her we work together and that nothing was going on between us. She was imagining things." Michael winked at his wife. Kate wished she could hear Marilyn's side of the conversation. "Kate will believe what I tell her. It's under control." This time, Kate gave him the finger. "...No, it'll be fine. Plan on it, both of you. We'll see you then." Michael hung up.

"Two more for dinner," he said.

"Marilyn wants to come here?"

"She doesn't want to travel to North Carolina to see her mother, or worse – cook. And going out in her words is "'so middle class'."

"Wait – the woman thinks, I think, you're having an affair with her and she wants to come to Thanksgiving dinner in our home with her lover?"

"Exactly," Michael said. "Do you see what I've been putting up with for months?"

"Poor baby."

"She made a great pitch about how much she loved the house and wanted to get to know you. It's all bullshit."

"And what am I supposed to say to her when she walks through the door? 'Sorry about that glass'?"

"Trust me, the subject of your temper tantrum will never come up. Marilyn will set the stage the way she wants it set. She'll pretend her lover is just a good friend, because she wants you to think I'm her lover. And then she'll act as if she and I are just business associates and not lovers at all, which we are – business associates, I mean. And I'm guessing she'll even apologize to you for not being in when you dropped by her office last Friday. Because on top of everything else, Marilyn has great manners."

"Fine, let her come. I can think of at least twenty million reasons to put up with her, but can we sit her next to your father?"

"Absolutely. Better yet, let's put Marilyn between my folks."

"Perfect," Kate said.

"Think you can get through it without letting on you know about the buyout?"

"I'll restrict my martini intake," Kate said.

"Thank you." He kissed her and Kate responded with more passion than she'd felt for Michael in a very long time. They knew they should get back to work. They should join the family and help with the cooking and cleaning. They should be taking out the rest of the serving utensils and polished silver and setting up the bar. Instead they locked the door like teenagers afraid of their parents walking in on them. They undressed each other slowly. Michael was shocked at Kate's bra.

"Where did you get that?"

"From Marilyn's stash."

"I warned you that's top-secret stuff."

"I saved her love notes for you."

"Smart ass." He lowered the straps and smoothly unclipped the back of the bra and softly cupped her breasts.

"What about the panties?" He asked.

"They really are smooth to the touch. Want to do a little market research?" Kate felt naughty and excited. Michael opened her jeans and slid his hand down and removed them. Kate led him to their bed and Michael pressed his body against hers and kissed her with the same tenderness he'd shown the first time they had made love. He removed the panties.

"Well?"

"Smooth doesn't even begin to describe them." He tossed them onto the floor. He kissed her again and they made love intensely, passionately, and quietly.

43

Kate was the first one up on Thanksgiving morning. The house looked like it belonged in a design magazine. The table was set beautifully and every room was full of fresh-cut flowers. She walked through her office and picked up the Elvis bobblehead. She put him in the center of the table. In a few hours, the room would be full of those she loved most and the house would hold the spirit of those who loved her. One by one everyone made their way downstairs. Breakfast was simple and quick. Kate watched as Jake helped pour cereal for Greg's kids. Edith manned the toaster, and Laura, Meredith, and Michael went for a quick run. Everything was staged and organized. Michael had predicted it would all get done, and he was right. In the insanity and sadness of the last few days, everything about Kate's life had changed. She was grateful for Michael and their children, she was grateful for Violet, for the time she had with her mother, and for the time she had left with her father. She was grateful for her life. She felt strong again.

Theresa and Frank went to the nursing home and picked up Tony. He was having a good day. They would be almost thirty around the table. Kate's trainer, Justin, called to ask if it wasn't too late to accept her invitation. People trickled in, family-by-family. Her sister Marie and husband Rick came with their kids. Theresa's son Little Tony brought his girlfriend Allison. Her daughter "Peanut" came early to hang out with Laura. Kate found the pies Violet stored in her freezer, already baked and ready to be warmed in the oven, of course.

Michael's mother, exhausted from days of working to pull the dinner together, had one too many martinis, and couldn't understand why so many strangers were coming for dinner. Michael explained that everyone was connected to the family in some way.

"But they're not blood, Michael."

"That's why we like them," he said.

Greg drove down to the city and picked up Steve Yeardsley. Kate greeted him warmly. Steve didn't bring up wanting to have sex with her, but he brought a bottle of wine. Kate invited him in, but he hesitated. Greg had her back and folded Steve into the group, introducing him to everyone there.

"Who is that guy again?" Michael whispered.

"Steve. Your replacement."

The doorbell rang. Kate opened to Marilyn and Susan. Marilyn introduced herself and gave her condolences about Violet. Michael had mentioned her passing. She recalled meeting Violet just the week before and she was so sorry she didn't get a chance to meet Kate that morning or at her office last Friday. Marilyn's polite manners and beautiful pale orange cashmere sweater and tweed brown slacks didn't intimidate Kate. She brought a beautiful centerpiece for the table, arranged in an expensive crystal vase.

"Kate, this is my good friend, Susan Adderly."

"Please come in."

"Thank you for having us," Susan said.

Susan was exactly the kind of person Kate would have chosen for Marilyn. She seemed kind, but quiet and completely in awe of her partner. They joined the family in the kitchen. There were ongoing debates about the Eagles Super Bowl prospects this season, the right temperature to serve the soup, and whether the turkey needed basting again. Sounds and phrases that sung out in familiar tones over the generations. Kate let her sisters and Edith spar. Michael introduced Marilyn to everyone as quickly as possible and made sure they had a drink. Edith took her head out of the oven, obviously very impressed with Marilyn's appearance and commandingly tall presence. She wiped her hands quickly.

"Mom, this is a business associate and friend of mine. Marilyn Campbell. Marilyn, Edith McAllister."

"A pleasure. She's so nice and tall, Michael," Edith said as if Marilyn couldn't hear her.

"Thank you," Marilyn said. "This is my friend Susan."

"I had a best friend named Susan growing up. You don't hear that name very often anymore, do you?" Edith was happy on three counts. They weren't Italian, probably not Catholic, and they were tall. Kate wasn't about to fill in the blanks.

When the moment allowed, Kate took Marilyn aside and apologized for the scene she made in her office. Marilyn was as warm and gracious as Michael predicted. Kate blushed when she confessed to feeling terrible that she had the wrong idea about Marilyn. Of course, Michael told her they were close business associates who shared several projects. Kate was fortunate she and Michael were so forgiving of her outburst. Marilyn assured her it was already forgotten. She never let on that Susan was more than a dear friend and the lie that was built upon a lie that was surrounded by a secret, kept peace and tranquility befitting the spirit of the holiday.

Kate called everyone in for dinner. She had one large square table made up of two eight-foot tables, and two six-foot tables. There was a smaller table off to the side for all the kids who were sixteen and under. Jake was in charge of making sure the little ones were fed and could leave the table ten minutes after dinner started. Michael said Grace, the Catholic version. Kate glanced at Edith when he instinctively made the sign of the cross. He added a few words about how much it meant to him to have everyone with them. He thanked his parents for coming out early and working nonstop since they arrived. He raised his glass.

"I'd like to make a special toast, to Violet." Everyone raised their glass and repeated "To Violet." They all drank. Greg fought back tears. Then they continued a tradition they'd started years ago. While the soup was cooling in their bowls, they went around the table and each one said something they were most grateful for this past year. Laura and Jake mentioned Violet, and Marilyn was grateful for being a partner in her firm. Greg was grateful for the long visit he had with Violet this past summer. Tony managed to say a simple "everyone." Her sisters mentioned good health, having each other, and the younger ones gave thanks for things like an iPad and Justin Bieber. Edith was grateful her golf team took first place in the fall league. Michael's father said "Pass." Steve Yeardsley mumbled he was grateful for being invited, and winked at Kate. They went around the entire table until it was Michael's turn.

"I'm grateful for this family, for my children, and especially for Kate, who is the heart of our family." Kate blinked back tears. She was next.

"My list is long this year. I hope no one's starving. Thank you everyone for sharing this day with us. I am grateful for Michael, and for you Dad – and Jake and Laura, Edith and Carl – and of course my sisters and their beautiful children – for our good friends and our new friends. I'm grateful to Greg for being a part of this family, but mostly I'm grateful to have had a dear, dear friend who shared and kept every single secret I ever told her, even at the very end." She glanced at Marilyn who had no clue what Kate was talking about. "Happy Thanksgiving."

Then she silently thanked God that her marriage had survived her insecurities and the doubt they had cast on Michael. She was grateful that she had only misplaced her faith in their life together and had not lost it altogether. Kate dried her tears with her napkin. Michael put his arm around her. The clanking of silverware against the china and the chorus of "pass the gravy," and "who wants more turkey," and "are the potatoes hot enough" filled the room. Kate ate very little. She was amazed at Marilyn's appetite. Justin asked about her workout schedule and wondered if she had her metabolism checked.

"No. I don't allow myself to gain weight. There's no reason for it, except laziness I suppose." Kate's sisters glared at Marilyn, but Kate couldn't dislike her. Every single face around the table was a part of Kate's story. And then the unexpected happened. Kate wasn't blocked anymore. Her column came to her in a rush of words and images. She knew exactly what she would write as the words flowed through her mind and she filed them away in her memory for later. She'd write her column after they all left and meet her deadline just as Violet had predicted.

In a life where one moment she learned she'd soon be worth a fortune and hours later lost a priceless friend, Kate McAllister decided from that Thanksgiving Day, she would stop being afraid. What's the point?

Penetration & Intrusion

By Katharine McAllister

Before you think I've downed one too many pumpkin martinis, or am suffering from a turkey and stuffing overdose, I want to take a look at what we really celebrate on the fourth Thursday of each November. Of course we're grateful for family and children, for good health and for some, good fortune. But what we are most grateful for; whether rich or poor, city or country, red state or blue state – if we are being completely honest with ourselves – is that the forces of fate haven't felled our own personal fortress. Our fortresses aren't made of stone and turrets, or surrounded by moats. They are, however, built over generations, like their historical counterparts. These bastions are made of flesh and blood. The mortar that holds them together is love, family, and friendship.

Our fortresses change over time. They begin with ancestors, great-grandparents, grandparents, then parents and our own families, one foundation, built on another and another. Our closest childhood friends, the ones who make us feel part of a special group as we ward off bullies, mean girls, tough guys, and the jocks, reinforce it. The fortress evolves to include our high school clique and college fraternity brothers or sorority sisters. The one you plan to spend the rest of your life with – your mate – lays the cornerstone. But this is the tricky part. If you're not careful, it can be eroded by suspicion and mistrust and self-doubt. But if you're lucky, you ride out all the misunderstandings big and small and the cornerstone becomes the strongest part of your foundation.

With arms linked together, you and your partner stand firm against the evil that threatens to penetrate and intrude on your security. The evil is called drug and alcohol abuse, the evil is called cancer, diabetes, stroke, and heart disease. The evil is the perils of wet leaves on a rainy autumn night. We fiercely protect the fortress door with prayers. We join gyms and eat healthier than the generation that came before us. We're certain our fortress won't allow the errant drunk driver, sex offender, or thief to break through our walls and disrupt the world we've created.

We are fools.

"Penetration and intrusion" is the technical term for putting your nose into someone's computer and sniffing around; it is a breach in security. But it pales when compared to the real security breach of losing our childlike conviction that nothing bad will ever happen to us or those we love. We don't dare think about it. The superstitious tell you that you are inviting trouble if you do. Trust me, trouble doesn't need an invitation. It is a rude guest who shows up at your door without so much as a phone call.

So what do we do? How do we protect our fortress from crumbling under the weight of the invaders? It's a waste of our precious time to try. If we stayed behind its walls and waited for them to come, we would never venture out on a blind date. We'd skip that wonderful restaurant in a reclaimed section of the city because of the crime rate. We'd keep our children at home and struggle to educate them, lest they be exposed to the challenges of bullies and social blacklists. We would become our own inbred society of imbeciles and the ever ignorant. Worse, we'd never accept those that are different. We wouldn't risk letting a stranger into our lives, that very stranger who might one day become a cherished friend.

We embrace and guard our personal fortress, dodging the latest intrusion now and then – the one that is more of an inconvenience than heartbreak. But it's when we step outside its walls and leave the drawbridge open, that we understand what it means to live. And there is no safe way to live. No one holds the secret to the perfect life, home, family, or spouse. Perfection is an illusion our fortress often creates.

Remember this when your son or daughter walks across your drawbridge with the person who may one day lay their cornerstone. They may not be your idea of the "perfect" choice, but worse things could intrude or penetrate your life than the intoxication of young love. Remind yourself that not all that is different is a threat. And that often what we fear may teach us some of life's most important lessons. Be grateful for your fortress, but don't become its prisoner. Happy holidays – I'll see you at the mall!

Acknowledgments

I want to thank the gifted and talented circle of women who supported and encouraged me from start to finish. To my sisters, Marie, Sandy, and Phyllis for a lifetime of unconditional friendship. To Laura Binner for her unwavering commitment to our weekly meetings and for being my first reader and to Mary Harris, Anita Brown, Kathy Borkowski, Celeste Sparano, Karen Wattles, Lori McCarthy, Shirley Graziani, Lisa Walsh, and Donna Lee Lista for their feedback and honesty. Above all I thank them for crossing my drawbridge and becoming family. I also want to thank my gifted editors, Laura Ford, Abby Plesser, and Laura Ignarsky, who magically made it seem like I haven't forgotten anything taught to me by Sister Mary Jeanette from her beloved *Voyages in English*. An additional read by Sharon and Vick Kelly gave added insight. I am grateful to Vick for that and so much more. And of course, there is Courtney Simon who was my remarkable television editor for years. Her grace, serenity, and friendship mean the world to me.

I am indebted to Jeffery McGraw for his expert guidance and that extraordinary afternoon spent at the Red Cat and to Louis Shaffer who was and is a constant source of inspiration. She blazed the trail and has been my cheerleader and cherished friend. I am grateful for the hours my assistant Michelle Guo put into organizing and becoming a part of my life.

I want to especially remember all of *my* children: Annie and Spencer, Art, Bob, Jenn, Kathy, Rob, Philip, Carrie, Tony, Maryann, Joe, Tony, Craig, Sara, Rob, Tommy, Aimee, Sean, Lizzy, Madison, Paige, Carter, Matthew, Christian, Callan, Jack, Madeleine, and Philip, Jr.. And finally to Mark for always being in my corner through it all and never once saying, "Get a real job."

About the Author

Judith Donato graduated with a degree in History from West Chester University. She has written eight television series, receiving seven EMMY Awards and three Writers Guild of America Awards. Judith has been named a Distinguished Alumni and Woman of Distinction at her alma mater. Following the most recent Writers Guild of America strike, she left a career in television and was struck with the inspiration for her first novel, *Lie Beside Me*. A background in telling multifaceted stories enables her to utilize her most enjoyable pursuit – observing people. She lives in suburban Philadelphia with her husband, two children and their dog, Rex.

Made in the USA
Lexington, KY
26 December 2012